# HOLY
# CITY

# HOLY CITY

## A NOVEL

## HENRY WISE

Atlantic Monthly Press
*New York*

FIRST EDITION

*Published simultaneously in Canada*
*Printed in the United States of America*

First Grove Atlantic hardcover edition: June 2024

Library of Congress Cataloging-in-Publication data is available for this title.

ISBN 978-0-8021-6291-5
eISBN 978-0-8021-6292-2

Atlantic Monthly Press
an imprint of Grove Atlantic
154 West 14th Street
New York, NY 10011

Distributed by Publishers Group West

groveatlantic.com

24 25 26 27   10 9 8 7 6 5 4 3 2 1

# HOLY CITY

**F**IRE WAS THE DREAM that broke him.

He sat stiff as a dead cat, felt for the handle of his pistol under the seat, relaxed. The sad night came back to him, one of many like it, riding indefinitely, listening to the angry word of God through a thin static distance, the voice somehow both austere and intimate, seeming to speak directly to him with piercing certainty. He listened because there was nothing else out here—no other radio station—between hamlets or villages or four-way intersections, some of which at one point probably had been towns, nothing to see between them but a country undulating in pursuit of some sort of equilibrium, a pulse one could assess only by covering its distances, surprising because the countryside felt dead otherwise. It was not the soft, green, junglelike vegetation of so much of Virginia, but a hard, coarse, spiky land. The lonely roads wended like snakes through close forest or open fields or woods felled entirely for their lumber, leaving the ground as naked and weird as a skinned bear. And as he passed the fading houses like craters, kudzu-covered or through-grown with wild privet and poison ivy and chipping of paint, out of a wood-paneled darkness came the dark, paternal, familiar voice, companionate and suggestive of violence, of guile, the voice clean-shaven, austere, piercing, and expectant, some local celebrity preacher in a countryside rife with bewildering crime.

Will Seems had returned from a decade in Richmond—the "Holy City"—to a land he had called home each year of that decade, a country he now saw was peopled by a kind of disparate lost congregation. Last year, a man had cut his wife's throat with a Buck lock-blade, shooting himself after with a Walther PPK, failing on both counts. His wife was able to stop the bleeding from her neck with a pillow before calling 911, and the man woke up in a hospital room missing most of his jaw and wearing handcuffs to boot. Then, a few months ago now, a man in Halifax County who had been stopped for a burnt-out taillight had shot the policeman dead and driven away without contest. Even now, no leads. But one of the strangest incidents had occurred only recently. A complaint had been submitted in town because of an odor emanating from a particular home. The middle-aged unmarried resident had wrapped her dead mother—deceased by natural causes—in winter blankets, leaving the body in the house for over two months. Will remembered the investigation they'd conducted, wearing masks that did little to mitigate the stench, counting out with watering eyes 116 air fresheners sprinkled over the quilts. The sheriff was glad enough to let Troy St. Pierre, the medical examiner, remove the corpse, but he and Will were stuck with the daughter of the deceased. When questioned, the woman could not explain why she hadn't reported her own mother's death, the only reason they had cause to arrest her. Will saw in her a sad and childish desperation that was not necessarily unique; he'd seen it in the faces of the county, a puckered, hopeless, dopey defeat. Will guessed she was so afraid of being alone in this world that she had considered the dead welcome company.

Will got out of his truck and stretched and made use of a tree, looking down at the flat water of the creek, the dream still nagging him, the taste of smoke refusing to fade. He couldn't keep doing this, riding late-night to wear himself out, ending up back at the creek to sleep and leaving early, before the fishermen came with their buckets and their lines. He'd smoked too much last night, tasted the cotton mouth now, remembered an acute craving for a Coke with vanilla, the way it was served at the nearest Waffle House up in Petersburg. He reached in the pickup and took a sip now of leftover coffee in an open Styrofoam cup he'd picked up yesterday evening from the Get 'N' Go, some cooked-down tired version of what it had been when brewed that morning, and now it was twenty-four hours old, and it seemed nothing had happened in twenty-four hours, but that everything and everyone had moved and breathed just that much forward.

He tossed the dregs at the ground and turned to see, beyond the plain white Baptist church, a pillar of black smoke coming from the direction of the Hathom house or, beyond it, the Janders place. He grabbed his cell from the cup holder, called it in, climbing in and starting the pickup and pulling onto the road as the phone rang.

"This is Deputy Seems reporting a fire in Turkey Creek." He rounded a bend. "It's the Janders house."

"Copy," Tania said. She'd worked for the sheriff's department longer than Will and had never seen a day in the field. "Fire truck is on its way. Wait for it, you hear me?"

Will slapped his phone closed.

Tom's truck sat in the yard, the tractor by the shed; the smell of old lumber and paint burning filled the air. Will slid through a dirt turn, pulling a parachute of dust into the yard, and saw now

3

the side of Tom's mother's house (he still thought of it as hers) on fire, melting inward like blossom-end rot on some strange fruit.

Will pocketed the phone. The fire had already consumed the right side of the house but had not reached the front door.

"Tom!" Will could feel the heat baking into his cheeks. "Day! Tom!"

It was too soon to hear a siren. The fire truck was twenty-five minutes out from the time he called if he was lucky. He breathed deep, kicked open the front door, a plume of hot black smoke rolling into his face. He crouched, moving through the house, unable to hear anything but fire. The flames roared over him, and pieces of ceiling fell nearby. He groped along the kitchen floor, the vinyl curling like antique documents, holding his breath as long as he could, until he stumbled into something. A boot, steel toe, hot to the touch. He found the other foot and pulled them both, making it to the side door, tugging at what must have been Tom's body. He was crying with smoke, coughed when he tried to breathe, found himself on his knees in the yard, trying to stand, trying to breathe, smoke in the bridge of his nose. Tears and smoke, tears and smoke. Finally, he returned to the threshold, pulled the body free, dragged it ungracefully down the three steps and into the yard, and fell beside it in the grass, coughing.

WHEN WILL CAME TO, Sheriff Mills was breathing heavily down at him, patting Will's face with his rough hand to wake him, and an EMT had a stethoscope on his chest. A bandage had been placed on his arm, and he felt the burn. Will could smell the spearmint from the gum Mills chewed compulsively, a habit he'd formed years ago in an effort to quit tobacco. Will sat up to see the fire truck hosing down the house in splintering rainbows beyond which, in the distance, he could see a bald eagle perched at the top of a pine tree.

"You all right, son?" Mills said. "You got some kind of death wish I need to know about?"

The sheriff helped Will to his feet, and they looked at Tom in the grass, his clothes blackened, face covered in soot. A look of eternal blankness, until Will realized why.

"Shit," Mills said, sounding it as *shiat*. "Eyes gone, melted."

Mills turned the powerful body over with catlike, delicate care and inspected Tom's corpse, looked at the steps smudged with dark matter and again at the body.

"Hold on, now," Sheriff Mills said to himself.

Mills took out a pair of latex gloves from his pocket, pinched Tom's shirt just under the left shoulder blade, so that it lifted like a tent, revealing a rift in the fabric and a dark wet stain, darker and more consistent than the soot. He spread the rift with two fingers and inspected the skin, finding soot-caked gash marks, maybe two, maybe three. Will put his hands on his knees in an athlete's resting position and looked down as Sheriff Mills let the soaked hot shirt fall back onto the soaked hot skin.

"Homicide," Will said, the word echoing, almost a question. This wasn't picking up drunks or issuing speeding tickets or nailing vagrants for trespassing on abandoned properties. "Who'd . . . ?"

Will watched the sheriff: quiet, thoughtful, composed. The man seemed to sharpen, brighten into a quiet efficiency, fully alive.

Mills said, "It's a miracle he didn't burn worse than this. You neither. Check his pockets."

No wallet, no phone. Nothing.

Will felt light-headed, empty. He began coughing again. The sheriff said, "Tape this off while I call Sheriff Edgars and Troy over here. Keep everyone out unless it's them. When they get here, I'll need you to take pictures. Camera's in my truck."

Will was heading for the tape when he detected movement behind the house, wishing he hadn't, but Mills saw it too.

"Head up the trees," Mills said. "I'll swing around from the field. Watch yourself now."

Will ran, his body a confusion of sweat and smoke and speed against the slow, muddled summer-morning heat and sudden, incredibly parching thirst that made it difficult to breathe. He ran like a setter on the scent, one thing on his mind, his legs blurring like water beneath him.

He tracked the runner to the edge of a tobacco field where it abutted the low muddy creek lined in thick trees and poison ivy. He stopped to listen for movement. Birds twittered loudly all around him in the trees, flew crisp against the white morning heat. He thought he heard a crash way out, maybe fifty yards up, into the field.

He began to run again, hearing only his steps thudding through his heavy body, in the direction of the noise, weaving around the large, heady tobacco plants, thick and green with summer and Jurassic-looking. He could hear tires popping the gravel, see a dull white cloud lift above the field like a floating spirit, and then felt through the ground an impact followed by a splash. The runner must have seen the cloud or heard the truck and changed his direction, deciding to brave the summer creek with its swollen oaks tall and sturdy at the cutbanks sprawling with invisible copperheads like roots.

Will followed, calling out, "Stop! Euphoria County Sheriff's Department!"

He came to the bank, and to his surprise, the runner turned to face him from the other side, dripping, no longer trying to hide, a man who looked aged and familiar, with a gray head and a power-ful farm-strong build.

"Will!" the man whispered loudly over the water and the birds.

"Mr. Hathom!"

Will had known Zeke Hathom for years; Floressa, Zeke's wife, had worked many years for the Seems family, and Will and Sam, their son, had grown up together.

"I didn't do nothing," Zeke hissed. "I swear."

"Better for you to come on in. If you're innocent, you'll be released."

"I come in, I'm guilty. Now come on, Will."

Will was about to say something. He trusted Zeke was innocent and knew he owed the man.

"Deputy," Sheriff Mills called out, stepping like the shadow of a ghost into the shade and removing his hat and sunglasses, run-ning his fingers through his short sweaty hair. "Arrest that man."

Will could see the fight go out of Zeke's eyes, cursed himself for hesitating to let him go.

"Please, Mr. Sheriff," Zeke said. "I swear. I saw the fire from my place. Saw it and came to help."

"Deputy."

"He didn't do anything," Will said.

"Read Zeke his rights."

Looking at the creek water, Will said, "Zeke Hathom," the first time he had ever called the man by his first name. "You have the right to remain silent. Anything you say can and will be used

7

against you. You have the right to an attorney . . . ," and on and on. Words that meant nothing to him right now. He couldn't believe he'd come back in part to help the man he was now arresting. He thought of Floressa, a mother to him after his own had passed, and knew this was a mistake he'd have to reckon with.

"Cuff him," Mills said, taking his handcuffs out and tossing them to Will.

"Mr. Hathom isn't running from us."

"Damn right," Mills said, swatting at something. "He knows better, don't you, Zeke? Come on over here. Don't make this worse on yourself."

Zeke crossed the water as if being baptized and held out his hands, together, gently, with a look in his eyes Will couldn't stomach, and, as if physically compelled by a force like water or gravity or heritage, Will clicked the cuffs shut just as gently, helping Zeke up the cutbank and into the field under the hottest of fires, even more puzzled and light-headed when Zeke whispered, tears in his voice, "I'm sorry, Will."

WILL STRUNG UP yellow caution tape to secure the scene, a desolate ruin gutted by fire and still steam-smoking, and Sheriff Mills deputized his gap-toothed cousin Buddy Monroe and another regular, Silas King, as he did when they needed more men. He muttered something about harm coming to that coward Seth Grady for quitting him. It was well known Will had been hired to replace Grady, who'd been a sheriff's deputy since Will could remember.

Within an hour, Sheriff Weenie Edgars drove up in a black Suburban with a couple of investigators from Tupelo County. Troy St. Pierre followed in the old white minivan he used to transport bodies. Since there were limited personnel in Euphoria, it was not uncommon for Edgars to assist in murder investigations.

"Hot damn," Edgars said. "Howdy, Jeff."

"Weenie," Mills said. The two sheriffs shook hands. "How're y'all?"

The other men nodded and put on gloves and eyed the atmosphere with disapproval, as if crossing the county line had left a bad taste in their mouths. Their posture made clear this was an inconvenience.

Sheriff Edgars was a short man with a barrel chest he thrust around like something he was proud of. He took in the scene, and Will realized this was his cue to exit, so he went to get the sheriff's camera, avoiding any conversation with Zeke in the back, then grabbing the film camera from his own truck.

Edgars said to Mills, "Talk to me."

"Well, we got a suspect. Caught him fleeing the scene. Got a body, stabbed in the back, under the left shoulder blade. No weapon, no ID on him, but we know he's Tom Janders."

"The football player?"

"Yessir."

"Goddamn." Weenie whistled through his teeth as if the recognition of the victim made the crime worse. "Homicide *and* arson. Hell of a time for this, ain't it, Jeff? I must've seen five signs with your name on 'em."

"Ain't no competition. But I want this to go smooth as can."

Sheriff Edgars smirked, hands in his pockets, toeing at nothing on the ground.

"I'll bet you do," he said. "But you and I both know that would mean calling State. You're understaffed and underfunded. Nothing but a green deputy sheriff and two part-times." He craned his head toward Mills, as if he dreaded the answer to his next question. "Call 'em yet?"

"I called you."

"How'd I become so goddamn lucky?" Edgars said. "Turn it over to State, and it's out of your hands."

"I don't like that. I want to handle as much of this as we can as soon as we can. I want Troy doing the autopsy, and I want to know whatever he finds out before sending away evidence. You hear that, Troy?"

"Yessir."

"Good," Mills said, winking. "Maybe you can use some of those connections in the state lab you're always bragging about to expedite our samples."

He turned again to Edgars. "You know about Sheriff Ramsey over in Mecklenburg. Busted up a drug ring almost a year ago. Them folks is sittin' in the courthouse jail yet, waiting on their lab results just so they can go to trial. That's how it goes when you call in State. I don't like the way they look down on us, those goddamn eggheads in the state lab."

Edgars raised his hand to placate Mills (he'd heard all this before) and said, "Where's the suspect?"

"He's sitting yonder in the back of my truck. Wet from the waist down, I might add."

Edgars squinted in that direction. "Who is he?"

"Fella by the name of Zeke Hathom."

"Hathom. Was he the one you called me about before? Wanted for B and E?"

"That was his son. Whole goddamn family of criminals."

"I reckon so. But it's no surprise, is it? What ever happened to that boy?"

"Nobody's found him yet. He's either holed up somewhere or he left the county."

"I'll bet that galls you. Well, anyway, you got one."

"I'm a little uncomfortable about it, though. Zeke is well liked. A churchgoer, works out at the sawmill. No record but a gambling here and there. Drunk in public when he was younger."

"Well. People ain't always what they seem; maybe he's just been lucky and it's catching up with him now. Luck can have its price."

They stood for a moment without a word, as if such a statement voiced an untidy profundity they needed to digest.

Edgars broke the silence: "Show us the body."

They walked over the tape toward where Tom Janders lay in the yard. Troy said, "Jesus Christ," at the missing eyes, put on a pair of glasses and gloves, took his bearings, looked at the gashes on his back.

"Your deputy moved him?"

"Yeah."

"Well, I guess it was either that or nothing at all."

Edgars got the EMTs to help bag the body, and Edgars and Troy walked with Mills to his truck to get custody of the body signed over to Troy.

Edgars said, "You said the victim didn't have no ID. You got anybody that could identify him?"

Just then, a green '93 Honda Accord, with its passenger side cratered in and the front bumper partly held in place by fraying duct tape, pulled up in a back-eddy of dust, and Ferriday Pace got out, the dust from her approach like a cloud mixing with the sour steam of the rubble.

"My house!" she yelled. "My house!"

She got past Will quickly, dodging the bystanders—Sheriff Edgars's men—like a running back. She was screaming, grief trailing her like blood or death itself. "Oh my god!" She broke down, sobbing.

Sheriff Mills made it to her and, as she attempted to dodge him, caught her with an athleticism defying his age, holding her in an embrace she fought, so that for several moments they appeared to be dancing in a stupefied sleep until she simply surrendered and cried in his arms. He could feel the tears through his undershirt, smelled the spray and sweat in her hair before she turned her face to him.

"Where is he?" she said. "Where is Tom?"

Mills looked into her face and moved his hands across her back. She tried to break free again, but he held her, talked to her as he might have a horse or a dog or a baby, in soothing, flowing whispers no one but she could hear. He stopped his gum chewing until she seemed to calm a little. Will watched, aimed, heard the shutter close before he knew he'd even aimed. Almost before he could think, he had taken several pictures. He'd previously thought Mills a good ol' boy who didn't think anything beyond the job. Here he was, calming a woman who was about to discover she had lost the father of her child.

"I've got you," Mills said, quietly, as if nobody was here but Day, who could have been his daughter or even granddaughter, and himself. She nodded, looking up into his square, timeless face, a terse fitness in the cheeks under his prominent cheekbones, tan under bright close-cropped silver hair, like a kid watching something for the first time. "Stay with me. There, there," he said. "We're taking care of everything. Everything's going to be all right. Everything is going to be all right."

She seemed to be in a kind of trance. Mills walked her away from the yard, where Tom's body lay. Soon enough she'd have to ID him.

"But Tom."

"Miss, he's not with us anymore. I'm sorry."

13

She collapsed in Sheriff Mills's arms. He nodded to one of the EMTs, who came over to make sure she was all right, but she gathered herself after only a moment.

Sheriff Mills said, "Where were you coming from now, Miss Pace?"

Will was listening as he walked over to the Accord and shut off the ignition. He looked into the back seat at a baby staring at him. Tom's baby, Destinee, her face like clotted cream. She cried the minute she saw his face.

"I was out," Day said. "I got a carful of groceries as I was coming back in town."

"When did you leave town?"

"Yesterday afternoon."

The baby wailed, a gummy, squawking, shouting cry.

Miss Pace went over and picked up the little girl, bouncing her up and down, the baby staring back and forth between the men.

"Come on to the station," Sheriff Mills said. "We'll make sure you've got everything you need, a place to stay, all that." Tipping his hat, he said, "I'm very sorry for your loss."

Mills walked to Will, and Day watched after him in a waifish daze. Under his breath, the sheriff said, "Thank god this didn't happen in town, where we'd be dealing with a crowd. I'll finish up here and take Zeke over to the magistrate and all that."

"You need my help?"

"You just finish taking pictures, and get on home and clean up and meet me at the office at ten. I want you with me when I talk to Zeke."

"Yessir."

"I'll keep Buddy and Silas out here. Good work."

Will moved around the still-hot, smoking ruins of the pitiful house as best he could, taking pictures of different angles, creating a POV film, which the sheriff liked for him to do. But he didn't think his efforts now would do any good. Fire was a criminal's best friend. He thought about Zeke. He'd arrested Mr. Hathom, goddamnit. That seemed like ages ago.

As Will was leaving, Silas gave him a nod, thumbs in his belt. "Way to go, bud." Will must have looked confused, because Silas had to explain: "Going in there and getting about the only evidence I imagine there'll be."

Buddy said, "Guaranteed it was over some money or some shit. These people always fightin' over money and drugs."

Will nodded, climbed into his truck, and leaned his head back and closed his eyes, almost falling asleep or disappearing. "Fuck," he sighed.

He took the back way onto the property, passing the abused cabins and trailers of his Black cousins, scattered near the plantation as if held to it by some kind of orbit or magnetism, temporal as well as spatial. He lurched through fields planted with tobacco and soybeans and surveilled by vacant plywood towers against the tall pines and parked behind the house, which could barely be seen from the road in summer for the trees, and in winter was a stark silhouette on a slight rise in the land. The yard had been overgrown for so long it looked like a wild tangled glade, hiding the sign with the year of its reconstruction—1819—and the name of the house—Promised Land Plantation—along with the "For Sale by Owner" sign that had been stuck in the ground by the road for over a decade now. The trees hovered close to the structure like old men, leaning with their age. The building was the single thing that seemed to emit a sense of pride in something long ignored or forgotten. Snakes often writhed into the house, sleek trespassers making full use of the broken foundation, leaving their long skins indoors in a tortured coiled loneliness, and sleeping in the cursive, illegible shapes of a maniac's writing, and he had to check for them under his bed every night. It was a house like a shipwreck. One window remained unboarded, simply because whoever had boarded it all up had not purchased enough plywood. That project, like the house, abandoned.

He slid out of his truck and shut the door, feeling old and raw and heavy and needing a shower. Kudzu cloaked some of the distance with a fecund verdant monotony, softening the often hard and spiky landscape like a kind of flesh over bones.

He took his boots off outside and beat them against each other, leaving them by the door. Socks flapping at his toes, he opened the back-porch door—an addition from the '50s where a game freezer like a rusted coffin buzzed—and made coffee. While it was brewing, he peeled off his ruined clothes and took a shower and shaved.

He dressed in his uniform with a mug filled and steaming on the counter and sat, hands paused over the top button of his starched, untucked shirt, looking at the sun hard already over the gray tired earth. He'd been counting on making a run to Richmond today, but with the investigation he doubted that would be possible. Sam would have to deal with it. This was going to throw everything off.

He'd been listening as much as possible to Edgars and Mills, heard Mills's comment about the Hathoms, about Sam hiding out somewhere or having left the county with a warrant out for his arrest. Will thought now about the night last month he responded to a break-in, caught the man, awkward and on the run with a backpack full and loud with monogrammed sterling silverware. Will had left his truck and tackled the man, who sucker-punched Will before the cuffs were on, then cursed and cried, then pleaded with Will by name. Will stood up, wondering how this man knew him, wiped off his grass-stained uniform, shoved the man into the back of the car, got in the driver's seat, turned on the interior lights, and looked in the rearview. In the light, Will barely recognized him. It was a shadow of Sam, but it was Sam sure enough. He'd heard things— the rehab, the warrants—but how could someone he'd known so well physically change so much? He knew about Sam's previous injuries, but this was different, and he had to remind himself he'd been gone for ten years. Sam was gaunt now, his face all scratched up, scarred, and bleeding, something Will would later understand could be an effect of cutting heroin with fentanyl.

"What the fuck are you doing?" Will said.

"Stealing spoons."

"You know you got a warrant out?"

"So either way I'm fucked. May as well keep doing what I'm doing till I get caught."

"Well, you're caught now."

"Fuck you."

"They said you were doing all right. I thought you were in rehab."

"I was sober for eighty-nine days, man."

"What happened?"

"You wouldn't understand. You're just like every other mother-fucker who wants to tell me what to do. I'll bet it's easy, you sitting there, to tell me how to live my life. Fuck you."

"How can you say that to me?"

"You left."

"You know I didn't have a fucking choice."

"Go on. Take me in. See if I give a fuck."

Just then, Tania came through on the radio.

"Will, talk to me. What's your status?"

Will pulled the radio toward his face, looked again into the rearview, whispered "motherfucker" upon seeing a bruise developing on his cheek, locked eyes with Sam. "Fuck," he sighed, still not pressing the send button to respond.

"Will, your status?" Tania said.

"No sign of suspect."

"Repeat?"

"No sign of suspect. I lost him."

"Copy," she said. He knew her well enough to hear the *what-the-fuck* in her voice. She'd tell the sheriff and catch hell for it. Then Will would catch hell for it. The sheriff was big on keeping headlines out of the paper unless they showed the sheriff's department favorably. And how the fuck would Will explain his eye or the grass stains on his uniform?

When Will turned around, Sam said, "Shit, brother. You're in it now."

Will glared back at Sam, opened his mouth to tell him to fuck himself, but Sam was laughing. Will couldn't keep himself from joining in.

He walked down the hallway now. The house was floored with wide boards smoothed over the past two centuries, pale where fine tapestries of rugs had once covered it. He walked past the parlor, with its moth-eaten French wallpaper from the 1830s, and climbed the stairs, entering his sister's old room and approaching a mattress on the floor next to a stack of books.

Will nudged Sam. "Yo," he said. "Coffee's up." He pulled the blanket away, shoved Sam again, and walked back downstairs to the kitchen.

He looked through the porch window out at the fields, the trees that broke them. It seemed a hell of vegetation, overgrown and yet somehow desolate, a desert of plenty. Will had taken Sam in because he wanted to believe the past did not have to control the future, and he wanted Sam to believe it too. People around here seemed to live in a cloud of defeat, self-wrought and inherited. Whites had the lost cause; Blacks had slavery. It would seem they should be pitted against each other, but they were really dug in behind the same trench, and the rest of the state, the rest of the country, was out there. Virginia was changing, leaving places like Euphoria County behind. He wondered why it is people return to the very things that guarantee them pain. Life, it seemed, might not be progressing toward an end but learning only to return to something again and again.

Will could hear the jingle of a belt, and Sam came down the hallway, scratching the back of his head, shivering, approaching through a golden dust floating in sunrays. Despite his pale left eye, his frantic blinking, the crooked nose and jaw, and the fact that he favored his left leg, he looked healthier now than what he'd been a month ago. Still too thin, awkward, and scarred, but the outside work had done him some good.

Sam nodded at Will's arm. "What happened to you?"

"Nothing," Will said, waving his hand. "How'd you sleep?"

"All right. You out all night?"

"Yeah," Will said. He didn't know if he should say more. He poured Sam a mug and handed it to him. "I'm going to need you to weed as much as you can in the watermelon patch. Careful with the vines. And the black-eyed peas can be picked. Prune and tie up some of the tomato plants. The graveyard looks good. Tobacco looks good."

"You said you was going to Richmond today."

"As soon as I can."

"You said today. Unless you got something I don't know about."

"All I got is some weed right now, but you can help yourself."

"I'm not talking about no weed."

"I'm going to go as soon as I can. Something has come up."

"You promised." Sam was close to tears.

"Sam, Tom Janders is dead."

"Dead?" Sam stepped back, instinctively raising his hands to scratch his face.

"He died this morning."

"How? I got to go . . ."

"You can't be going out there for any reason. Tom's dead. There's nothing you can do about it."

"But what about his mama? What about Day?"

"I'll look in on them. But if anybody finds out you're here, you and I are both in deep shit. Take care of the garden today. I'll see if I can slip away. But in a murder investigation . . ."

"Murder? Murder? Who the fuck gonna kill Tom?"

Will couldn't believe he'd let that slip. He was tired, sloppy. But he would not risk telling Sam his father was their primary suspect. If he did, Sam would leave without a thought. If he didn't get caught, he might well overdose (he was lucky enough to be alive as it was). It was best he didn't know. Will was able to tell a truth without saying anything about Zeke's arrest: "I don't know. Promise me . . . promise you'll stay here as we agreed. Just until we can figure all this out."

"You still got my cell?"

"That's a part of our deal. You can't go calling people up right now. Calls can be traced."

"Fuck, man. Where's that weed at?"

So Will left for the courthouse. He remembered Tom emerging from out of the tobacco, out of the past thirteen years, carrying Sam. It was Will's fault, and he closed his eyes, then as well as now, against this world of broken sins.

FLORESSA HATHOM came to the courthouse in Dawn in time to see Sheriff Mills bring her husband in front of the magistrate, Judge Allen, a sleepy man with a red nose, white hair, and a face like a closed drawstring bag. The purse draped over her shoulder looked tiny against her as she stood in Sunday clothes, her hair straightened, eyes red and worn out. Will Seems came in a few minutes late, and sheriff and deputy gave an account of that morning's events—Will Seems finding Tom Janders's body, calling it in, spotting Zeke fleeing the scene, and the pursuit and subsequent arrest—and the judge issued a warrant to hold Zeke in custody in the Euphoria County jail, without bond, at least until the arraignment on Friday, day after tomorrow. None of them—not the judge, not Zeke, not the sheriff, not Will—acknowledged Floressa's presence. It seemed to her they were all ashamed.

She dabbed her eyes with a handkerchief outside the courtroom as they took Zeke away. A few minutes later, she pushed through the doors of the sheriff's department.

"I want to talk to Zeke," she said.

Before Tania could say anything, Sheriff Mills came out of his office.

"Mrs. Hathom," he said.

"Take me to my husband."

"We haven't had time to question him yet."

"You know they were friends. Ask anybody."

"Haven't you ever heard of friends getting into an argument?"

"This ain't that. I saw Zeke last night. He wasn't angry at Tom."

"Mrs. Hathom, we have a responsibility to look into every possible cause of Tom's death. We'll get to the bottom of this, I promise."

Floressa saw Will then. "Put a uniform on a good boy and it change him."

"No, ma'am," Mills said. "This is a good man doing his job."

"I reckon what they say true," she said. "Like father like son."

She glared at Will, her eyes seekers of weakness, seekers of softness and strength.

"Zeke innocent," she said, addressing the room. "Everybody know that man don't have a mean bone in him. Sometimes I wish he did. I got to be mean instead."

"You're going to have to let us do our jobs, Mrs. Hathom," Mills said. "Once the lab results come back, we'll let you know."

"I tell you, Mr. Mills, ain't always evidence the most important thing. There's what you can't see. There's what you believe. Your faith in the law because of the justice it represents."

"Can't operate by belief in this line of work. That may work in a nice white chapel." He held his hand up as if swearing an oath. "Now I believe in God; I was raised a God-fearing Christian. Belief has its place, but you gotta balance faith with a healthy doubt. Otherwise, you float away."

"So you doubting Zeke, a man ain't never hurt no one 'cept when drunk and attacked first."

"Anyone is capable of anything, Mrs. Hathom. Worrisome as it is to admit it."

She was going to object, but then she looked at Will.

"I guess that is true," she said. She faced the sheriff again. "When I come back later, I expect to see him."

She turned and marched out the door heavily, as if carrying a great unseen but physical burden.

"Deputy," Mills said.

Will followed Sheriff Mills back into his office and sat down and watched Ferriday Pace sitting there, pretty but disheveled, clutching the baby to her, looking out of her lightly freckled face with huge, fathomless shadow-eyes through a stray lock of strawberry-blond hair she'd teased into loose curls. She looked, in a way, like a child. Having lived away for years, Will had seen her only a couple of times and at a distance, at the supermarket or across a parking lot, but something about her was familiar to him, caught his eye. He'd met Tom two, three weeks ago and been struck hard with a sadness he expected was due to something at home. Maybe it was just the area: Euphoria County seemed for most of its residents to tighten like a vise, and you were either crushed or pushed out under the pressure and set out for life somewhere else. Back in high school, Tom was going places. Now, with some puzzlement, Will wondered how he had settled for the woman in front of him, noticing all the while an intense and luckless sorrow similar to Tom's. She was twenty-eight, younger than Tom by three years, but something about her emitted age and hardship. She had a bruise on her cheek that had been covered with makeup. There was a quality of dressed-up shame about her. She put herself together like a little girl who can make cheap clashing materials shine by sheer willpower. Her fingernails had been painted a glittering purple at the Vietnamese salon where she worked, her V-neck shirt hung low, and her jean shorts were cut so short the front pockets poked out from under the frayed edge, revealing her lightly tanned but pale freckled skin. Her forearm and ankle displayed tattoos, already greened with age.

Sheriff Mills began, "We just want to ask you some questions. We are not interrogating you. You understand you have the right to speak with an attorney if you so wish?"

"I'm a mama now. I ain't got nothing to hide."

The absurdity of her statement caused Mills to pause his gum-chewing for a moment. She spoke like a country girl, neither white nor Black but raceless, and had a kind of self-consciousness Will had rarely seen but took as a sign that she had experienced a great deal.

Sheriff Mills said, "When was the last time you saw Tom?"

"Yesterday morning."

"Tuesday, July nineteenth," he said, jotting it down. "And where were you last night?"

"I was out of town," she said with an upturned intonation, seeming shy or embarrassed, making that statement into something resembling a question, as if awaiting approval. It seemed she was about to cry again. She covered her face and wiped it with her hands. Sheriff Mills adjusted himself.

"Where? Why? Help us fill in some blanks."

"I don't want to say," she said.

"It'd look better if you did. Your beau was murdered."

She stopped bouncing the baby, closed her eyes as if in prayer. "I thought it was a fire."

"We found some evidence that suggests otherwise. Please. Tell us what you know, who might have done this, where you were, so that we can help you."

She sighed, looked at Mills, and patted the baby on her back, readjusting a cloth on her own shoulder. From out of her purse, one-handed, she brought her wallet and produced a folded paper and handed it to Will as if passing a note in class, all the while watching the sheriff.

"Well?" Sheriff Mills said.

"A receipt for a motel," Will said. "The Rebel Inn."

"What were you doing there?"

"I went back home to see my people."

"What people?" Mills said.

"Out there to Sassafras Ridge. Granny, I call her. She's not blood, but I call her Granny."

Mills seemed to smile to himself. "You mean that old palm reader in the Snakefoot?"

"That's why I don't want to say," she said. "You just gonna laugh."

"What'd you see her about?"

"I visit her sometimes."

"Why stay the night out that way? Shoot, can't take you an hour to get back."

"I got tired. The baby was needing to feed. I can park at a motel if I want to."

"Were you and Tom having problems?"

"No, sir. I just got tired is all."

"Did you let Tom know at any point that you were going to be away?"

"I sent him a message, I think. I can't remember. The baby was crying, and I had to feed her and put her down. I knew he'd be playing cards out at Arnie's Lounge, losing all his money, not that it matters now."

The baby was crying now and piped up shrill. Day then looked up at the sheriff as if she were asking something only he could understand.

"Excuse me, sirs. She could use some feeding now," she said, two tear streaks on her face and a tremor in her voice.

She reached up to adjust her bra, and the men stood gravely in unison, walked to the door.

Mills said, "We'll just be outside."

At the threshold, Will turned back. She was already watching him.

"Did you go home at all between the time you left and when we saw you this morning?"

"No, sir. I was gone all night, until I came back to the house and found y'all there, my house all aflame"—her voice began to shake—"my man dead and gone."

"Deputy," Mills said, and they shut the door and walked out to Will's desk in the main office, over by the old radiator against the windows, the shades closed. Will moved a stack of files aside. Tania went about her work across the room.

They paused awkwardly, as if holding their breath.

Will said, "You know Zeke didn't do it."

"No, I don't."

"I know the man."

"That's not good enough. We have to wait for the results. You know that."

"I know it looks bad for him. But there's got to be more to the story."

"You can't assume that. You been sheriff's deputy over a year. You know better than to cloud the facts with bias."

"Yessir, I know."

"What were you doing out there anyway, calling in a fire out in goddamn Turkey Creek?"

"I was just out; fell asleep out there."

Sheriff Mills chuckled to himself, shaking his head. "You're living hard, it seems. Guilty conscience? Bad dreams?"

"There a law against insomnia?"

"You keep in mind that someone less considerate would make a point of finding out how come you were out there, on that side of town, why you've been looking through all these criminal files, like you're trying to memorize something. Oh yeah, don't think I don't notice."

He stared at Will. The wet sound of his chewing and breathing and thinking. It seemed he wanted to say more but shook his head like this was a great pity and Will hadn't caught on as to why.

"You got baggage, son," the sheriff said finally. "But you handled yourself real good out there today. You may have got us the evidence we need. Call up that motel and confirm Miss Pace was there, and let me know what you find out."

Mills surveyed the room, remembering some of the changes he'd seen, his days as a deputy, the way it all used to be, back when his daddy was sheriff. Southside could be rough, and this job brought you in touch with the thresholds of good and evil. But back then, investigating led you somewhere if you put in the work.

Now, it seemed the harder you looked, the worse you got lost. He saw in Will Seems something he'd been missing in his department for years. He was an old soul, one of them. He'd do all right. If he could just pace himself, learn how to work on the team.

"That Mrs. Hathom was right about one thing," Mills said. "You're a lot like your daddy."

"He ran away," Will said. "I came back."

"Yes, you did. And I'm wondering if that's got something to do with why you can't sleep in your own house. Now hold on. I'm going to need a report on my desk first thing tomorrow morning."

Will got up. "Yessir."

"You look like you got somewhere else to be."

"I thought we were finishing up."

"Not by a long shot."

Will cleared his throat. "Sir, Silas and Buddy are out at the crime scene, and Troy has the evidence. Could I take the afternoon?"

The sheriff looked at the ground. "I'm gonna forget you asked that. We need to talk to Zeke, search the Hathom house, find anybody who saw Tom last night for questioning, you need to write that report, and right now, I need you to go over to Mrs. Claudette Janders's house and give her the news."

"Sir?"

"Rumor will be spreading fast," he said. "She has a right to learn from us about Tom's death. And see if she'd be willing to take in Miss Pace for the next little while as all this gets resolved. When you get back, we'll start in on the other stuff."

Sheriff Mills whistled something, stretched, and stood up. "Tania, darlin'. Get Will that address."

"Yes, sir," she said. Mills turned for his office, knocked, went in.

"Congratulations," Tania said as Will approached her desk. "For getting Tom out I mean."

"I wish I hadn't been there."

"I know," she said, a look of pity on her face. "You just got to remember, you didn't put Zeke there. You did what you had to do."

She looked up from her desk, and it hit him, as it sometimes did, and he looked away. Tania had grown up in the county one year behind Will. She'd gone to community college and student-taught before attending the academy but was still, after a couple of years working for the sheriff's department, working dispatch, organizing files, even getting lunches. Will felt some guilt about having been hired after Mr. Grady had quit, when the obvious decision would have been to put Tania in the field.

She cleared her voice. "You ready? Need a pen and paper?"

"You can tell me," Will said.

"Fifty-two Walker Court Road," she said.

"Fifty-two Walker Court Road."

Will stepped out, glad to be away from the office. He put on his hat and looked out over the town. He could see the back of the statue commemorating Confederate veterans—stalwart and dark as a shadow under the shade of two magnolia trees in front of the white-columned courthouse of Dawn, Virginia—and out into the baking sun and the pale cracked sidewalks. There was barely anyone on the road, even approaching the lunch hour. Fifty-two Walker Court Road. He began walking toward it, thinking the exercise would do him good, but was sweating through his undershirt by the time he reached the road adjacent. It was met by two streets on either end of the lawn and paralleled by another, forming an absurdly grand yet brief town square, vacant except for the starved library (open but always empty), the pharmacy, and Antoinette's Restaurant. This was the town he'd held in his dreams those years he'd been in exile. All this had shaped his understanding of the world. It all started here, and coming back had been like digging out the dirt pinning a coffin in the ground. He remembered growing up here with a vividness he didn't even have for this morning. He remembered going into town and seeing it because there was nothing to do, driving the farm-use pickup too young and getting groceries at the Texaco or Gulf and nobody caring, the slackness of time he used to feel as a kid, the bright white innocent wasting of it, as if it would always be there like a great comfort, the way you take for granted mountains or land of any kind, the feeling that the world somehow made sense if you just let it spin. He used to lie in his bed in Richmond, close his eyes, and see it: home—the living piedmont swamps and the ugly scalps of new pine growth after brushfires and logging; the sounds of wild quail warbling at the edges of fields in the exploding thickets; the vague impressions of life on a series of roads all looking the same; the austere plantation silhouettes alone in their worlds of flowing red horizons, tobacco barns, and smokehouses; that heavy resinous fragrance of tobacco, like sweet, profound raisins; the cotton in the flats to the east poking out like warm soft stars. He'd attempted to bring back a past innocent and familiar but found himself a stranger to the present, ever guilty. Had leaving Richmond been a mistake? Had he been running away, lying to himself and his father when he claimed he'd come back to make things right, to face things instead? Euphoria County seemed at times to be a tangent, like an unmaintained road going nowhere. Many of the neglected houses were inhabited by vagrants and users, those who lived tobacco's tragic legacy, and the shops on the square had mostly given way to a similar vacancy. And so the place that had for so long haunted him now appeared itself to be haunted. And here he was again, riding tall pine-lined two-lanes through the boonies, cresting into hamlets like mistakes, listening to that angry word of God since there was nothing else.

He walked on. A Ford rumbled past—a truck he'd probably seen before but didn't recognize now that he was half foreigner—a long antenna wagging like a fishing pole from the top of the cab, arms hanging out of the driver's window and the passenger's, one Black and one white. Two hounds roamed the bed, sniffing the air and sliding when the truck sped or slowed. A solitary finger raised up from a tired arm slumped over the wheel, as if triggered by an uncomfortable reflex, as the truck passed through the stop sign, and Will waved back, smelling the ragged smoke floating out of a cigarette rolled with flue-cured tobacco.

He trudged on to Walker Court Road and realized he had not thought anything about how to deliver his message. This was a first for him. This whole day had been a day of firsts.

He passed old houses with little yards. One cluttered home rotting and virtually paintless, trash bags over windows, had two sedans parked on the lawn, one jacked up, both adorned with custom paint jobs and immaculate chrome rims. Nearing the little yellow house where Tom Janders had moved his mother a couple of years ago, he could see people gathered there on the porch. The street ended in a sandy track, and it was backed by the tall old woods that had not been developed yet and probably never would be since over the years anyone who could find a life elsewhere left. Will took a deep breath. He paused, uncertain he should continue, but he reasoned that he owed it to Tom and pressed on. But instead of the prayer he'd been trying to work toward, he heard a deep, hoarse voice from that strange and awful realm: "You don't belong here."

THE SKY HAD BEGUN to fill in with a relief of clouds, and a little wind started up. Their faces turned, and Will could see they already knew. He was merely to be the voice, the face to associate with the news. Their eyes were hard, with generations of anger welling in them. They opened out like dark water, and he could see her there at the end of this procession, a woman crowned by grief. He hoped for some tenderness and welcome but saw that she was not going to supply it.

"Young Seems," Claudette Janders said.

All the folks in town, white or Black, called him "son" or "young man," treating him as if he had returned the same age he had left, as if, stunted in his exile, he had to somehow catch up or fall behind. What did it take to earn respect, to be a man in one's home, where other men's tall legacies lay like vehicles discarded in a field? The white men met up for coffee and breakfast at the gas station. He could barely look at Mama Jay—mother it seemed to the entire county—who served up a simple country breakfast of scrambled eggs, greasy crispy bacon, biscuits and gravy, fried apples, grits, and fried fruit pies. She sold road maps and gas station T-shirts customized on Hanes blanks, reading "Mama Jay's Get 'N' Go," along with a variety of spicy pork rinds, red pickled eggs and wienies and pigs' feet, newspapers and lock-blades, a samurai sword, made-in-China Confederate flags. These men who had stayed in town on family tobacco money or quiet law practices met in the morning, former high school jocks wearing loafers, khakis, and polo shirts, sunglasses hanging from straps around their necks. They fished and hunted deer and turkey and what quail there still were and mounted what they killed in their houses and offices, had put on a comfortable weight since high school after marrying their ornamental prom dates—who'd remained beautiful and aged easily and gracefully, as sedentary as catfish, as trees—and Sheriff Mills somehow was one of them, though he stood apart as a celibate, monk-like figure, married, it seemed, only to the law. Will Seems had known all along he couldn't be a part of their fellowship, which required both feet to be firmly set in this world of Euphoria County, of Southside, Virginia. Anyone with outside perspective was suspicious, and he'd been gone ten years. These were the men he used to see at the old deer camp, the men and their sons filling the bunks in the old cinderblock hut, men who boasted of their woodsmanship and ability to kill, and then on the way home tossed empty beer cans or trash out of their pickups.

"Mrs. Janders," he said. "I have some bad news. Tom is dead."

He heard it himself, how his own grief had clipped his words into a directness that sounded tactless and harsh. He felt as if he'd jumped into a creek from a tree but had not yet hit the water.

"I'm sorry for your loss," Will said. "He was a good man."

He suddenly found himself caught by emotion, barely able to get through his own words. He stood there, wanting to say something about justice, his memories of the dead.

He held back from blinking to prevent his own tears, she and the moment blurring like water until the seconds like a collective eternity passed.

"I know," she said without judgment or attitude. No comfort or closure either.

Will wanted to say so many things about Tom, but his skin and office made it impossible. His tie tightened like a snake around a branch, and he found breathing came hard. At one point in his life, when he was young and innocent, he had believed one could explain anything, that any truth would eventually surface above all else. How many times had he heard *The truth shall set you free* and believed in its sanctuary.

"He send you out here to tell me," she said. "He send you, but he don't come himself."

"He's in the beginning of a new investigation."

"But y'all arrest Zeke Hathom. Son, don't you owe that family? Ain't that why you come back, why you lurk around?" He looked away. "But you ain't accomplished nothing. Nothing but giving me news I already know."

"The signs led to Zeke, ma'am," he said.

"What you know about signs? Let me tell you something. You can see the signs, the signs can be there, but if you don't know how to read them, ain't going to do nobody no good."

"We had to arrest him," Will said.

"You don't believe that," Claudette said. "You know he didn't stick no knife in my boy's back." So she'd heard that too.

"Mrs. Janders," he said. "I promise we're looking into this as thoroughly as we can. I promise we will—"

"Don't make no promises. Promises be the cause of lies."

The porch congregation muttered its agreement.

Will put his hat back on having nothing more he could think to say, touched the brim, and turned, but she called him out. "What gives you the right to wear that uniform? To tell me this?"

"Someone has to."

"Might as well be you. Every man who ever harmed another has said the same thing. I don't want to hear no promises from you. Ain't fair to claim the future. You wear that now. But anybody can see you are divided, and a house divided cannot stand. You white people got the luxury to do what you think is right, go home, close the door on history you celebrate and think you can live your life outside of it. You think you have the luxury to leave and return. But no one is that free. You a part of this all too." She paused. "And you know that. That's why you came back, son."

"I came to give you news of Tom. I'm sorry for your loss. Good-bye, ma'am."

"Sit down," she said. "Come on here, son. Sit."

Claudette stood up from her chair. Will didn't know what to do. He had been raised to abdicate his chair for a woman, not take one, even at her bidding. Claudette told someone to bring her a plate with all the fixins.

He could see then that some of them had brought over food, a great feast, ridiculous in that it was to console a woman who could not have consumed it in a month and whose sadness would have prevented it even if she could. His mother had been the same, her food always there, forced on him, that burden he now missed with an acute nostalgia. He could not have set out on a one-hour drive

37

without her loading him down with her sweet potato biscuits and ham, her lemon tarts, her devil's food cake. He thought of such waste, of food, of life, of love.

The paper plate sagged, translucent under the grease and weight of the food when it was brought out, and Claudette then handed it down to Will Seems, the plate laden with fried chicken, collard greens, angel food cake, deviled eggs, pulled pork, coleslaw, catfish, turnip greens, broccoli casserole, macaroni and cheese, green beans, buttermilk biscuits, preacher cookies, shaved Virginia country ham. His mouth watered, and suddenly he was incredibly hungry, like one of his famished ancestors, bootless and starving, infantrymen nameless upon the first battle they survived, for whom home had become a memory like a bayonet in the back, prodding them forward with the lofty hope of returning.

"Eat."

"I can't, ma'am."

"For Tom."

"Mrs. Janders . . ."

"Don't disrespect a grieving woman. Don't disrespect my dead son."

The others had seemed to constrict like a python, spectators and arbiters all, and so he began, ridiculous, a spectacle, the butt of some joke. Each time he slowed or stopped, he was told, "Eat," by someone. He'd begun politely, looking around at their eyes aimed solely on him, but then knew he could never finish the meal as he'd been raised to if he took his time, so he became more ravenous and uncouth with his eating, less discreet, shoveling more food in his mouth before he had swallowed the previous bite. He wasn't sure what he felt—comfort, guilt, fear, a belonging—in this hostility as they watched with intense personal investment, about hunger themselves like fasting monks and nuns. He cried as he ate with growing momentum.

Claudette said, "You need this good food to sustain you on this path toward truth."

He was filling up rapidly. The food was delicious and rich, pared by the long-calloused expedient communal hands of Christian women with tears in their throats, but he was unable to enjoy it.

Claudette leaned toward him.

"I knew your mother. I know you know right from wrong. I know you have a good heart. I know you want to do right by us. And here's a secret: Your guilt—that thing you running from—can be your virtue. This food is more than victuals; let it sustain you spiritually. But you going to have to fight! Do not lose sight of what is at stake. This is a war. Good and evil. God and devil." She put her hand on his head, and suddenly, in a huddle, they all reached in to place theirs on him as well. "Go now. Serve the Lord, who has brought you back to seek the justice you represent. Use your office for good to thwart your enemies and the enemies of the Lord."

They began to hum and buzz and sing a strange hymn, impromptu and imperfect and holy.

Afterward, Claudette said, "Where they going to stay?"

He'd forgotten he was supposed to ask.

"You tell them to come on over here to stay with me," she said. "I need them. I need my people. We got to stick together."

"Yes, ma'am," Will said, standing awkwardly. He turned and walked away, down the street, past the neighbors in their yards or on their porches who watched him as if he had committed the crime.

He walked on in some kind of trance, the food heavy in him as if he'd been filled with lead, with a great thirst, tired, stains on his khaki uniform, a strange shame crawling through him until he realized he was filled more than anything with a hate, a hate for what, but now, he could not say.

T HE MOMENT WILL RETURNED to the courthouse Sheriff Mills hollered out, "What took so long? We got things to do!"

Will used the sink to dab a stain on his shirt and run a wet comb through his hair, and then they walked down the hall to the interrogation room. He stood back and watched Mills pull up a chair across from Zeke under the room's bald bright single light. Mills took out a stick of gum, unwrapped it, added it to the piece he'd already been chewing, then offered one to Zeke, who sat, staring straight ahead without emotion, something he'd no doubt learned during Jim Crow that you didn't see in younger generations.

"What say, bud?" Mills said.

"Nothing, Mr. Sheriff."

"Listen. We've got a few questions for you."

"I need an attorney."

"Well, now, sure. But we're trying to help you. See, you talk to us before lab results come in, that'll mean a lot to the judge. So, bear with us a minute. Why were you there at Tom's house?"

"Tom's my neighbor."

"Doesn't answer my question."

"I got up early, saw the smoke, knew it wasn't a brushfire. I started walking that direction—you know, to get a better view—and before I knew it, I was running. I knew it was something awful."

"How could you tell all that?"

"Saw smoke coming from that direction getting thicker and blacker, like it was burning up a whole lot of stuff in one place. Brushfire covers a lot of ground."

Will said, "He's right about that. I saw it, too, and knew something was wrong."

Mills stared at Will without response. Then he continued talking to Zeke.

"Can anyone prove you were home when the fire started?"

"My wife."

"Where was she? Did she see the fire?"

"She in the bed."

"See, that doesn't help you."

Sheriff Mills finished writing something in his notebook, then leaned over his elbows to look closer into Zeke's face. Under the glare of the naked light bulb, his face looked eyeless.

"So, then what?"

"I got there, and smoke was coming out the side of the house, and I seen Tom's truck. I didn't know what to do, but I was worried someone might be inside. So I pushed open the kitchen door—way I've always gone in—saw . . ." He paused here, his lips trembling. "Saw Tom dead on the floor."

Sheriff Mills considered this.

"So you ran a quarter mile to Tom's because you could tell there was a fire, found Tom's body, and then left it to burn. Is that right?"

"I need a lawyer."

Mills tapped his pen against the table thoughtfully. "Zeke? Why didn't you call us?"

"I was scared. But Mr. Mills, Tom was my friend. I had no reason to do something bad to him."

Sheriff Mills looked over to Will, stood up, and said to Zeke, "You'd better be telling the truth, old man, 'cause I don't give a hot flash how close you were to Tom. All I care about is what happened. I'll remind you we saw you running from the scene of the murder."

"But why? Why would I do that?"

"Lord knows, but we'll find out," said Mills. On his way out, he said to Will, "Take Zeke back to his cell and meet me in my office. You probably want to catch up anyhow."

He chuckled and walked out.

"Will," Zeke said when the door closed. "You believe me, don't you, Will? You're family."

"Mr. Hathom," Will said. He sighed, finally meeting the man's gaze. "I've got to know, is there anything you didn't mention just then?"

"Like what?"

"I can't help you if I don't know what happened."

"You talk like you don't know me either. God, my God. Is there anyone in this world that ain't a stranger to me?"

"Did y'all have some kind of beef?"

"You've known me your whole life. Have I ever given you a reason to think I'd kill a man? Floressa been like a mother to you when you needed it most. My boy won't never be the same because of you. But I never held that against you."

"This has nothing to do with Sam."

"It does too. You stayed by him, went with us to the hospital; up until your daddy moved you away, when the world tried hard to tear y'all apart, you were a friend to my boy. You ain't the type to turn your back or stand there and watch. I'm asking you, don't turn away from me. What would your mama say right now?"

"Well," he said, swallowing, his throat dry and cold. "She revoked her ability to say it, didn't she?"

Zeke said, "Well, why'd you come back then? Why come back if you don't care?"

"I ask myself that question all the time," he said. "It never gets any clearer."

"That's bull. Maybe it ain't easy coming back, maybe it's complicated as hell. But you know you here for a reason."

"It may not look like it, but I am trying to help you out. Trust me."

"If I'm going to trust you, you're going to need to trust me."

Will sighed. "Okay. Why don't you tell me who was there, who saw Tom last night."

"Try Arnie's Lounge, out Possum Creek. That's where we'd been before he dropped me off at home."

"Did he take you by his house on the way? Did you see any cars at his place?"

"I didn't notice. He just took me on home."

"Did anybody follow you? Maybe someone who'd been at the Lounge?"

"What I remember, that road was just as black as hell. But there was a couple guys from Charlotte County we'd been playing with. They was mad because Tom won a lot of money. They was talking trash, but we watched 'em leave."

"You know their names?"

"No, sir," Zeke said. "But Arnie know."

Will indicated they should go.

"Will, can I ask you for a favor?"

"You can ask."

**F**LORESSA WENT TO SEE Claudette that evening, taking a pecan pie with her, still warm from the oven.

"You didn't need to bring me nothin'," Claudette said.

"I know," Floressa said. "It won't do no good."

A dark flat layer of cloud floated over a peach-colored sunset, so that, when you glanced up, it felt like you were looking down into a separate world. A slight wind blew pleasantly out of the west, a welcome change from the hard blatant heat. Claudette offered some iced tea, but Floressa insisted she'd stay only a moment. The two women sat on the porch.

"How's Day doing?" Floressa said.

"She asleep."

"She holding up okay?"

"Hard to tell. She ain't saying a whole lot."

"Lord," Floressa said. "We got to do something."

Waving a folded handkerchief around, which she would use to blow her nose and wipe her tears whenever she broke down, Claudette said, "What's there to do? Ain't nothing bringing my baby back."

She blew her nose again.

"Listen here," Floressa said. She had that gleam in her eye Claudette knew too well, knowing she couldn't resist the woman's enthusiasm, which was a force like a thunderstorm. Floressa spoke eagerly, quietly. "There's a woman, a private detective up in Richmond who got a reputation."

"What reputation?"

"For getting at the truth, no matter what. She used to work for Richmond PD, but she got fired."

"That don't sound too good."

"It was because she was gonna do anything she could to put a bad man in jail. And that's what she done."

"I don't know. Ain't nothing gonna bring my Tommy back."

"I know that. But what about justice?"

"You think Pastor Marcus might could get us some donations?" Claudette said. "Hate to ask."

"Already asked him," Floressa said. "He said to call her to arrange something, and I did. She said she can come tomorrow if you say okay."

The two women were very old friends. There was a whispering excitement, an undeniable hope now hanging over the grief like a star. It couldn't bring Tom back, but it could protect Zeke. Later, when they were alone in their separate beds, miles from each other and their husbands, this subsided back into the dark hopeless grief that had shot up like a weed with Tom's murder. *Murder*, Claudette thought in bed, a vile word that made her weep for all the mothers who'd lost children to it, thinking of all the people guilty who were not caught, thinking of how easy it was to destroy yet difficult to make something grow. Justice could not replace the dead. That was something people didn't seem to understand: Justice now did not make up for past wrongs.

"Okay," Claudette said. "Okay."

"Good. I'll call her tonight. If she anything like the way she sounds on the phone, she's the real deal."

**B**ENNICO WATTS tossed and turned most of the night. She saw the dark shape of her husband cowled in the thin sheet like a stiff and crawled out of bed and went downstairs to the kitchen in her bathrobe to make coffee. She hadn't been sleeping well anyway, and the call she'd received last night had not helped.

Custis seemed always to be able to sleep hard and without difficulty. The week their girls had gone back to boarding school after their spring break, he had approached his wife of seventeen years and asked for a divorce, papers and all. Another failure. He was in the prime of his career, and she had lost hers. *Never marry an attorney,* she said to herself. She began to go down that old road to self-pity, wondering why no one had ever warned her, but she caught herself. She didn't appreciate people who wanted or claimed to want the ability to do things in life yet never seemed to step out of their crippling role as bystanders. She tried every day to live deliberately.

Bennico looked at the pleasantly lit kitchen—recently remodeled—and it seemed so silly, all the things that were significant only if the marriage worked. The way he'd pay for anything just to appease her, get her off his back. Who really gave a shit about granite countertops, stainless refrigerators, and tile backsplashes

49

when somewhere in the city someone was stalking some poor young girl, where a father or uncle was undressing a daughter or niece, where a crew of young men was planning a drive-by, where someone was overdosing?

She slid open the door to the back deck and stood at the wooden railing, looking into the thick green forest behind their property. She saw a deer and spoke aloud to it, and the bright beautiful red doe looked up, made what seemed to be eye contact, then bounded like a spirit over the fence and down toward the creek.

At first, she had wanted to fight the divorce, tooth and nail, but after the surge of anger and betrayal, she couldn't help but think, *Of course. It had to be this way.* Anyway, what did she want with a fair-weather husband? All those poor women out there, all those victims, who suffered because of sons of bitches who followed their fickle testicles, who lay with you when convenient, then stood up and left you those tainted years of illusion to hate, those years of your life to wish back, to wish away. She was suspicious, afraid that, in some subconscious and primal way, he wanted to leave her because he was white and she was Black. That's really what pissed her off as she broke apart her Glock 26 on a dish towel, reassembled it in a matter of seconds. It was the wasted time and the energy you'd spent and lost completely now that it was over. The time that, by a simple decision by the goddamn quitter to stick and be a man, could have been all worth the effort and struggle. *Well, fuck him,* she thought, reloading the clip and racking the pistol. *He won't get any more of my fucking time.* She would not pretend it would be easy, that it ever had been, but she believed in moving on when things didn't capitulate to you. Control only what you could control. It had always frustrated her, living in the South, the way people seemed not to care about efficiency. They preferred to be dazed, for the days to pass them by, to be victims. That had changed some in Richmond, which in recent years had been dubbed Happiest City in America and the Next Nashville and a little version of Austin, and now you saw everywhere RVA stickers on cars, advertising a sense of new pride in being recognized for something other than the Confederacy, and outsiders, Yankees, had given the town a shot to the arm. The reality was, they were changing the city as Richmonders sat on their verandas and watched with their empty mouths open.

After being fired from the Richmond Police Department's Major Crimes Division for conducting an illegal search, although it had led to the incarceration of a serial rapist, Bennico had seemed prone to defeat. But a woman couldn't stand idle; she had to make things happen. It made no sense to her how someone breaking the law to uphold it could be vilified more than an out-and-out criminal. Her colleagues, after she was asked to pack up her things and leave the force, turned their backs on her, as if she'd never worked there, as if all the good she'd done amounted to nothing. Such was the world of today, and it was a hard and devastating truth that circumventing bureaucracy for true justice could be condemned by those employed to uphold it.

In a way, she was relieved to be out of that job. Working for the city was a paradox: You tried to solve cases, but often protocol meant to protect everyone got in the way. It was worse now. Everyone had cameras, and police behavior could be recorded and manipulated and shown in segments lacking context. She was working for herself now, able to pick and choose cases. But it was mostly dull work, much of it dealing with infidelity, which she felt incapable of approaching without bias. So when she received a call last night from Floressa Hathom, regarding a murder and a local sheriff's department that seemed to be uninterested in finding the perpetrator, Bennico's heart began to beat with a hope she hadn't felt in some time. It was the real thing again, an investigation that mattered, and no chief to report to.

Sneaking into the bedroom, she gathered some clothes, packed her bag, and when Custis turned over the other way to cover his ears with her pillow, she slammed the drawer shut and walked downstairs, deciding not to tell him she was even leaving. She left the house and drove from the West End through the city she'd grown to love but couldn't wait to leave, and south across the river, going twenty over the speed limit, a pace she kept all the way into the coyote-colored country of Southside.

W ILL SAT at his desk, finishing his report, when Tania walked in, put her purse on her desk, and looked at him, in a T-shirt, his hair messed up, completely focused on his work.

"Morning, Will. Been here a while?"

"Couple hours," he said, in a manner that suggested he didn't know.

"You want me to put on some extra coffee?"

"Please. Thank you, Tania."

He sent the document to the outdated printer at a wooden desk between the coffee and a file cabinet and stretched as he waited for the feeble pulse of Wi-Fi to transmit the job and print.

"This thing seems to be on its last legs," Will said.

"Printer or coffee machine?"

He laughed.

Tania said, "Well, I've already brought it up twice, but you know he's not going to get another one until it stops working just when you need it most."

Will grabbed his report from the printer and went back to his desk, made some marks on the draft, applied some changes on his laptop, and sent it to the printer again. He poured some coffee and read it again, said to no one in particular, "Well, it doesn't have to be *Huckleberry Finn*."

Tania gave him a manila folder and a paper clip. "Want me to give it to him?"

"I'll do it. I need to talk to him anyway."

He was putting on his uniform shirt when Mills came in a little before eight.

"Is that your report?"

"Yessir."

"You look a little better than usual this morning. More civilized."

Sheriff Mills took the report and sat down.

Will said, "Sir, I've been thinking about the issue of a motive. For all I can figure, Zeke had no reason to kill Tom."

"Motive or not, Sheriff Edgars's team found a burnt kitchen knife, and Troy's running it to see if anything shows. We'll go from there. Sometimes you got everything but the motive, and you have to piece that part of it together."

"But we don't have everything else. Zeke was just in the wrong place at the wrong time."

"You say. Any evidence to support that?"

"No, sir. But according to Miss Pace and Zeke, Tom was at the Lounge that night. I think we should follow up on that. Talk to whoever saw him."

"Well, go ahead. I've got to be here for a little while, but if you find out anything, I'll help you follow it up. But don't be surprised if all you get out of that junkyard is blank stares and stale beer and, if you want to pursue it, possession of marijuana charges and maybe even a little gonorrhea. In short, keep your hopes low."

"Yessir."

On his way out, Will said, "Thanks, Tania. Call me if you need anything."

Sheriff Mills took out a pair of reading glasses to look over Will's report, grunting and chewing gum, marking it with a pencil. "Goddamnit," he said under his breath, taking off his glasses and pinching the bridge of his nose. His deputy couldn't seem to stick to the plain facts, and so his reports were always too long, too detailed, crowded with subjectivity and unnecessary observations. The sheriff was glad for a break when Tania transferred the call from Troy St. Pierre.

"Troy! Talk to me."

"We've got the initial results."

"Well?"

"We'll go over the autopsy report when you get here. I've sent samples off to the DFS in Richmond with a request to expedite, but you may well be waiting two to four months. Do you think Tom's mother or Miss Pace would come to ID the body?"

"I don't see how Mrs. Janders could stomach it. Then again, I'm not sure Miss Pace could either, but I'm going to bring her, as she lived with Tom and bore his child."

Mills cleaned the passenger seat before he picked up Day and made sure she could leave the baby with Miss Claudette. The young woman looked as if she'd had time to go to the salon. She wore plenty of makeup and had bright, freshly painted fingernails. Mills made clear to her what they were doing, that she would be seeing Tom's mutilated corpse, but he wasn't sure she understood. He'd seen shock cause denial before.

In Troy's office, she rocked back and forth, clutching herself, as if she had only just realized that the baby was not with her. She and the sheriff sat in two metal folding chairs while Troy, behind his metal desk, explained what he knew. Tom had died somewhere between one and five on the morning of July 20. The cause of death had indeed been the knife wounds in the back, not the fire. The investigators believed the fire had been started on purpose—an attempt to cover up the murder. Among the ruins of the house, a knife had been found, burnt but not destroyed, traces of Tom's blood on the blade. Furthermore, the only discernible fingerprints on the knife were Zeke's, but what was even more curious was that his prints also appeared on Tom's belt. Amazing how fire—usually believed to be destructive—could sometimes preserve, almost fossilize evidence. In short: They had all they needed to press charges against Zeke.

"What's that, Miss Pace?" Sheriff Mills asked.

"I said, Zeke. Zeke Hathom."

"It seems that way."

"I always took him to be a good man," Day said, hugging herself.

Troy turned to her. "Are you ready?"

She sat still, a blankness to her that caused Mills to admire her composure. He adjusted his tie, shifted his belt, looked away. The thought of her having nothing, now that Tom was gone, angered him. Let anyone in his county take advantage of a woman like that, and they would have to answer to him.

Troy escorted them down the hallway to a cold room lined with small doors stacked like bricks, as if the very foundation depended on the dead. He opened one and rolled out a body covered in a sheet and looked up at Day.

"I'm sorry about his condition," he said. "Be forewarned."

She breathed in, nodded, and he lifted the sheet and she was crying, staring down at Tom's eyeless face.

"Baby," she said. "Oh, baby."

There was something more than grief in the way she looked at Tom. She felt the deep wetness running through her, clenched her hips together, looking down at his remains, remembering that last time, knowing there would never be another. *Oh, baby.* She could feel Tom watching her now, waiting for her in that space where he existed like an echo. *This is the last time I will see Tom Janders's body.* Now, the true grief.

"We need your verbal for the record, Miss Pace," Troy said.

"Can I . . . ?" she said, touching the sheet.

She lifted back the cloth and looked at his groin, held her hands to her face. *This last time.*

"Yes," she said, covering him again. "That's him. That's Tom."

"For the record, please say his full name."

She coughed out "Tom Janders" through tears.

Mills put his hand on her back and gave Troy a look. She'd done enough.

"Miss Pace," Mills said. "Miss Pace. That's all we need. We can go now."

The wetness had grown and spread, and she felt something else, a little sickness spreading through her stomach. Suddenly she fled the cold room with the same agility Mills had seen her charge the burning house. They found her in the hallway.

"Are you all right?" asked Sheriff Mills.

She nodded, clutching herself, her face raw and red and ugly and blotched with her crying.

"I'm sorry you had to see this," said Troy. "My condolences."

Mills turned to Troy. "Is that everything?"

"Yes, sir."

"When will the body be released for burial?"

"We can begin preparations today, if that's what the family decides. We'd be happy to do it in-house. Miss Pace and the mother of the deceased can call me to make arrangements."

Troy handed her his business card and a brochure for the funeral home he owned on the other side of the building, where the facade attractively and solemnly looked over a magnolia-lined street.

She seemed to shake herself from some dreamworld reality, crossed her arms over her chest, looked up at Sheriff Mills, and began to weep again, a sadness Mills could understand: He had experienced a similar loss. He didn't make a policy of holding the sweethearts of victims, but he allowed his arms to embrace her in a fatherly manner, saying, "There, there," patting her back. Mills could feel the wet of her tears through the collar of his uniform shirt, smelled a fragrance of earthy, sleepless female grief beneath her makeup and perfume. When she seemed to be through the worst of it, he said, "Let's get on."

The road undulated and curved gracefully somehow through a graceless landscape of tired crops yellowing with drought and wide lakelike creeks and swamps with bright red banks and catfish the size of children. The car hummed, thumping over the dips and cracks in the asphalt of the highway.

Mills broke the silence: "What I don't understand is why would someone want to kill Tom. Of all people."

She looked from the flowing outer world to the sheriff, whose taut face had a rugged kindness in it, like an old house, timeless but hard marked by time.

"You can talk to me," he said. "I want you to know that."

She scanned his face as one might a field or a horizon for sign of weather. She wasn't sure.

"See," he said, somehow watching her while keeping the cruiser between the faded lines. "We need a motive to understand the crime. I wasn't aware Tom had any enemies. Thought everybody liked him. Might be you know different."

She looked away, eyes scrambling over soybean fields that had replaced tobacco, dark tall ominous trees like shadows of nothing along the hilltops along the horizon. She could not control her tears, nor could she have explained them. She clutched her stomach as if she were cold, felt that empty sickness that somehow seemed to fill her. She didn't want to answer questions. She just wanted to pick up and forget all of this. Move on. She wanted to leave and go somewhere else. She wanted to dance in some nightclub alone in a crowd of strangers who would not judge her, who would not know there was anything to ask.

Sheriff Mills pulled off the side of the road into a gravel patch, trees hovering over them against the bright sunshine. She looked at him now with a knowing glance, now beginning to understand. It gave her a feeling of assurance and power, like driving a familiar car on a familiar road; she knew this role. She would fight; she would lose. She didn't ask what this was about because she knew, and she didn't want to give a man of the law more power than he already had.

He unclicked his seat belt. She waited, sitting straight.

"How'd you get that bruise?" Mills said.

She immediately covered her face with her hands with a sudden insecurity the sheriff had not seen before. He looked her in the face.

"I need you to trust me," he said. "I'm trying to help. Don't you believe that?"

"Ain't nothing free. I know that."

"It's not like that. Don't you remember anything? Don't you remember me?"

He sighed again, opened the door, and they could hear the smooth roar of a passing car like a strange wave. She could feel his disappointment and waited now for him to reach for her. She began to feel it again, that sickness, that wet, as she prepared herself and began to accept it, that familiar trait all men possessed, the desire and ability to invade and shape. But instead, he heaved himself out of the vehicle in a rustle of starched cotton and creaking leather, leaned back in with his elbows against the door frame, looking out over a piney field, razed to an ugly bald scalp, lined by trees in the distance. She took the opportunity to touch herself up, dabbing at her cheek with foundation from her compact.

"Up yonder," the sheriff said, "my daddy and mama brought us up in them tobacco fields until he turned deputy when I was six, and we moved and he could look men in the eye and they nodded back at him. Back then, all a man needed was courage and a gun. He said to me, said, 'Jefferson, I figured out how to live the American dream.' He said, 'You gotta break into it like a house. Nobody'll ever give it to you. It's the only thing you got a right to steal. And I'm taking it, not for me, but for you and your mama and brothers and sisters.' He was a good man, but worked and worked those fields for all those years, which his daddy had done, and for what? The Big Man. That kind of life went nowhere, like piss in a stream. 'Scuse me. But when he was deputy and then sheriff of the county, he had something. Opportunity to mean something, to do something. I always have wanted that too. Still do. I ain't asking you questions because I want to get in your business. I want this to be resolved. I ain't living for me right now. I'm living for you. For everyone else. For my daddy's name that used to be worth less than the dirt he plowed and planted. I don't care what you done and where you're from. I am not the Man. I grew up poor, and I give everyone a chance to prove themselves. That's what I mean to say to you. We ain't so different, just 'cause I'm wearing a badge. Here," he said, handing her a handkerchief.

She took it, clasped his hand for a moment, said, "Thank you," realizing she actually meant it, though she didn't exactly know what for. It was something she'd known forever, like a recurring dream or a debt, something strange and familiar.

She said, "I'm scared."

"I won't let anything happen to you. Euphoria's gonna take care of you. Now, tell me what you know. Anything."

She swallowed, looked down, suddenly timid and demure.

"All I know," she said, "is Zeke borrowed money from Tom a while back. He came around, said he couldn't pay it back yet. Tom said he'd be needing the rest the next month because we had a baby on the way. I don't know if that means anything to you, but I don't know nothing else."

"When was this?"

"Three months ago, maybe? Sometime in April? The baby's seven weeks old now."

"What was the money for?"

"Zeke's son, Sam. They sent him to a rehab or something. I don't know all about it."

"Of course!" Sheriff Mills said, with sudden clap of his hands that startled her.

So it was a loan. Zeke had borrowed the money, couldn't pay it back. There was an argument. Tom was an athlete, and Zeke was a man of comparable size—although older—so a struggle made sense, and the outcome was believable. Zeke killed Tom so that he would not owe him anymore. But Zeke was wrong. He'd have to pay that poor young woman every penny. There was nothing Sheriff Mills hated worse than the thought of a defenseless woman.

He started the car and drove back onto the road. For a while, it was just him thinking, chewing.

"What are your plans after all this?" he said eventually, having calmed down. "You going to stay in town?"

"I don't know. This place. I got to get away from here. Ain't never had a chance."

"But this is your home."

"My home wasn't no place to be proud of."

"Hmm," he said, seeming to disapprove. "I thought you might stay. Go back to working."

"I'm a mama now."

There was a pause. "Don't you remember?" he said.

"How could I forget the way you'd walk into the Lounge, look me up and down, like you wanted to eat me. But I ain't looking for another man."

"No, before that. Don't you remember? Didn't your mama tell you anything about me? I always been there, watching you."

"I knew you were trouble."

"No," Mills said. "I was watching out for you, like I am now. I was watching over you."

S HERIFF MILLS DROPPED Day off at Miss Claudette's, returning afterward to the office in a fit, hollering at Tania about needing to see his deputy.

"He's out at the reservoir. Someone disappeared last night coming back from fishing. Body hasn't been found."

"I don't give a wet cigarette what he's doing. That's Virginia Game and Inland Fisheries' responsibility. You tell him to get here ASAP."

When Will came in, Mills had his back to the door and was fixing his hair in the mirror. "What you got?" he said.

"James Abernathy, thirty-eight years old, from North Carolina. He fell overboard last night and never resurfaced."

"Well, it doesn't surprise me. That lake's like a goddamn foreign planet." He looked at Will in the mirror. "I don't need you to waste your energy on a crapshoot like that. Let those VGIF boys take care of it."

"Alonzo called this morning. They were short-staffed and needed help."

"You hear that?" Sheriff Mills said to an audience that was not there. "*They're* understaffed!"

He handed Will the autopsy report and grabbed a notebook and a paper bag, the top of which had been rolled shut, and motioned for Will to walk with him.

"You still think he's innocent?" the sheriff said.

It wasn't really a question, and Mills didn't wait for a response. He pushed open the door, and Will followed him into the blank room where they saw Zeke under that skull-white solitary bulb, sitting at an old schoolhouse desk. Sheriff Mills pulled up a folding chair leaning against the wall and sat it backward, his legs straddling the back of the chair where his arms rested.

"Zeke," Mills said slowly, as if considering the way it tasted to say his name. "We got someone says you owed Tom some money."

"I need a lawyer." Zeke stared at Will, who glanced away.

"You got your arraignment tomorrow morning. I imagine you'll be taking a court-appointed attorney, which they'll assign then."

"I'll wait."

"You'll talk now. When are you gonna learn what's common sense? The sooner you cooperate, the easier things will go in court. You understand that?"

Zeke nodded, but didn't look too sure.

"Okay then," Mills said. "Tell me about this business of owing Tom."

"He helped my boy Sam go to a rehab up in Richmond. Ain't no secret."

"You know where Sam is now?"

Zeke shook his head.

"We know he ain't at your place because we already searched it." Mills got up out of the chair, began pacing back and forth in front of Zeke, whose wide eyes followed him up and down the room. "Heard you couldn't pay the money even after Tom said he needed it."

"That's a lie. I paid back every cent."

Mills stopped pacing, put his foot on the chair, and leaned toward Zeke. "What if you're the one lying? You got a receipt?"

Zeke looked like he was trying to laugh but couldn't move his face.

"You think it's funny?" Mills said.

"You can ask anybody, any of the boys—Herb, T-Man, Arnie, Maurice—that . . ." He stopped.

"How would they know anything? What you been up to? You better finish your statement, or I'm going to arrest every blessed one of them."

Zeke swallowed, looked at the ceiling as if something there would help him. "Anybody tell you, Tom had that money I paid him back. He played with it that night. Won a lot of money."

"What were you really doing at Tom's house the other day? You can tell us. We already know."

"I told you. I saw the fire and went to see what was going on. I didn't do anything to Tom. I swear."

"Then explain this." From inside the paper bag, Mills brought out the knife in a plastic evidence bag. Zeke's head slumped forward as if it had snapped. "And these prints—yours—also appeared on Tom's belt. What the hell's that about? Well?"

Zeke looked directly at Will, as if Will had been interrogating him. "His pants was down. I tried to get 'em back on to cover him up."

66

"Then you just left him there to burn," Mills said. He looked at his deputy. "Don't make much sense to me. Does it to you?"

Before Will could say anything, Zeke said, "I won't say anything else until I get a lawyer. I shouldn't be talking."

"It's understandable why you'd kill him," Mills said. "Shoot, you don't have to pay money to a dead man. Times are tough. Where's the money? Where'd you hide it?"

Zeke sat straight and looked at nothing, said nothing.

"Well you're right about one thing," Mills said, placing a notebook in front of Zeke. "You sure as hell do need an attorney. Now, you should think about confessing. You do it soon enough, your attorney might even be able to get you a plea deal. A confession from you now is better than proof of guilt in court."

Zeke said, "I swear before God, Mr. Sheriff."

"You gonna have a tough time in court," Mills said. "Judge don't take kindly to perjury."

Mills nodded to Will. "*That's* motive."

As Will walked out, leaving the sheriff to escort the prisoner back to his cell, he could hear Zeke crying for God, a scratching, miserable sound.

Shortly after, Sheriff Mills came back to his office, where Will waited for him.

"I want that confession before the arraignment," Mills said. "Yes, I do. And I do believe he'll write it."

"Sir, I tracked down Maurice Newman at the landing today," Will said. "He confirmed Tom won a pile of money. We searched Zeke when we arrested him and his house and didn't find anything. Doesn't it stand to reason that Zeke might be telling the truth, that the person who killed Tom has the money? His wallet and phone? His ID?"

"How much are we talking?"

"Maurice said it was upwards of five thousand dollars."

"Bullshit. I've been in that shithole, and I don't believe those fellas would ever get up that much to play with. That's why I don't bust 'em. See, that's the kind of information you get from those low-lifes at the landings, drinking a forty by noon and smoking blunts all day, shooting craps and playing poker at night. Tobacco was good for people. You got your media and all talking about equality and equity and whatever the hell, and yet the best thing for everybody was being able to work. The same people who cry about how things are are the ones made it that way. Anyway, you should know better than to take information from friends of the accused."

"Even Herbie Toones said it was true."

"That bag of shit."

"He didn't get along with Tom, and he confirmed Maurice's story."

"Have you forgotten we caught Zeke Hathom running from a crime scene? He could have buried the money, thrown it in the woods. Pretty hard to trace loose cash. Either goddamn way, his prints are on the murder weapon. You know what that means? GUILTY."

"If he did kill Tom, how could he be careless enough to let us find the murder weapon yet careful enough to hide the money? This has all been too easy. Zeke was just in the wrong place at the wrong time."

Mills tapped a pen against the palm of his hand. "You call that motel?"

"Yessir, I did."

"Well, what they say?"

"They confirmed Miss Pace checked in that night."

"What did you find out at the Lounge today? Any possible suspects?"

"Everybody who was playing cards with Tom. And they all are saying something about a couple guys from Charlotte County. Something about them talking trash after the game."

"They threaten Tom?"

"Something like that. We should follow up on them."

"All right," Mills said, with a wave of his hand. "Track 'em down, talk to 'em, and report back."

"Sir," Will said. He knew he might be on the verge of saying something rash, but he couldn't hold back any longer. "Why are you railroading him?"

"Beg pardon?" Mills said, squinting up into Will's face.

"You're sending me out to interview murder suspects, like you could give a shit. This stuff about these Charlotte guys might actually be a lead. If you wanted to get to the bottom of this, you'd already have looked into them."

"Watch your goddamn tone. 'Scuse me, Tania."

"It's not disrespect; it's just, I can't see why you're so set on Zeke. If you polled everybody white and Black in this county, you'd come back with one hundred percent or close to it saying Zeke's innocent."

Mills narrowed his eyes and cleared his voice. "Listen here, son, and listen good. A trial ain't a popularity contest. It's not a vote. I don't give a mound of coon scat that people like Zeke Hathom. *I* like Zeke Hathom. But you got to admit, there's evidence that Zeke did it and a motive that would satisfy many a jury."

"Since you've given up, I'll just keep looking then."

"Seems!" Mills called out, standing, and Will turned at the door. "The next time you raise your voice at me, I'll have your badge so goddamn fast you'll think a ghost took it off you."

"You want to take it, take it," Will said. "But until then, I'm going to keep doing my job."

With that, he pushed out into a gust of summer heat.

S HERIFF MILLS STEWED all day over what to do about his smart-ass, back-talking deputy. He had reasons he didn't want to actually take his badge, but something needed doing. Never in all his years as sheriff had someone on his payroll talked to him like that, not even that shiftless Seth Grady. Probably had to do with him living in Richmond all those years, getting his education in a city going liberal in a red state going the same way.

So he went to Mama Jay's the next morning, getting out of his truck with "In God We Trust" across the tailgate and nodding toward a cluster of three men in do-rags and oversize T-shirts, saying, "Howdy, boys," pulling the glass door open, triggering the bell. His presence was met with an uproar from the boys sitting at the tables over by the wood-paneled dining area.

"Ain't seen you in some time," Taylor Hart said. "What's been keeping you?"

He told the boys he'd taught Will a lesson yesterday afternoon, and they bet him he hadn't. Someone even said, "Like you taught Grady?" which made him turn around with that hard scowl. It was Nick Squire, smart aleck. So Mills told them:

"Will gets in that old pickup his daddy used to drive around here, and he's leaving work. And I followed him. Sure did. Flipped them lights."

Mills told them the story, but here's how it really happened:

Will Seems saw the lights, heard the brief notice of the siren, and pulled over into the grass off the broken single lane, which bisected the fields of corn on one side and tobacco on the other.

The sheriff grabbed the roof of his patrol car and hauled himself out, straightened his belt and corrected his holster, and put on his hat.

"Sheriff," Will said as he got close, looking around at the sheriff's car.

"Turn your ignition off," he said. "Don't pretend you didn't hear me."

The quiet was filled with cicadas like bagpipes at a funeral, searing and suffering, living and dying. A slight wind blew against the thin gauze of sweat that covered both men. The dust caught up pale and transient and ghostlike. Will opened the door and started to get out.

"Get back in the truck," the sheriff said. "License and registration."

"What's wrong here?"

"Nothing, you got your license and registration."

Will got out the papers.

"You know how fast you were going?" Mills said.

"Are you serious?"

Sheriff Mills shifted his weight and looked off, as if he was thinking real hard about something or had seen something distracting on the horizon.

"You were going fifty-six in a thirty-five," Mills said with a wave of his hand, as if the numbers were arbitrary. "That's reckless."

"This is fifty-five."

"Back there."

"Bullshit."

"You got some little attitude, and I'm not sure I much like it. You think you know more than me about the law? You think you can tell me how to keep a county safe I been protecting since you were born?"

"I didn't say that."

"You been suggesting it mighty hard for a greenhorn. That poor young woman tells me you been watching her. That true?"

"I'm doing my job."

"Son, you got some secrets you been keeping. I don't care that you go out there and sleep in your truck. I don't care what you got going on behind closed doors in that house. Long as you come to work, and when you do, you take orders from me with a smile. You leave that poor woman alone."

"Zeke didn't do it." Then, looking up into the sheriff's face, shaded by his hat, Will said, "You know that, and I can't pretend he did."

"Well then, you being out there in Turkey Creek to call it in could make you a suspect. Should we go that route?"

"Sure, but you're always saying you don't want publicity that 'don't reflect the department's true potential.'"

The sheriff looked hard at him, a relaxed blank hatred undisguised in his face. A copperhead writhed its way out of one field and into the road, and they both saw it. The snake lay still, licking at the dust in the air with his forked tongue. The sheriff went over to it, and it tucked its head under a leaf; like any good copperhead, it was loath to move if it believed itself hidden.

Just as Will was about to say something Sheriff Mills put his heel down fast on the snake's head, and something—blood and venom—leaked out of it, and its body worked like a whip, wrapping around the sheriff's leg, quivering and working as he put all his weight down. With his pistol he removed the snake's earnest grip, but the tail kept working, and he just stood there like the goddess on the Virginia state seal, Will thought, with her foot on the fallen tyrant. *Sic semper tyrannis.* Thus always to tyrants. Only this seemed the reverse.

"Son, you're gonna learn a thing or two. This is my jurisdiction, and you work for me, and I see something I don't like, I'm gonna do something about it, and you've done got a speeding ticket, and you're gonna pay a fine or give up your goddamn badge for a while. Either way, I don't care."

Mills began walking back to his truck but wheeled back around: "And don't you ever again use my words against me!"

The boys laughed so hard Mama Jay come out from the back and said, "Now, what could be that funny?"

Jimbo Rawles said, "That Seems boy."

"Well," Nick Squire said, his coffee in Styrofoam before him on the table, both hands resting around it. "He pay the fine?"

"Goddamnit," Sheriff Mills said, and Mama Jay laughed, no one else.

"*That's* funny," she said, disappearing back into the kitchen.

**B**ENNICO WATCHED as the countryside shed itself of years, decades, and only the pure defunct heart of whatever it was—Virginia, America—emerged like a meat beneath a skin, a map of everything that fed it, made it. The trees and vines hung over the road, untamed and untamable, and she drove through the quiet of their fecund mottled shade.

The radio went static, and she found only one station dark and clear, the desperate word of God howling through a preacher's furious tenor. She turned it off after a moment and felt what she saw: a solitary double-wide silhouetting a naked rise, an unbrushed horse searching the dirt patch of yard for grass; some hamlet's or town's main street that appeared to have been permanently vacated, where a storefront advertised Coca-Cola and Red Wing boots and CB radio work; a Confederate flag whipping against the nothingness of dark sky; a Gulf gas station absolutely broken by saplings, faded as if whitewashed except for the rust, like a trail of bullets, across the medallion of its sign; a tilted wooden church open mid-sanctuary where the roof, beams and all, had caved under some invisible weight. She had the sensation of sinking deeper and deeper underwater, compressed within the depth.

"Okay," she said aloud.

She had long held the belief that understanding a crime—or any action—had almost as much to do with the setting as the act itself. It was a part of the process, a kind of preparatory meditation, seeing it unfold, approaching something, whatever it was, the act of casting a net that would eventually draw closed and hold what was important enough to keep.

She got off the main road and found herself on broken black-top turned to a faded rebellious gray, a country lane winding past fields of tobacco plants like soldiers in file, each as tall as a grown man, and houses and trailers alike, defeated alike. As she crossed from one tobacco field to the next, divided by a dirt track, she saw the burnt rubble of a house that looked familiar. She also saw a cruiser parked down the lane. The online *Southside Telegraph* had included a photograph, though she'd seen nothing at all—not even an article—in the *Richmond Times-Dispatch*. She shook her head. *You know how you can tell you're on to something real? Because it isn't news in the big papers. If it was, it would be too late.*

In her reverie, she almost missed the address Mrs. Hathom had given her. At the red mailbox to the left of the road she skidded to a stop and turned right and came to a small house with a bowed porch and a wide field behind it. A large-boned woman wearing a blue bandanna over her head appeared behind the screen of the front door.

"Mrs. Hathom?" Bennico said.

"Bennico! You're early. I wasn't expecting you till later."

"I thought we'd go ahead and get a move on."

Bennico got out with her backpack slung over one shoulder.

"You're packing mighty light, ain't you?" Floressa said.

Bennico withdrew her Glock 26 seamlessly and without sound, and showed it, barely the size of her hand, like a toy, as if it had been the reveal in a magic trick.

"You got that right, Mrs. Hathom."

"You ain't planning on using that, are you?"

"You can't ever know. I usually punch above my weight class."

Floressa shook her head.

"I don't like guns in my house."

"I'm guessing you don't like your husband being in jail, either, but here we are."

She stepped up onto the porch and into the house.

"I'm sorry, I ain't finished cleaning yet. You can have my boy Sam's old room until we get you set up."

"When do you think that'll be?"

"I hope tomorrow."

"Sounds like we're blowing in the wind here. I don't like that."

"What do you expect me to do? I ain't been able to reach him."

"He getting cold feet?"

Floressa didn't answer. "Sit down. Can I get you something to drink?"

"If you think he's getting scared, I'll go find him."

"Give it another day."

"Mrs. Hathom, I don't think you understand what a day can mean in an investigation like this. This isn't the first time I've dealt with a flake, and I won't let that stop me from doing my job. I don't need him."

"You might. He's going to be your partner on this. We ain't negotiating on that."

Bennico leaned back, staring at Floressa with a flat disgust in her eyes.

"I work alone."

"Not this time, you don't."

"You said he was a source, not a partner."

"His name is Will Seems, and he's deputy sheriff here. He arrested my husband."

"And you think you can trust him?"

"We go back a ways."

"I'm not splitting my fee with someone else."

"You won't."

"You're gonna trust a man working for you for free and getting paid by the department you don't trust? People tend to be loyal to who pays them."

"You let me handle Will Seems," Floressa said.

Bennico closed her notebook with a flick of her wrist and stood up.

"Where you going?" Floressa said.

"I'm not waiting around for Deputy Seems to get started."

"You don't know the area."

"Time for me to find out. Mrs. Claudette Janders live alone?"

"Did. Tom's girlfriend and daughter staying with her now."

"Well, get her over here tonight. I want to talk to her alone."

At the door, Bennico turned. "He doesn't know anything about this, does he?"

"It don't matter."

"It does to me. I don't like secrets."

With that, she shut the door and left with a kind of urgency that seemed ridiculous against the tired, stolid country.

CLAUDETTE KEPT a tidy property. The shag carpet showed vacuum tracks like rows in a field, the kitchen floor and counters smelled of lemon, the bushes were neatly trimmed, the sidewalk weeded. Tom had seen the potential in the house and helped her move in. He'd painted the outside, fixed some of the drywall and molding inside, painted the walls, and worked hard to turn what was a dingy house into a bright home she was proud to live in. She'd retired from the hospital over in South Hill and had come to enjoy retired life. She read the newspaper in the morning, tended a small container garden out front, swept the porch. But after Tom's death her space had changed. People were always checking in on her, unannounced, and she had more food than she knew what to do with, covering her table and counters in disorganized heaps. Day and Destinee were living with her now, and toys and pacifiers and cloths and a stroller were to be found in the living room, not to mention the TV was always on, Day lying comatose, hungover, it seemed, on the couch, makeup faded and hair matted, suddenly not the young woman who'd come straight from the salon, looking like she was fixing to go out, but a freckle-faced girl—with an ugly bruise on her cheek from that car door—in a dead man's threadbare high school sweatshirt.

No judgment here. Claudette felt sustained by her granddaughter, holding the child, seeing her sleep and cough and smile, and
it brought tears to her eyes every time she heard her wake and cry,
felt her tight innocent grip. Claudette didn't know Day very well,
but she was concerned the young woman had not gotten dressed
in two or three days and had hardly eaten anything. Claudette understood. She too found it hard to get out of bed. She'd look out the
window, like any other day, and every little thing would remind her
of Tom, and she'd lose all her motivation to accomplish anything.
A hopelessness filled her like hunger.

When Tom's father had left them, all she'd had to place hope in
was Jesus and Tom. Now, the thought of her son filled her with an
unbearable emptiness. It was a curse that she did not want to think
of her own son because she couldn't stand it. But Claudette, ever
practical, turned that grief to hope. She hoped she and Day would
bond over their common love and loss, over little baby Destinee too,
but so far, Day hadn't said or done much. At least in Destinee was
hope for some future with Tom still in it.

Claudette was holding Destinee that evening, tickling the child
so that she bubbled and cooed, and Day did not once even turn to
watch. Claudette couldn't understand a mother so uninterested in
her own child, especially after losing Tom.

"Day," Claudette said. "Honey, you got such a blessed life. I
know it doesn't seem like it right now."

Day didn't move.

"Listen here, girl. I know what you going through."

Day turned her brown-green-blue eyes Tom had found so in-
toxicating without apology and seemingly without care.

"No. You don't."

"Oh, honey. I don't mean no disrespect."

Day again gazed into the fathomless TV.

"Everything is going to be all right," Claudette said. "God has a plan."

Day kicked the blanket off and stood up, walked toward the bedroom.

"Come on, Day! I'm trying here. He's my loss too. We should help each other. Tom would want that."

"How do you know what Tom would want?"

"Well, I think I'd know. I held that boy when he was big as Destinee. Fed him, raised him up. And I think he'd want us to help each other."

"He doesn't want anything anymore."

"He still exists. He exists here, with us. In Destinee. And I believe he's watching over us with the angels."

"Yeah?"

"I know what you need, Day. You need belief in something beyond this."

"I'm going to bed."

"Let me fix you some tea, get you something to eat. I know you want to hear about our plans for justice."

"What do you mean?"

"Deputy come by here, said they picked up Zeke. You think that man killed Tom?"

"Sheriff says that's what the evidence says."

"Well, Zeke didn't do it, and Floressa and I done hired someone to look into all this."

Day buried her face in her hands.

"Day! It's good news."

"I don't want no trouble."

"Well, trouble comes around sometimes. And trouble's what you got. But you got to deal with it. We got to deal with it."

"It's hard enough as it is to move on. Now it's going to dig everything back up. Claudette, Tom ain't coming back."

"You ain't the only one who got a say. I know we can't bring him back to life," Claudette said, choking up a little. "But I ain't about to sit by and let Zeke Hathom take the blame. Come on. We lost the same man. Let's get together on this."

"I'm going to bed," Day said. "I can't deal with this shit right now."

"Watch your language in my house."

"Yes, ma'am," Day said.

The truth was, Claudette didn't feel she knew anything about the woman before her, even about Tom in the last year since Day had moved in with him. Living just a few miles out of town, he'd nevertheless seemed to inherit an inner distance that had troubled her. She'd hear things from folks who went out and spent their money at that place out by the sawmill, the Lounge, gambling and drinking, but she put her worries into prayers. She'd implored him to think on his soul, wept when he refused to marry at the church or marry at all.

His excuse: "She with child, Mama."

"God don't care. Life is life."

"Church ain't about God. It's about judgment and pretty hats."

She'd slapped him then, a small violence still echoing.

"Let's pray," she said to Day now. "Won't you pray with me, Day?"

"I'm tired, Claudette."

"Call me Mama."

Day looked at her then with tears so thick in her eyes she might have been blind.

Claudette reached out her hand and said, "Do me this favor. Pray with me."

Day stared at the woman. What good would prayer do? But she took her hand.

"Kneel before our God," said Claudette, and Day did so, the only other times she'd knelt having been to administer fellatio. "Lord, we love you. We love your light of truth, your mercy, your wrath. We fear you. We fear for your son Tom. We fear for our community. Help us, Lord, in our path toward justice. Help us find who did this terrible thing, so that we can raise up your Word as truth. So that we can . . ."

Day had withdrawn her hand, stood up.

". . . Lord, help your child Day as she navigates her doubt. Help her to understand it was not you who killed Tom. Help her return to your light. Amen."

Day went into her room, leaving the baby with Claudette. She buried her head in her pillow, cried into it until a depleted numbness crept through her. She remembered the Saturday nights she would already be there at the Lounge, waiting on Tom to show up. She'd watch the door to the front of the house, where cars and trucks were parked just as fucked up as the folks who drove them. She'd watch the door, say to herself, *Okay, Day, the next man comes in is gonna be Tom Janders, and if it is, you're gonna get lucky. But if you're wrong, if you guess Tom and someone else comes through that door to the world out there, you'll be responsible for some kind of bad luck that's gonna come to Tom.* She knew it didn't make sense, as if by guessing right or wrong she could change a goddamn thing in this world. But in that plantation house, its peeling porch columns barely holding up the porch roof, where the walls were torn and you could see through holes in them into other rooms, and the music thumped, and lights lit up like Christmas Eve inside, and cigarettes and weed with their spirit smoke floating like genies, like in the movies, and the music always moving through you, keeping you where you wanted to be and who you wanted to be, yes, maybe she could do something with her mind, make him come through that door. And if it wasn't him, and she said to herself it would be, she'd reason it didn't count. She'd known deeper than the wish that it wasn't going to be Tom. *That don't count, Day. Go easy.* But even that game seemed like somebody, something was watching it play out, keeping a tally of the tallies unwritten that she erased in her head. Somehow, she knew all those little guesses amounted to some count that was there—fake or not, because what is false is also true—existing somewhere.

And then, he'd step in. The way he'd have his brown hat slanted, on hot days his sleeves rolled back so that you could see in his strong arms what it took to work at the sawmill, and he'd move like everything was a dream except for her, as if they were attached by some invisible chain.

But it was her own damn fault, her idea to secure him by pushing for commitment. Well, she'd gotten it, all right. Lying on the bed, she remembered convincing Tom and then going to Granny's in the Snakefoot for something to make it true, and then Destinee began. Granny had said, "You going to get more than you want, maybe."

"I don't care," she'd said.

She took out Tom's phone, looked through his texts again. Some unsaved local number had sent him more texts than she had. Texts like, "can't wait to c u tonight," and, "where u at," and, "tonight my night off. U want to ride?" She wanted more of him, somehow. These were the threads of an existence she'd been a part of. She considered texting the number, but that might not be smart, and she decided against it.

She looked at herself in the mirror, a sight that horrified her, and touched the tender bruise on her cheek. She needed to shower and touch herself up. She'd let herself go.

*You got to go back*, Day said to herself. *Granny helped you get into this; she can help you get out.*

**W**ILL ARRIVED AT the courthouse just in time for Zeke's arraignment on Friday, July 22. The court appointed Zeke a defense attorney, a man Will had encountered before named Davidson, who tended to bow while wincing behind round gold-rimmed glasses. In court, the evidence Mills was able to present—Zeke's fingerprints on the knife handle and Tom's belt—along with the lab results, made a compelling case against Zeke. The judge ruled that there was probable cause and that, as Zeke was being charged with first-degree murder and therefore might be a threat to others, he would be held without bond in the Euphoria County jail. The judge reminded Zeke that his attorney would be able to schedule a bond hearing, but Will knew how unlikely it was for bail to be granted in a first-degree murder case. Will couldn't help but feel the guiding principle of American criminal law—that one is innocent until proven guilty—had been subverted. The charges against Zeke seemed already to have defeated him and shamed his family. What did it matter that he was not guilty if the charges themselves had already done such harm?

Will took Zeke back to his cell. Neither spoke at all. Will wanted to leave the man with some hope, but he couldn't think of anything to say that either would believe. Besides, he had other things on his mind. He returned to the sheriff's office quickly. Tania gave him a look and stood up and walked over to the sheriff's office and knocked on the inside of the open door.

A rustling sound, weight shifting in the swivel chair.

"Well?"

Tania pretended not to watch as Will stepped past her and into the office and began to close the door, but Sheriff Mills said, "Ain't no secrets here. Leave it. What you got to say for yourself?"

Will sighed—uncertain what he was going to do until now—and placed his badge and gun on the sheriff's desk.

"What in the hell, boy."

"I'll take the suspension."

Sheriff Mills stood, his trim figure somehow imposing as well. "You walk out, and you'll wish to hell you hadn't."

Will stood still, looking off through the blind slats and out the window at nothing.

"You know what I think?" Mills said. "Things start to get real, and you don't want to deal with it. I think it has something to do with whatever you're hiding, whatever you really came back for." Will turned to leave, only to hear: "Just like your daddy. Quit the game when you don't like it anymore. Coward."

Will's back rose, and he turned around and was facing Sheriff Mills now.

"Step back," Mills said, with a kind of jovial antagonism. "Seems is pissed!"

Through a curled lip, Will said, "You ever say that again . . ."

"What now? That a threat?"

But Will had already turned, muttering something, ignoring Tania—not even seeing her—and walked straight for the doorway.

87

He thought he could hear Mills say something to Tania but couldn't be sure. He could barely stay upright enough to make it there, and when he shoved open the door and felt the bright white heat, he took some small comfort in its familiar smothering embrace and hurried to his car, finally able to make a run.

**D**RIVING TO RICHMOND was always a retreat for Will. What should have been forward was backward. Instead of the thick piney woods and derelict garages, the occasional filling station and the low-lying swamps he passed, Will watched something unfold from a great distance in time like an eighteen-wheeler coming head on in the wrong lane.

He was playing basketball with Sam Hathom on that late summer day under the crooked hoop against the white barnlike Baptist church, the broken parking lot providing the only blacktop nearby. It was June of 1998, and they were sixteen. In the late afternoon heat, they peeled off their shirts to keep them clean and let them dry, playing endless game after game, that pinprick summer feeling, sweating through their burning shoes, the ball covered in palm sweat and dust, their bodies smudged from hours of play and looking the same dirt color, Will a little darker, Sam a little lighter. The tradition was to play here—they could walk from Sam's house—until they couldn't stand it, then go swimming in the creek. So, after playing for several hours, they sat against the shaded side of the church, sharing the last half of their water bottle, sweating even in the long shadows at the end of the day, replaying their moves. Eventually, they threw their still-damp shirts over their shoulders and walked roadward, the half mile feeling like a forced march.

Will remembered how silent it was that day, muffled in the ether or humidity, whichever it was. Often, you'd see men, out of work or after work, fishing for cats and bass up and down the embankment with their buckets and their lines, but on this day there was no one, as if they had been forewarned. The boys got in, barefoot, watching for dull-eyed copperheads at the banks, muddying the water with their steps. They were looking forward to the dinner Mrs. Hathom was making—fried chicken, shaved Virginia country ham, macaroni and cheese, turnip greens, and coleslaw—and started telling each other how hungry they were. Will's mother had begun sleeping during the day, keeping to herself, and he hadn't seen her smile in weeks. Two years later she would pass, and Mrs. Hathom would embrace Will, smother him outright, cry for the family and for Hannah as if they had been siblings, and only this would temper the rage and prepare him for the long grieving that does not end.

They swam the dark waters that held the colors of the sky like a dimension. Then, without clue or warning, they could see a new darkness in that reflection, looked up, and saw a row of figures standing on the embankment, charred silhouettes towering above them in bright tank tops or without shirts. They stood like a row of trees, each identical and without individual features, backlit by a red dusk so that each of them looked actually black, pitch as iron, dark as the inside of a fish.

"Hey, yo," someone called down in a voice so hoarse it sounded like it hurt to speak. "Little nigger."

Laughter on the bank.

"Who that?" Sam said.

The speaker's teeth flashed white as he spoke. "Who's this Casper-looking motherfucker? Who is he, and what the fuck he doing out here?"

"Will," Sam said. "My friend."

"He look like a faggot. He your faggot?"

Laughter from everyone but the speaker. Will no longer looked up at them but stared at the riverbank where water met clay.

"Nah," Sam said. "We just friends."

Will stood still, as he'd learned to hunt, thinking of nothing, focusing on nothing. It would pass. In an hour, they'd be back at Sam's house. Soon, they would be eating.

"Come here, white boy," that rough voice commanded. "Come on up here."

Will looked up to see the boy again, older, his bright teeth smiling down from that shadow black. He didn't move.

"Where you live, Casper?"

"Dawn."

"Bet you got one of them big old houses. Who's your daddy?" Everyone on the bank laughed. "Come on now."

"Bill Seems."

Will looked at Sam, but Sam would not look back at him.

"Bet he a doctor or a lawyer or a big old swinging dick," the boy said.

The boy walked toward the bank, reaching his hand out.

"Come on, Casper," he said. "Come on out of there."

"That's okay," Will said.

"So that's how it is," the boy said, looking around at his comrades. "Come on," the boy said to Will again, waving him over vigorously. "Don't be a faggot."

Will reached out and was pulled up in that awkward handshake by a tawny, sinewy strength. The hand gripping him was calloused and lean, with a texture like brick. The boy pulled Will up so hard he almost lost his footing in the clay of the cutbank.

Suddenly the black circle formed around him like a forest. Will couldn't see the creek now, couldn't see anything but night fast approaching. The sky had gone colorless, clear, and only the shapes and the eyes and the teeth flashed like the stars that were beginning to shine in the true sky.

"Let's fight," the same boy said in that rough voice Will still heard when he closed his eyes. "I never fought a white boy."

"Why?" Will said.

"'Cause you here, and we here."

The shadow figure got into a relaxed stance, the grass underneath him oddly bright in that paradise glow at the end of a day, and Will could see him dancing around in a comical shadowboxing routine, pretending to be hit, to stagger, to fall. Everyone laughed.

"Come on," he said, a rough, intimate love in his voice. "Bet your daddy taught you some moves." This was the moment. The moment he could have known this would never end. He stood there, like a dope, unable to feel his legs. If he could only go back. But would he act any differently? All uncertainties began here.

The gang tightened around Will. Whatever it was that was happening had already begun, set in motion like a car accident.

Something—the boy's hand, it must have been, which Will couldn't see—hit the side of his face, and Will's ear was ringing. He lunged in the darkness, felt the force more than any pain at first, found himself kneeling in the grass, tasting the iron of his body and the underwater shame. He covered his head, not as much for protection as to hide, hearing that rough bass voice that he would remember longer than he would his own mother's: "I'm your fucking daddy, you white faggot. I'm your daddy. I fucked your mother, and you got my nigger sweat and blood and jizz running through your veins."

The boy saw Will beginning to rise, and he walked over, and Will stayed put.

"Who's your daddy, white boy?"

Will said nothing.

"Say it. Who's your daddy?"

Will couldn't talk. He closed his eyes, heard steps, felt a shoe pressing his neck down.

"Say it."

Will mumbled something.

"What?" the boy said. "Speak up."

A strange voice broke the moment. Sam? He yelled in a pitch so different than Will had ever heard that he didn't recognize it at first.

"Why you being a punk!" Sam said, and Will still wondered if he was talking about him or the other boy. "Leave him alone, mo'fuck. He ain't done shit to you."

"What you say, nigger?"

The shoe lifted from Will's neck. The attention shifted.

"You heard me," Sam said. "Leave us the fuck alone. Goddamn. Ain't done shit to you."

"You're talking like a man now."

Will felt sick as he began to stand. But before he knew it, the boy seemed to dance, and he saw Sam disappear, black within the black, a disorienting movement of colors of their neon clothes

93

glowing like fragments of a sunset, like the flag of some strange exotic country, a kaleidoscopic disorientation of sound and vision.

Will had been roughed up, but he wasn't really hurt, though he'd tried to convince himself he was. He wished now he had been hurt. He wanted to help Sam but couldn't move. He stood there, watching, frozen, statuesque, planted here and only here, glowing yet invisible, unimportant now. He heard sounds he had never heard before but would now give anything to forget, that dull rhythm like a snake heart, those groans of pain and the giving of it, and when they left like shadows he couldn't see through his own tears, their invisible festivity and laughter, the loud screeching of the insects, witnesses, and as suddenly as it had commenced it was over, and they were running, and the sound he could hear thirteen years into the future, now on the road to Richmond: the babbling of someone without teeth to even cry for help.

THAT WAS WHEN he realized someone, a shadow, appeared at a sprint out of the field, out of a rustle of tobacco, out of nothing, and chased off the stragglers, yelling after them. The voice belonged to Tom Janders, who was older, a senior at the time, an all-state cornerback and wide receiver on the public high school team, someone who was going to shake this county, and everybody knew it, white and Black. Tom ran back to where Will knelt over Sam. Sam lay there naked, clothes torn from him, and Will saw teeth like drugs glowing in the grass and attempted to collect them in his shaking palm. He thought Sam was dead. Tom shoved Will aside and picked Sam up like he was nothing, checked for breathing, and ran back through the tall tobacco toward the Hathoms' house. Will followed blindly.

Tom was out of breath when he'd reached the house, calling anyway, "Mr. Hathom! Mr. Hathom! It's Sam! Sam's hurt!"

And Mrs. Hathom howling up at God, yelling prayers as they got into their car and took Sam to the hospital. Will could remember the panic in her step, the smell of burnt food in the yard.

"Who? Who done this to my boy?" Mr. Hathom kept saying, yelling over Mrs. Hathom singing and praying in the car, but the question wasn't clear exactly: Who did this? Who would let this happen? Who was to blame?

Sam had four broken ribs, a broken jaw that had to be set and wired shut, a punctured lung, and partial blindness in his left eye. Several operations were required, and still, Sam was destined to heal crooked, like one of those finger puppets slumped and attached only loosely by strings. The doctors said that if Tom hadn't shown up when he did, Sam probably would have died.

Out in the hallway, Tom pulled Will aside. "What happened out there?"

Will said, "It was because of me. It was my fault." But how could he explain? How could a coward have the courage to say he was a coward?

And Tom Janders had put his hand on the back of Will's neck, a hand that seemed capable of accomplishing anything, and he looked Will in the eyes with a bravado of athletic confidence he hoped would instill the genuine form of it in Will, and said, "Don't nobody guilty but them motherfuckers. They was looking for trouble. They gonna get it, here or after. They gonna get it." Will had thought many times about these words, and they echoed even more now that Tom was dead. Then, for the next few years, Will had believed that justice would take care of itself. Feared it. Justice. And then he knew it was true because his mother was dead, and he knew that it was because of him, because he had brought it on her. That was part of his punishment, he knew. It took him a few more years to come to the belief that justice had no meaning, only consequence. And it did not just happen. It never just happened. It had to be made to happen, forced. "Justice" was unnatural, a word that meant something in a courtroom, a thing that could be reached only outside of one.

WILL CURVED AROUND Richmond and made his way down Hull Street, a nondescript, flat expanse of road, part industrial, part jungle. Junkyards, car dealerships, strip malls, fast-food joints, vacant lots busted through with weeds. He passed the Bill's Barbecue where he used to go after work on summer days when temperature and humidity raced to reach one hundred, his T-shirt filthy and sweat-wet and scratching him with the fiberglass from the insulation warehouse.

At the old Lee's Mufflers and Auto Repair (named for General Lee and not the owner), he turned down a slim lane through an explosion of overhanging trees—an unmarked turn you'd make only if you knew something was behind Lee's—and the warehouse opened up, a cinder-block and sheet-metal building like a green barn with a loading dock on one side, a wide concrete area for preparing deliveries on the other, and always, behind every box and even sometimes in the offices upstairs, lurking and sound-less, snakes.

He walked in through the big open area, past Joe, who had an amazingly wide head, eyes half-shut, smoking a Newport.

"'S'up, Will," he said, and they bumped fists. "You looking for Caleb?"

"Yeah."

"Shit. He out on delivery."

"They're not running you on delivery?"

"Caleb won't let me drive for another two weeks. Says I waste company time."

"What he got you doing?"

"Supposed to sweep this floor like you used to do." Joe looked around, for the first time opening his eyes, cheeks rising in a tired mirth, "But that mo'fuck ain't here. And he won't know the difference."

Joe and Will had always gotten along, despite the fact that Joe had pulled Will aside several times and told him not to work so hard because it made him look bad. Bar none, he was the laziest man Will had ever known. Will had been on deliveries with Joe, and the man had perfected a distant insolence that infuriated Caleb—the warehouse supervisor—and made a virtue of wasting time. Joe didn't make any attempt to explain or deny this. It was understood: You sent Joe out on a delivery that should take an hour, and he'd be back at the end of the day. Will could remember Caleb shouting in through the radio, the incoming beep and static anger pouring through the speaker of the phone, and Joe, leaning over the big wheel of the truck, would draw a Newport from a pack, put it in his mouth, press the lighter in and wait for it to pop out, light up, pick up the radio (Caleb would have called in three times since the first "Joe, where the hell you at?"), and Joe would sigh smoke, smiling with his eyes at Will, say, "Hey, Caleb, we just dropped off, on our way back. 'Bout to stop for lunch."

"Lunch! Y'all ain't been to lunch this whole time?"

Joe wouldn't answer. Will would watch him in awe, the way it seemed nothing could worry him, even losing his job.

"Ten-four," he'd say eventually, although there was nothing to understand. "We on the way."

Then they'd stop for lunch, sit and talk in the parking lot, get something else from the menu, head back. Will never would have taken his time the way Joe did, and he thought Caleb probably sent him with Joe thinking he'd be able to hurry him up. But Joe was going to do it anyway, and Will ended up hiding behind that. The way Joe could stretch out a day was impressive, and he'd tell Will all about his philosophies and his perspective on current events. "You know what the problem with the country is?" he'd said once. "TVs in bedrooms."

"How do you mean?"

"My ol' lady don't never get out the bed. And you see me. If that woman would turn off that TV during the nighttime, I'd be a better man for it. I would. I know I would."

Standing now in the warehouse with Joe, Will said, "Weasel here? Nari?"

"Weasel out too. Nari back there. Man workin' too hard."

Will went back to the area by the loading dock where Weasel could usually be found working with steel—galvanized, stainless (which would cut your fingers off, yet he worked without the chain-link gloves), and any other kind, at big two-man stations he handled alone. He drove for NASCAR at some intermediate level.

One of the two Salvadorans, Nari, was sewing custom insulation at his station. He always looked strangely academic, laboratorial, his glasses resting on the end of his nose under a crane light as he worked. Without stopping, he looked up, painfully shy, nodded his head slightly, and continued sewing. Despite the heat, Nari always worked in his white pants and sweatshirt.

Will went into the bathroom, an old, stained commode in a room that smelled like the green industrial soap bar at the sink that felt like sharkskin. He shook off and zipped up and turned and looked in the mirror and washed his hands and said, to those eyes that viewed him now, "Fuck you. Fuck you."

He dried his hands and walked out, passing Joe, who looked asleep leaning against a post and certainly hadn't moved.

"I'll see you, Joe. That floor looks better already."

As Will was leaving, Caleb drove up in his pickup truck with "Dixie Insulation" across the door of the cab.

"Will Seems."

"Hey, bud."

"What are you doing back in the Holy City?"

"Just in town. Thought I'd swing by, see if you were here."

"Well, here I am. Come on in for a drink."

"What you got?"

"Got some peach. Top of the line."

Will's first taste of moonshine was not in Southside, where it should have been, but in this very warehouse. He was eighteen, had just graduated high school. Caleb was from Southside too—Mecklenburg County—and had taken pride in busting Will's 'shine cherry with a cherry batch in an Aquafina bottle over lunch in his office. Will was still filled with a gratitude that he'd survived an afternoon of climbing ladders to retrieve insulation and helping Weasel with some of the steel bending and cutting.

"It's too early for me," Will said now. "But I did want to ask you something."

Caleb nodded, swung around, and parked his mammoth new white F-250 perpendicular to the warehouse. Will followed him into the cavernous opening of the loading area.

"Joseph Goddamn Baker, what in the shit makes you think you can sit in my goddamn chair!"

Joe immediately stood up, grinning at Will as Caleb cursed him on out. Will sat up against a bench in the plywood office, about the size of Zeke's cell at the jail.

Sandy, one of the secretaries up front, called, and Caleb picked up.

"Yeah, put him through." A moment passed and the call came in. "Hey, dickless. I mean Earl." Laughter. Will saw Joe outside, pushing the broom in pitiful little sweeps, a Newport dangling from his lips, a sad figure indeed.

When Caleb was finished, he turned in his chair to Will. "What's on your mind?"

"I ask you a favor?"

Caleb nodded, of course.

"I got a buddy who might need a job."

"He got any experience with asbestos?"

"No experience with insulation."

"Look, man. I'd like to help, but I can't be taking on someone who's not going to know his ass from a tire. Can he drive?"

"I'm just talking about some warehouse stuff. I know you could use some help around here. You hired me in high school."

"When does he want to start?"

"I don't know yet. It might be a last-minute kind of deal. His name is Sam Hathom. I've known him his whole life. He's recovering, and I'm just trying to give him something to help him get back on his feet."

"Well. You send him to me when he's ready and we'll find something for him to do. But he shows any evidence of a relapse, I'll have to let him go. He does okay, and I think I could keep him busy."

"I understand," Will said, standing up and shaking Caleb's hand. "Thanks."

"Sure you don't want a nip before you go?"

"Wouldn't be right, not having to cut steel after."

Caleb's explosive laugh filled the room, and he slammed his fist against his desk.

"We can put you back there."

"Maybe next time."

WILL DROVE the old parallel cobblestone streets flanking tree-lined park medians in downtown Richmond, passing the phalanx of grand Monument Avenue houses, which at Christmas displayed two-story trees in their two-story hallways, residential blocks following a straight trail of Europeanesque monuments erected in honor of Davis, Maury, Jackson, Lee, and Stuart. The statues punctuated the city with a brooding homage to the Confederacy, and they were a part of whatever it was that made Richmond unique. No city in the South, or beyond, was quite like Richmond. One did not feel the city was some backwater of racism; Richmond exuded culture and was alive, buzzing, vibrant, getting younger and younger, and the statues stood constant and prophetic against sweeps of sudden change. Not so long ago, back in the '90s, Richmond had been one of the most dangerous cities in the country, in competition with New Orleans for murder capital of the United States, but Richmond had a strong economy and had fared better than many Southern towns. Over the years, Will had seen childhood friends from Southside migrate to Richmond, sometimes coming for college and then always staying for jobs. Will saw them, the mostly white faces from the private school, and he met them at parties and for drinks, the small Southside clique strong anywhere, like a cluster of expatriates in a foreign land, even here, not two hours from home.

He cut over and drove slowly, east on Cary Street through the cheerful midday crowds, buskers and beggars standing around the doorways of cafés and restaurants and corner stores. He noticed the bright sunny legs of young Virginia Commonwealth women and recalled his own time at VCU, the house parties in the Fan and the neighborhood bars along tree-lined streets, the late breakfasts hungover with classmates whose names he had mostly forgotten, and the lazy almost carefree sunny Richmond weekends, the life he was trying on for size. The young women from good Richmond families and no families from elsewhere. The brief scattered relationships, gone every one.

In Church Hill, Will took a one-way street and crossed another slowly, looking down it like a rifle barrel. No one was behind him, and the cross street seemed empty. He took several one-ways until he'd looped around two blocks from where he'd started and came to what should have been a flashing stoplight but had been shot out and stopped anyway. To his left, a dead field of trash and broken concrete behind a chain-link fence, and on his right, a group huddled on a corner in front of tenement homes of chipped white brick over a century old. This was a blind spot from several angles. He saw shirts lifted to reveal handguns sure to have been filed numberless. He rolled down his passenger window and leaned over and said, "Bundle of pure," slipped a wad of bills up through it as the bundle fell on the passenger seat. The man, whose face he'd never been able to see (everyone on the corner wore white T-shirts, black jeans, white bandannas, and he could never know which one he was), stood at the truck and said, "B appreciate the bidness." He knocked on the door, and Will drove off, watching the side streets, even though he knew, despite Richmond "cleaning up," that cops didn't come here.

Will shoved the bundle behind his seat and drove back through downtown toward the highway. He didn't know yet what he was going to do, if he was going to honor Zeke's request. He almost passed by, but before he even realized he'd made up his mind, he was walking into his father's law practice.

Gladys said, "Hey, Will. How you been?"

"Hey, Gladys. He here?"

"Son," Bill Seems said from his office in his old deep, husky Southside accent that would have suggested to an outsider the sophisticated low-country way of speaking that existed farther south, looking over his reading glasses. He'd become a lawyer when Will was in middle school after deciding to get out of tobacco farming, which had been a Seems business for almost three centuries. It was a decision that had taken years of thought and planning, and Will remembered well how hungover his father had been after passing the bar, and Will had even thought "the bar" had something to do with drinking. Will remembered his father's torn clothes, raw knuckles, his sour animal smell, lying in bed with a washcloth on his head, which served to prove the local belief that you had to live rough to have a good time.

His father's accent always suggested precisely what Bill Seems was—learned, well-read—but not far beneath his slacks and button-downs and loafers and the pages he'd read, he was a Virginia boy, a country boy, born and raised a hunter and fisherman, at home on a porch with a dog by his side. He spoke in a brusque manner, gruff but warm somehow, a nuance that Will didn't notice much in his own generation, particularly in Richmond, where the mild accents of city boys and girls were wearing off. Bill possessed a slow and easily unnoticed efficiency. He seemed more of a forgetful professor than a lawyer, a man who'd lived the better years of his life and the worst and appeared to be comfortably in the home stretch. Will heard a jingle of excitement and saw the white speckled head of Annie, his father's beloved two-year-old setter, who came from back in the office and trotted to Will, tail whacking the desk, and Will indulged her by rubbing his hands over her soft white head, remembering the hours they used to spend pulling burrs out of dogs' ears in front of a fire after cleaning birds they'd shot that day. At one time, his mother would have cooked those birds to perfection, despite her dislike of hunting, wrapping them in bacon sometimes and stuffing them, or marinating them overnight in a blend of vinegars and serving them up grilled over a hickory pit with a side of guilt.

Bill said, "Come on in, son."

Will looked around at all the accolades, time spans of years represented each in turn by paper behind glass, a picture of himself holding his father's twelve-gauge duck gun when he was nine years old, remembering his first lesson on how a gun could kick like a cow. They used to hunt the blinds and the flooded timber back of the farm, with or without the hunt club, setting out the wooden decoys his daddy would carve and paint himself when he had the time, and Will could remember that and hunting with setters in the lowland fields bordered by loblolly and longleaf pines, loving the coveys living like warm beating hearts in flattened nests of grass and briar. Despite these tributes to their traditions, Will had always felt that, when his father had turned to the law for a profession, something of his essence had been sacrificed.

Will said, "I don't know if you heard." Bill looked at something on his desk, fiddled with it, examined his hand. "Zeke Hathom's been arrested for homicide."

"I read a short piece about it this morning; not much detail," Bill said, holding up the newspaper. "I always thought he was a good man."

"He's innocent."

"Then trust in the law. If he's innocent he has nothing to worry about."

"If he's got the right representation."

His father squinted at him. "What are you doing here during a homicide investigation? Aren't you a little busy?"

"Zeke has asked me if you'd consider representing him."

"What's the evidence suggest?"

"Zeke was seen fleeing Tom's house, which was on fire. Tom was dead—stabbed in the back—and a murder weapon was found with Zeke's fingerprints on it. The arraignment was this morning. He's being held without bond and charged with first-degree murder and arson."

"I won't even ask you if he can pay the attorney fees that would be required." Bill petted Annie and seemed to be talking to her. "Here's the real question, and I ask this not because I doubt Zeke but because anybody is capable of anything: How can you be sure he's innocent?"

"Zeke Hathom, Daddy. Don't we owe that family? What happened to Sam couldn't be pursued because nobody could or would ID anybody. But this. We can help."

"Put yourself in my shoes. You've got to build a case. How do you know he won't be able to plea? They might be able to reduce his sentence. That's probably going to be the best he can do, unless hard evidence can be found—or a confession—that someone else killed Tom. But that seems unlikely. Has the court appointed him an attorney?"

"Kevin Davidson."

Bill nodded. "What's the sheriff say?"

"He says we caught Zeke red-handed. What we did was, we caught him at the scene, but that doesn't mean he did it. He was running away, but who knows why he was there? He says he saw the fire and came to help."

"And you're willing to try to thread that needle?"

"I want you to."

They stood facing each other, two versions of something neither understood.

"A man's supposed to be innocent until proven guilty," Will said. "I think that's what Mom would have said."

"So that's why you want me to go sacrifice myself."

"Never mind," Will said, tired. "I shouldn't have even asked."

Mr. Seems exploded with sudden desperate fury. "What are you trying to prove?" He gestured wildly so that his tie came out of his coat and his suit wrinkled like water on the creek in the wind. "Going back down there to live. Becoming a deputy. Coming at me with this. You didn't go back for your mother or for Sam. You went back for yourself. You went back to wallow in your grief. To prove something to me. Well, you can't dig her back, goddamnit." Spit flew as he raised his voice, and Annie sat up, concerned. He wiped his mouth with the back of his hand, smoothed his tie, and buttoned his coat. The wind had passed. "If you can't let it go, at least let me. Say what you will about your sister, at least she's done that."

"I knew this was a mistake. Zeke asked for you. He doesn't know anyone else or trust anyone else, and his attorney is a joke. But the problem with you is you've found a way to live with yourself. I haven't."

"And that makes you superior, somehow. A saint. That's the tone your sister took before she left."

"Well, maybe you should have listened to her," Will said, more to himself than to his father.

I T WAS DARK, or darkening, the air at Promised Land so thick with humidity that it seemed to glow.

That afternoon, in the garden, Sam had begun to shiver despite the heat and came inside the house and went up to his room where he lay now on his mattress. It was the second day, and he felt it in his stomach, the fever scratching up and down his spine. He wrapped himself in his sleeping bag and slept restlessly, on and off.

Overall, the outside work had been good for him, and the scabs he was scratching open just a month ago were healing. But some days were bad, like today. He didn't know where Will was. He scraped a bowl with antic desperation for any resin he could burn for a secondhand high, but he felt no benefit. Anyway, it wasn't weed he needed; it was H, for "hero." China White, dynamite. Finally, he recognized the rattle of Will's motor as it turned off the main road and grew louder, passing the trees along the fields toward the house. Will turned off the ignition, hearing the flatline beep when he opened the door until he removed the keys, shut the door, and stepped across the creaking porch to the gasping screen door. The solid back door clamored shut, causing a shudder through the house.

Will climbed the stairs, walked into the room.

"I thought you might not come back," Sam said, close to tears. "I knew you would—I mean, I knew you should—but I started thinking, what if something happened to you? What if you didn't come back?"

"I went to Richmond."

"Good," Sam said, sitting up. "Good. Everything okay?"

"Sure. Think I got you a job."

"A job?" Sam said, reaching for the belt by the mattress and tightening it around his bicep and smacking his forearm as Will prepared the heroin. "You serious?"

"Where I used to work off Hull Street."

"How's that going to happen? Can't even leave here without getting arrested."

"I'm working on it. Maybe the judge can help. If you got a job lined up, maybe he'll cut you some slack."

Will took out one of the baggies with a *B* stamped on it, a circle beginning and ending at the top of the letter, so that the letter appeared to be part of the circle.

Will said, "Why do you always want me to go to him?"

"When I came to Richmond, working, that was where I got my first taste outside of prescriptions people was selling. After I ran off from rehab, I went back to B. It was like my heart had the GPS. God, I can't believe I made it that night. How much you get?"

"Enough for a little while, but we're going to start weaning off, like we agreed. It's time we move from daily to every other day, like we've been talking about. We're turning a corner."

Will carefully put the white dust in the spoon and lit the bottom until it turned wet as tears. The smell he had never breathed until he'd arrested Sam. It was a condensation of something natural that man had manipulated. He put the syringe needle in the fluid and drew it up into its chamber, a cloudless, placid liquid, appearing benign. Sam's dentures made a clicking noise. Will helped him up, could smell the odor of a man who hadn't showered in days, the natural oil on his scalp sour with sweat and summer.

Sam said, "They find out who killed Tom?"

"No."

Sam was just starting to get healthy, beginning to accept the idea of sobriety. If he knew his own daddy was their suspect, he'd run off and relapse, and that would be that. He might never get another chance to sober up again. Will just couldn't tell him.

"What's wrong, Will?"

"Nothing."

"Bullshit. Something eating you up."

"Forget it."

Sam looked pale even in the slanted shadows of the dark house, scrawny. Fingers shaking with a violence that Will would have associated with Parkinson's before seeing Sam after all those years.

Will spoke now to him almost as a mother would. "Have you been feeding yourself? I left those cans of soup and beans last week, and there's all the stuff from the garden."

"I felt sick."

"It's this shit. You know that."

Sam nodded at the floor. "The sickness is the cure. Sometimes I wonder, what's the point of living just to live without?"

"One day at a time, brother. Forget the rest of your life. Live for every day."

"That's what my sponsor in rehab used to say. Ray. Good dude. But you could see in his eyes, he wasn't alive. He was just sober. He was just breathing, like I am now. But you ain't never been hurt. Sometimes, I wonder if this is all that bad. I'm just doing my thing."

"Be real, dude. It's the same as suicide."

They had talked about it before, and Sam had loved Mrs. Seems like family. Will knew Sam understood, and it helped that he had known her. The fact was, these days Will depended on Sam as much as Sam depended on Will. They were trapped in a shared past.

"Come on, man," Sam said. "Don't go there. Come on."

Will gave Sam the injection as one might treat a sick child or grandparent or even lover. Almost immediately, his friend calmed and held his arm and lay back on the mattress. Will took out his knife and opened up a can of beans and put it by the mattress where Sam lay in a relaxed state, staring at nothing. Then he covered his friend up with the blanket. He sat and watched Sam for a little while.

Eventually, he heard his own boots creaking on the steps, the spiral staircase like a rifle barrel aimed at heaven above. He turned back at the door, looked up at the ceiling, at the plaster walls cracked and bare, and the hanging wallpaper in the parlor where his family used to eat meals. It had once been warm, the windows allowing the golden sunlight in. He remembered a time the house had been beautiful, and he would fall asleep listening to his mother's voice as she'd play the piano. At one time they'd been happy here. But happiness was as elusive as guilt. Where did it start? Where did it end?

He opened the door and walked out. Tonight he'd return to the familiar creek where he had failed, watching over everything as if he could do something about it.

FLORESSA SAW Will's truck parked by the swimming hole down the road from the church. She shook her head, said a prayer, and leaned the door open against a doorstop so that she could bring in the two buckets of flowers she'd picked up from the supermarket in Chase City.

After she had made the arrangements on the altar (a folding table covered in a white linen cloth), she drove away in her Crown Victoria to Dawn, felt the tires crunching gravel and dirt, pulling her sedan along the ruts that had been set before her until she hit the main road, looking back once to see the red cloud behind, risen as if in indecision, in the balance of something's whim. But she was happy now that Bennico Watts was in town, staying with her in Turkey Creek. She came to the square and parked across the street from the courthouse.

Part-time deputy Buddy Monroe took her back to Zeke, who had heard a flat, solid shuffling of feet. *Floressa. Lord God.* He was too ashamed to see her. She sat down, trouble in her eyes, and said, "Have you heard from Will about his daddy?"

Zeke shook his head.

"I'll talk to him," she said.

"Everything all right?" Zeke said.

"She's in town."

"Does Will know?"

"Not yet, baby. We're going to talk to him tomorrow."

"I don't know, Floressa. I'm worried. He ain't the boy who used to hang around with Sam."

"Yes, he is," she said. "He is too. You leave him to me."

They heard the keys approaching.

"All right, Mrs. Hathom," Buddy said. He was a little scared of Floressa.

"All right what," Floressa said.

"That fifteen minutes is up."

"Shoot," she said, turning. "Why are you here, anyway? Where that Seems boy?"

"Suspended," he said, smiling. "Thought everybody knew that."

"Suspended!"

He showed his teeth now, partially rotten. Sugar definitely, meth maybe.

"Traffic violation."

"Traffic violation!"

She stood and blew Zeke a kiss and followed Buddy down the hall toward the main office.

"Sheriff pulled him over and gave him a choice," Buddy said, talking back over his shoulder at her. "Suspension or a ticket. He took the suspension. You ask me, that boy ain't got more sense than your old man."

"Maybe he got sense enough," she said, a little out of breath. "One of these days, that badge going to bite you."

"I'm a sworn-in bona fide deputy of the law."

"Y'all got problems. Sheriff pulling over deputies instead of fighting crime. Only people you ain't catching are the ones who need to be where my husband at right now. Don't you touch me."

"I got a mind to put you back there."

"I dare you."

As she moved out through the door, she couldn't help smiling at the thought of Will Seems taking that suspension just to spite the sheriff, but it bothered her a little too. That wasn't going to get them anywhere. She thought of him out there, alone with all his thoughts, living out there on his family's property like a hermit, and she wondered . . . She worried about him, remembering the way his mother had passed. Her own heart had gone out to the boy as if he were her own. Boy had some redemption in him, something his mother had also had. That was a sad business. Her heart ached with the memory of all that had happened, all that had been lost between the two of them.

WILL'S GRANDMOTHER CALLED and invited him to Saint Luke's Episcopal Church in Dawn, which his family used to attend regularly. "We'll come by and pick you up."

"I'll meet y'all down by the gate so you don't have to drive up," Will said.

"We'll be by at ten thirty and have a picnic after the eleven o'clock service."

"Yes, ma'am."

The Episcopal church was a mighty brick edifice surrounded by magnolias and pines in an open area at the end of a gravel drive. As had hunt clubs, churches had stayed segregated, not by mandate or really by choice but just because that was the way things had always been, and people didn't want to swap churches. There may have been twenty people attending in a church built for over two hundred. Most of them were old. The youngest, aside from Will, was middle-aged. Will remembered playing in the courtyard here with his sister, who was now living up north in Chicago, and with the other young kids, most of whom had since moved away.

After a service in which the bookish priest focused on the tired theme of forgiveness, Will's grandfather said, "We've been thinking about you, son. About that man y'all took. Wasn't he Mrs. Hathom's husband?"

"Yessir."

"It was all in the *Southside Telegraph*," his grandfather said, shaking his head.

"Horrible," his grandmother said.

She had packed a wicker basket with fried chicken and coleslaw. She spread out a blanket in the grass, but Will and his grandfather stood leaning against the tailgate. They had taken off their jackets and could feel the sun on their white button-downs through which sweat showed like grease. The old man was someone Will respected but pitied. He was the kind of man who had a strict sense of honor, someone who might actually challenge someone over an insult. But those days were long gone. The world had never stood still enough for him to find a way to live in it.

"It's terrible seeing the way things have become," the old man said. "It's no better in Emporia. Son, why didn't you just stay in Richmond? You had everything."

"No, sir, I didn't."

"I'll never understand your generation," he said. "It's never enough. Everybody seems to bounce from one thing to another. Anything but plant their feet where they are and stand tall."

"Jed," Will's grandmother said, but he didn't stop.

"Somehow it's all changed. What used to be a good countryside to raise babies and grow them into servants of the state and the country is now . . . Well, just look at it."

"What are you doing about anything, Jed?"

"Surviving, Gale. Goddamnit." A strange moment of silence passed before the old man said, "Should've brought us some fishing poles. Why the hell did you come back to this place? We're old—no use us leaving just to die. But you. You got your whole life to live for."

Will knew the only thing that would satisfy them. "I was called back."

His grandfather nodded. His jaw moved, as if determining whether he could swallow what was in his mouth.

"Sure enough? Well, you got to keep in line with Him, pay attention to signs. You see the young folks these days. There's no God in anything. And what do we got now? Empty houses, empty people, but a fine spread of crime. I can't see what use the Lord would have for you to be back here."

Will was sick of this kind of talk. He understood that his grandfather was afraid. It was the fear talking. He knew the real reason, and they were circling it. Bitterness could only mask it for a time.

"You look tired, honey," his grandmother said, touching his cheek. "Are you liking your job okay? I worry about you. It's a brave job."

"Yes, ma'am. I'm on unpaid vacation." His grandparents didn't understand. He said, "Suspension."

"Oh, Will," his grandmother said. "That's not funny at all."

"You best keep your head down," his grandfather said. "No telling what'll come around the corner. For all you know, it'll be Satan himself. I begin to wonder, if man's made in God's image, if we shouldn't just be afraid of God Himself."

They ate. His grandmother's chicken, thickly breaded, seasoned with black pepper and salt and cayenne, cold and refreshing on a hot day.

"What's your plan?" his grandfather said, licking his fingers. "You gonna go on staying in the house?"

"Yessir. I aim to fix it up. Start the farm back up."

The old man chuckled. "That's a lot of work for a full-time lawman."

"I won't be a lawman forever."

"She'll always be there." The old man looked away quickly, as if surprised at himself for opening that door, and Will could see the twitching side of his face now. He held his hands to his eyes as if shading them. Will hated to see his grandfather sad, as he had seen his mother in those last months, not knowing how to save her.

"I think He called me back for her."

Will felt bad about lying. God had called no one to do nothing. But he hoped it would bring them some comfort to think there was a purpose to it all.

"Let's go see her, Jed. Will. Let's go see your mother, Hannah."

He tried to think of a reason they couldn't go, something that would make sense, but they had a right to see their daughter's grave. He could only hope Sam would stay out of the way. He had no way to warn him.

They packed up and rode out to Promised Land.

Will forced the key into the rusty Master Lock and lifted the heavy, dented metal gate so that it swung high enough above the earth and let it rest against the far fence post. His grandfather drove the truck forward, rattling over the cattle guard, the soft sound of hard dirt under the tires as Will got in the bed and knocked on the window, and the truck moved forward again, and Will couldn't remember the last time he'd been a passenger somewhere, riding in the back of a truck, warm wind in his hair, the way they used to. He stared up through the trees, the skittering of cicadas rising out of them like heat waves over tar, the strong sun heavy white against the boughs of the cedars, and up at the house. He couldn't see any sign of Sam yet. The truck pushed through the long heavy grass, leaving it compressed in two trails behind them like a wake in some green marsh, and came around to the back of the house—where they could see the manicured pathway to the slanted brick wall against the slanted hill, nothing higher around them—so they could see the fields angling away gradually like the sides of a tent from the peak.

His grandfather killed the truck motor, and the doors opened, and Will watched his grandparents, old but still agile enough, slide down out of the truck, beeping until the doors shut.

"Well," his grandfather said. "Guess I didn't need to bring that Weedwacker. You been keeping it up, Will. Good on you. Last time we was here—before you moved back—it was like she'd been forgotten."

"I won't let that happen," Will said.

Will led the way, scanning for Sam and looking out for snakes in the sunny path or hanging over the wall. They came to the graveyard, and Will opened the gate with his father's family name centered so that *SE* and *EMS* were divided when the gates opened. He held out his arm for his grandmother and led her in.

His grandmother cried when she saw it, her hand gripping Will's shoulder.

"Oh, William," she said. "It's beautiful."

The headstone, indeed, looked wonderful, with fresh flowers lining it, some beginning to wilt, the grass throughout the walled graveyard trimmed neatly. There were many old, very old stones, chipped and covered with lichen and moss, darkened with time and difficult to read. All Seemses, dating back to the early 1700s, including the sixteen with the Southern Cross of Honor beside their headstones. (The current house at Promised Land dated back to 1819, the year the previous version, built in 1791, had caught fire and burned to the ground.) She had a bright grave, the words "Loved by all who knew her" carved underneath her full name, Hannah Elizabeth Lee Seems, and the years she had lived, 1956–2000.

"Oh, William," his grandmother said again, her arm through his as if at a cotillion.

They stepped forward and offered the new bouquet, his grandmother taking the older flowers away, holding them in one hand, arranging the new ones before the grave. His grandfather crouched, his face closed, hand over his eyes again. Will heard him breathe through his nose, a sound like the tension of a screen door opening or like a doe blowing at a threat. They, like he, would never get over it, but Will was too angry to cry. It was a hate that filled him. She had done this to them, and Will knew in some way it was because of him. They would only learn and relearn to live with it, because there was no other way, but he also knew it would never be over. She would never really die.

His grandmother gripped Will's hand. "I'm so proud to know she knows she's loved. I'm so proud you keep it up. It means everything."

When his grandfather stood, he was raw-eyed and weak-looking, as if he had just stumbled out of a bar or had been whipped good.

"Thank you, son," he said. "You loved your mother very much. Not like your—"

"Jed."

They turned to face the grave again, and his grandfather said a prayer to Hannah: "We don't know why you did it, Hannah, but we love you just the same. The pain you felt is now over. We'll love you forever. Think about you every day, sweetie. Every day. Amen."

They walked back to the truck, and his grandfather cleared his throat. They stood around the tailgate, looking ashamed. Will wanted them to go. He wanted to be alone in the dark empty house, alone with the dead fresh on his mind, alone with pain like a cat going to die, private personal griefs welling in his chest. He wanted to pull chaos out of deep shadows, make something out of it, rise from himself.

His grandfather said, "Let's look inside. I'll help you see what needs doing. I got a little bit of time these days, and while you're off at work, I can get Jerome Davis and Terrell Bloom to come over and help you get settled."

"Some other time. It's not ready for company."

"I can see that," the old man said, walking toward the house. "You might've at least removed the boards from the windows."

"You'll be needing some furniture," his grandmother said.

"I've got the dining room table and chairs, the piano."

"But you need beds, linens, coffee tables."

"There's no hurry," Will said, calling after the old man. "Grand-dad, I don't need help."

"You been here close on a year," his grandfather said, "and it don't look like no one lives here. See you got a crop of tobacco in the ground. You raising it by yourself?"

"It doesn't take all that much once it's in the ground," Will said.

His grandfather chuckled to himself, pushed open the heavy door to the house, a gasping sound of stale spirit air churning the motes of dust in the deep dark hallway. Will hoped it would be too dark to see anything much (only the back porch windows and cracks in the boards and the solitary unboarded window upstairs let in light), but his own eyes adjusted after a moment.

"It's like a damn crypt," his grandfather said. "You need some light, son. You need to pry off those boards."

Will scanned for Sam, walked ahead of them into the parlor. When he turned, he heard the sound of a foot on the stairs and rushed back into the hallway to see his grandfather four steps up.

"Granddad!" Will said. "Come downstairs."

"Hold on. I just want to take a look."

Will said, "I don't think it's a good idea to be climbing the stairs in this heat, in this darkness. They're not in great shape."

But the old man kept climbing. "These stairs were built back when things were made to last."

"Jed," his grandmother said. "It's hot enough down here. You got to worry about your heart."

Will watched his grandfather's back in terror as he saw him straighten and draw his M1911 pistol.

"Granddad!" he shouted, bounding up the stairs.

"Don't shoot, Mr. Lee! It's me! It's Sam Hathom!"

"What in the hell?" Will's grandfather said, looking at Sam standing against the hallway wall, white squares like tan lines where pictures had once hung.

The old man looked over his shoulder at Will. "He's here by your design?"

"Yessir," Will said.

"What, because of his daddy?"

"He's just staying with me is all."

The old man holstered his pistol. "I don't know what the hell's going on here, and I don't want to know. I see now how you got that crop in."

He turned, descending, pushing past his grandson like a stranger at a bar. Will could see his grandfather had sweat through his shirt.

"Granddad, I can explain."

"I said I don't want to know."

He followed his grandparents outside to the truck.

"Granddad, Grandma." They turned, and in their eyes he could see he'd lost something else. "Please. Don't say anything about him being here. Not to anyone."

"I don't like this," his grandfather said. "That boy doesn't look well. Is he on drugs?"

"He's sick, and I'm taking care of him."

"Bull," his grandfather said. "You're lying, to us and to him."

"You knew about his condition."

"I'm not talking about no condition. You see the look on his face when I mentioned his daddy? Does he not know?"

"Please . . ."

Will's grandfather raised his hand and turned away. Will kissed his grandmother's cold, fragile cheek. She reached up and combed his hair with her fingers, looking at what she was doing rather than in his eyes.

"Will, I worry about you and the decisions you make. You can't depend on good intentions to protect you."

"Yes, ma'am. Please. Please, promise me you'll keep this between us. No talk at book club, or at the grocery, or . . ."

"Okay, honey," she said, a wariness in her face. "I won't talk. But I don't like it."

He helped her into the truck and watched them jolting away, following the low patient contours of a hard, undulating land that had shaped them all, their bodies and their dreams.

Will found Sam upstairs, pacing. "I got to get the fuck out of here. What kind of dumb shit was that, bringing them in here?"

"I couldn't stop them. Don't worry. You're safe. They won't talk. I made them promise."

"What Mr. Lee mean about my daddy?"

"I don't know," Will said.

Sam looked hard at Will, as if making a decision.

"I know how your grandma can be," Sam said. "I sure hope she don't blab at all. If she does," he said, a little smile forming, "you gon' be fucked."

"Me? Me! What happens to me happens to you."

"Nah, man. It ain't the same. Who holds the drugs? You. Who got a job to hold? You. I'm living free as a crow, just floating over paradise. Ain't got shit to lose."

THE THREE WOMEN, Claudette and Bennico and Floressa, waited at the Hathom house for Will to arrive. He came in civvies and gave brief nods to the three women sitting at the kitchen table.

"Bennico Watts," Floressa said, and Will reached out and shook her hand. "Will Seems."

"What's this about?" Will said.

Floressa said, "Sit down." He slid the chair out, sat with his elbows on the table, hands clasped. "You want something to drink, honey? We got some juice, some sweet tea, some Coke."

"I'd take a Coke, please, ma'am," he said.

Tom's mother stood up and filled a glass with ice and got out a two-liter RC Cola and poured it over the ice. Will felt bad for accepting anything. Miss Claudette put the two-liter back and shut the fridge and brought him the glass with a napkin under it.

"Thank you, ma'am," Will said.

Floressa smiled. "Miss Claudette and I agreed we want you and Mrs. Watts to investigate."

Will was already shaking his head. "I got a job, and my best chance of being able to help Mr. Hathom is to keep it."

"Son, it's all over about you got suspended."

Will looked away, taking in the house he had not set foot in for over a decade. It was more familiar than the house at Promised Land in its current state.

"Claudette and I want this, and you gonna do it. Bennico here's a private investigator from Richmond. You've got the badge."

"Why her?"

Bennico said, "These women filled me in about this resistance to investigating Tom's death. I won't stop until I expose the facts."

"It's bad business to go into it with preconceptions."

"Isn't that what's going on here? Arresting a convenient suspect? Hurrying along a case to keep up appearances?"

"Now, wait up," Will said. "I don't know about all that. I'm doing my job."

"You keep telling yourself that and you'll go far around here. Right in line to be sheriff someday."

Will leaned back and folded his arms across his chest. "What the hell do you know about things around here?"

"Enough," Bennico said.

"Oh," Will said. "You're one of those."

"Those what?"

"Activists. Getting into things and leaving a mess for others to clean up."

"Will," Floressa said. "Don't you want to help Zeke out?"

"Of course I want to help. But if I get caught doing this, I won't be able to."

"What kind of law enforcement is it when you can't stand up for the truth? Your job is to serve and protect, ain't it? Use that badge for good."

"How do you expect this to work? I can't exactly bring her into the office."

"Y'all met in Richmond. She's visiting you for a little while. It's that easy. You share what you know with her, she does some snooping. You ain't dating nobody, is you?" Will looked down. "So there won't be no problem."

Will said, "She's wearing a wedding ring."

Bennico took the ring off her finger, after staring at it a moment too long, and said, "Anything else?"

"What about your husband?"

"He's leaving me."

"But you're . . ."

"What, Black? It's okay. I was born this way."

Will laughed uncomfortably. "*I* don't care about that. But people might not believe we're together."

Claudette spoke up. "How come you to say that when my boy had a baby girl with a white woman? It does happen. You just got to get over that."

"Well, where is she going to stay?"

"With you."

"Fuck no."

Floressa slapped his hand.

"Nobody would believe someone's staying with me out in that house. It's still got boards over the damn windows."

Floressa said, "Don't you see it's the only way this will work? You can't be meeting out in public to discuss this."

"Don't put that on me. I didn't invite her, you did. I don't need this right now."

"Well, we do."

Bennico said, "What are you hiding?"

"Is this an interrogation? What the . . . ," he looked at Floressa, ". . . hell."

"You better realize something, son," Claudette said, calm compared to Floressa. "Mrs. Watts going to investigate with or without you. It's done. We got our own law around here, and it's called God's truth. Remember what I said when you come to my house? This is a fight. We prayed over you. You can't put them blinders on no more."

"You don't understand."

"*You* don't understand," Floressa said. "She going to stay on with you, and you gonna treat her like the gentleman I know you is. The gentleman your mama raised you to be. Everybody know you go out there and sit in your pickup out by the creek nights. Seen you. I know you care about all that's happened to us. Well, here's a chance to act."

"I got things I need to do," Will said. "On my own."

"I know you didn't mean for Zeke to be in this mess," Floressa said. "I know you're a good boy. We got a history, Will. Of loving each other in all this pain. But you owe us—this whole community—and you damn well know it, and I believe that's why you came back. So you're going to do this, not even because I'm telling you but because you know it's right. You got that?"

Floressa reached out and put her hand on Will's neck, a touch that triggered something old and repressed. She petted him as someone might a beloved horse or dog.

"Answer me, William Cuthbert Seems, III."

He could feel something deep within him unlock as Floressa ran her coarse, pink-palmed hand up and down the scruff of his neck, and he looked at her with all that internal pain, and she could see how it had gone to seed and bolted through him, that his wounds were real too. He was a link to her boy and to the past. She had needed to see that pain that was in him, that deep pain. She needed him to hurt so that she could comfort him. He was as pale and transparent as he'd been as a boy. She could see him now, hair like corn, sitting beside Sam through the car ride to the hospital, remembered that dark night, the crops tall by the road in the car headlights like startled promises, tears along his face in the white light when they had arrived at the hospital.

"See," Floressa said. "I knew you cared. Your mama was a good woman full of pain and full of love. She had a heart the size of Euphoria County, so big it had to break. She's gone, but we ain't. We always here for you, baby."

Claudette said, "Son, you got to go on back to Sheriff Mills and get you back your badge. We counting on that. You got to do whatever it takes."

"Yes, ma'am."

He stood up, looking like a boy again.

"I got to ask you something," said Floressa. "You been talking to my boy? Do you know where he is?"

He stared at her with that confused, young, hurt look in his face.

Her laugh was forced and weary, her face turning to an expression similar to Will's.

"You never could hide a bruise, Will Seems, nor tell a lie. You tell my boy, if you can"—she teared up again—"his mama loves him."

T HAT EVENING, Will guided Bennico out to the ruins of the Janders place at dusk, toeing through the rubble with flashlights illuminating a bleak scattered scene that offered little in the way of evidence or hope of any kind. He explained everything to her that he knew, that he'd witnessed: stumbling over Tom's body, cuffing Zeke, Day returning to the house in a panic of tears. Will pointed to where he'd found Tom, and where they'd seen Zeke at first. Tom's truck was still in the yard, and as they were leaving, Will put his hand on it as if there might be an answer in the gruff texture of the surface rust.

They stopped at the Hardee's—the only place open after nine—for some chicken and biscuits to take back to the house.

"You throwing a party?" Bennico said.

Will looked at her. "Promise me something," he said.

"What?"

"Promise you won't say anything about what I'm about to tell you."

"What is this, middle school? Fine, I promise. What is it?"

"Someone else is staying with me."

"Well, if you're seeing somebody, we should come up with a different story."

"He's an old friend."

"So what's the big deal?"

"He needs to think we really are together."

"You don't trust him?"

"No, I do. But he's Sam Hathom, Zeke and Floressa's son."

"Floressa was right." She watched him carefully. Shaking her head, she said, "No way. You're lying to her. That's fucked up."

"You promised," Will said, an intense glare fixed on her.

"Okay, okay," she said, looking away. "But I still say it's fucked up. Does Sam know about the murder?"

"He doesn't know his dad is our main suspect."

"What kind of friend are you? He deserves to know that if you ask me."

"Sure, he deserves it. But we can't tell him. He's not ready."

"Well, this is bad. I don't know how you expect us to talk about the murder if he's going to be around."

"I didn't plan on any of this," Will said.

"Neither did I."

"I guess we'll have to wait for Sam to go to bed before we can talk about anything."

They drove the dual dirt tracks, the tall grass brushing the undercarriage of their vehicles. It seemed to Bennico they were off-road a long time before reaching the house, which emerged as a looming tree-crowded shadow. They walked in under the buzzing fluorescent light of the back porch, where moths moved like an indecisive tornado, and into the dark house, which had an old spicy smell from all the hardwood fires that had cured it like Virginia ham.

"Yo!" Will called out.

They came down the hallway and saw a dim light in the parlor to the right and found Sam reading in one of the ladder-backed chairs, up against a dining table on which a kerosene lantern flickered.

Will turned to Bennico. "No electricity in this part of the house."

The room was something out of another, previous world. In the lamplight, the room seemed grotesque, with its ornate fireplace and the moth-eaten antique wallpaper with a mural of Romanesque ruins that played out all through the room without repetition. Sam was hunched over his book on the table and craned his head up, and Bennico could see marks all over his face like burn marks, pale spots where skin had scabbed over and healed. He stood, awkward, like a tree grown around some obstacle. Even his jawline was crooked, and he appeared to have some trouble seeing and blinked rapidly in a strange reflex of nerves, as if trying to clear his vision. Sam looked like he'd never seen a woman.

"No need to stand," she said.

"I didn't know we were gonna have a guest."

"Well, last-minute plans," Will said. "This is Bennico. We started dating in Richmond, and we figured it was time for her to see the place."

"See *this* place?"

Bennico said, "He told me not to have high expectations."

"You eat yet?" Will said, leaving Sam and Bennico in the parlor to get some plates.

When he returned, Sam said, "I got to talk to you, man."

Will glanced at Bennico, a look she was not meant to notice.

"Talk here," Will said. "Over dinner."

"Naw. I told you, it's about that business we got."

"After supper," Will said. "Eat something first."

Sam had begun rubbing his arms and neck and shoulders, and looked anxious, even while eating.

"Why you want to come here?" Sam said to Bennico. "Euphoria County is about as far as you can go to being on another planet from Richmond."

"Things are getting serious," she said. "It was time. Ain't that right, baby?"

"Yeah . . . honey," Will said.

"I can see it's serious by the way y'all look," Sam said, forcing a laugh. "Shit."

Will and Bennico glanced at each other.

"So," Bennico said. "You're familiar with Richmond?"

"I've spent some time there. 'The Holy City,'" he said with a great deal of irony, using air quotes. "The holiest."

"Well," Bennico said, "if it's so bad here, why are you here?"

"Shit."

"How long you been living here with Will?"

"He hadn't told you? Too fucking long," he said, obviously an attempt at humor that didn't land. "Shit, I don't know. I can't remember. Dude has my phone. I don't know what fucking day it is."

"Been more than a month," Will said. "Really rolling out the carpet, aren't you?"

"You got a carpet?" Sam said, looking around. "Didn't think so."

"How do y'all know each other?" Bennico asked.

Sam looked at Will. "I thought I was a little more important than for you to not tell me you got a girlfriend and for you not to tell her about me. You a secretive mo'fuck."

"I wanted her to meet you first," Will said. "These things are usually better in person."

"You haven't even taken the boards off this haunted-ass house, and you think this is the place for your girlfriend to see? I'm calling bullshit."

"It's the house I'm going to fix up and live in. It's my family place. It shouldn't be a secret."

"You okay with this?" Sam asked Bennico.

She shrugged. "Will's told me all about the house. I wanted to see it. You know, the before and after."

"Will," Sam said.

"You've barely eaten anything."

"I got to talk to you."

"Okay," he said. "Fucking hell. Excuse us."

As they got up, and Will walked past her, she grabbed Will's hand and pulled him down to her for a kiss. Will looked like he'd seen a ghost.

"See you in a minute, baby," she said to him.

"You bet . . . sweetie."

He went upstairs with Sam, scratching his head.

Bennico waited at the table until she heard a door shut. She stood up, took the lamp, and walked over to the wallpaper and studied it. An idyllic, pastoral scene of couples lying about and picnicking, dwarfed by great ancient ruins. She'd never seen wallpaper that could be considered art. In the room, a couple of strange sculptures stood on the mantle. There was an old sideboard, and a kind of chifforobe in the corner, and a spinning wheel by one of the windows. She walked out of the room and looked up the tall stairs. She could hear only muffled talking and commotion. She walked into the room across the hall from the parlor. It was almost entirely bare except for a settee by a fireplace and a grand piano.

All around the room, she could see pale stretches of wall and floor where furniture and rugs had once filled what now appeared to be a massive cavern of a room. The grand piano had been covered up with a blanket. Her footsteps echoed; the house seemed to gasp and breathe, as if a sustain pedal had been pressed down, releasing the possibilities of sound.

She came back to the foot of the stairs and looked up, took her shoes off, and left the lantern on the banister rail. She slipped up the stairs, listening. She heard what sounded like a paper bag being packed away, and when she heard steps, she quickly slipped downstairs. At her shoes, she saw something moving. She lowered the lantern.

Will came to the head of the stairs to the sound of hammering, Bennico saying, "Go on. Get away. Shoo."

She was bending over, smacking at something with her shoe, and then he could see the snake seething, wending down the hall. Bennico threw her shoes, one at a time, after it.

"It's just a black snake," Will said. "They keep the copperheads away."

He picked up her shoes and handed them to her.

"Well," she said. "I don't care if he's a good snake or not. I don't want him coming after me like he done."

"I told you this place might not suit you."

"I don't care if it suits or not. If it doesn't, I'll just have to make some changes."

Will rolled his eyes as she slipped her shoes back on. He went back upstairs, said something to Sam, closed the door, and came back down.

"Is Sam okay?" she said.

"He's going to bed. Come on, let's get to work."

He showed her the darkroom in the basement with its uneven dirt floor and broken chinks in the foundation. A couple of photographs still pinched by clothespins hung from a string, and others were crudely framed or pinned to the walls, all curling with the humidity, photographs he'd taken, sketches, all colorless—stark black-and-white, employing a kind of chiaroscuro, an emphasis on shadows and the blankness behind them, light and dark. Black trees lining the swamp, bleeding in wet spidery reflections down the paper, across the image of brief light on the visage of dark water, clouds thin and running like blood down a thick sheet of paper sky, evoking the essence of a fall evening in some ancient essence of Virginia.

Will grabbed a stack of photographs and took two off the line.

"Let's go out on the porch where we can see."

Outside, he handed her the stack and let her look through them.

"These are pictures I took of the crime scene on Wednesday."

She picked up one of the Janders house, steam and smoke rising from the rubble, black against a bright sky, and sun slanted against the treeline, a kind of apocalyptic dusk or dawn. But the focus was on a waifish, grieving woman, hand to her face.

"Does the sheriff have copies of these?"

"These are mine. He doesn't know about them."

She held up a particular picture that had been catching her eye. Will had probably looked at it twenty times. A man—the sheriff obviously—was holding the same woman. The emotions captured, faces crisp, movement of legs and arms blurred, a chaotic balance achieved by the photograph.

She said, "If they weren't for an investigation, I'd say these are personal."

"What do you mean?"

"I'm not stupid, is what I mean. So this is Tom's baby mama."

"Yeah. Ferriday Pace when she returned to the house."

"What do we know about her?"

"She's from the Snakefoot is about all."

"Snakefoot?"

"We call it Snakefoot Swamp. Think of it as the forgotten back-side of our fine forgotten county, a place where descendants of escaped slaves and white trash coexist. Anyway, Day used to work at Arnie's Lounge, an old house that serves as a bar and casino, where she and Tom met. Pretty soon after, she moved in with Tom. Ten months later, they had a baby girl. There was some talk about that."

"Why? Because they weren't married?"

"That, and people said she only moved in because Tom got her pregnant—he told me that as well—but if that were the case, it would have been less than nine months after she moved in until their daughter was born."

"I don't see what the big deal is there. Could have been a miscarriage."

"From what Tom told me, I believe he'd have left her if she'd lost the child."

Bennico said, "I'm going to have to meet her."

"Hold off on that for now."

"Shoot. You hold off if you want."

"If we're going to work this, you're going to have to listen to me sometimes. I know this area."

"Well, I know some things too. And I don't like to hit the brakes, especially before things get started. You may not like me or my style, but I make things happen. You can be assured of that."

"Fuck. Just hold off on that for the time being. Tomorrow I'm going to have to go in for my badge. I'll probably be tied up until late afternoon—if he gives me it, that is. I'm hoping I'll be able to track down a couple possible suspects, guys who lost a lot of money to Tom the night he was killed. After that, we'll go to Emporia and talk to the coroner."

"I'm going to need to see the body," Bennico said.

"Of course."

Bennico sifted through the other photographs, every single one with Ferriday Pace in it. She shook her head but decided not to press the issue.

"How old's that baby girl now?" she asked instead.

"A couple months, I guess."

"Where was Miss Pace that night?"

"A motel called the Rebel Inn."

"You sure?"

"She had a receipt, and I called the motel."

"Did you know him well?" Bennico asked.

Will nodded. "At one time, anyway."

"When was the last time you saw him?"

"Ran into him two or three weeks ago."

Ran into him. Will had followed him, hit the lights, instructed him to take his next right up a dirt road that led to a small clearing with a small house no one had lived in for years. Will observed Tom's eyes, tired, like a setter that's run himself sick through briars and thickets. Tired but shrewd.

"Tell me something, man," Tom said, squinting through the smoke from his cigarette and scratching his head. "Why you digging into all this? What good's it going to do?"

"But you can find out," Will said. "Even if you don't know who it was."

"How it make sense for a man of the law to be asking me for information?"

"Look at me. I can't exactly go undercover."

"I get all that. What I'm asking is why you looking into this now? After all these years? Sam gone. Disappeared. This ain't gonna benefit him. Unless you know something I don't. If not, just let it go."

"I can't."

"If I do this, what are you gonna try and do?"

"I don't know."

"I see. You came all the way back to put on a uniform. But you didn't come back to serve and protect, did you? You came back to search and destroy."

"You're the only one who can help, who can understand."

"A'ight man," Tom said. "I'll see what I can dig up for you. But you better promise me, no matter what I find, you won't do nothing stupid."

There was a strange feeling in the pit of Will's heart, a feeling none of this was real, finally seeing Tom again and how he'd aged and become just another man who could have accomplished who knew what. It was as if the real Tom had been kept alive only in Will's memory.

"How did he seem to you?" Bennico said now. "Any indication something was wrong?"

"It looked like he was living hard. You should have seen him in high school. He was going places. But that's what this place does to people. You leave and disown it, or you stay and suffer. Eventually it gets to you. I think staying's really what killed him. I'm convinced of it."

"Then how come you're back?" Bennico said.

"I didn't ever want to leave."

"You got to explain that," she said, wheeling her hand in the air. "Come on, I got enough to figure out as it is. Don't keep me guessing when you know something. Don't make me ask every time."

Will looked away.

Bennico said, "Like pulling teeth with you. Why did you leave if you didn't want to?"

"That's not relevant."

"Shit," she said. Will seemed to be as likely as not to indulge her, and she couldn't figure out when he would, what was off-limits, or if there was a logic to it at all. "You're trouble."

"Once again, I didn't ask for this shit."

She thought about slapping him. Instead, she controlled her breathing and said, "Tell me how Sam is taking all this news, of Tom, and all that."

"He's fucked up over it. Everyone is."

"Will, you got to let him go. Floressa needs him. Do what's right."

"I can't let him go. Can't give him a reason to. I'm helping him."

"By dosing him?"

She believed him capable of anything then, the way his gray tired eyes filled up with new young hate.

She said, "Boy, do you realize how much trouble you could be in right now? Come on, don't act surprised. I'm a PI. Sam's got marks all over, like he's been cutting it with fentanyl."

"We don't do that anymore," Will said, a little puzzled that he'd included himself in Sam's actions.

"It's not right. Now tell me, why are you dosing him here, in secret? I thought you were his friend. You can trust me."

Will sighed. "Sam has two warrants out for his arrest. One in Euphoria, one in Mecklenburg. I arrested him breaking into a house about a month ago. To see the shape he was in . . ." He shook his head, looking off. "We were old friends. I made the decision then and there to bring him back here, help him out. He wouldn't have been able to handle jail."

"You don't have the right to make that decision. Didn't you go through some training to be in law enforcement?"

"It's not a right. It's a responsibility. I owe him."

"What the hell for?"

He pulled out his wallet, removed a photo of him and Sam when they were younger, maybe thirteen. "That's us. It's because of me he looks like he does today. It's because of me he's got that addiction. It's because of me."

He recalled for her the summer of '98, the beating, enough of it anyway.

"Were you hurt at all?"

"Not like he was."

"Well, why the guilt?"

"I didn't protect him."

"What could you have done?"

"Something. Anything."

"Did you come all the way back here for him?"

Will stared out into the dark. "Not exactly."

"Don't bullshit me. It is why you came back. To protect him or do something for him."

"We need each other."

"What happens when they find out you've been hiding him?"

"Maybe it won't matter then."

"You're dangerous," she said. But she startled him, reaching out and holding his hand in her rough grip. "Whatever you are trying to do, whatever you're planning, I can help you."

He pulled his hand away and stood up, glaring down at her.

"I don't need your fucking help, and I sure as shit didn't ask for it. I had a mother once, and she's dead. Don't try and take her place. Your room is upstairs, end of the hallway."

He snatched his photographs and left her on the porch, running her fingers through her loosely curled hair, not understanding where this sudden anger came from. He fired up his truck, felt the thin and troubled comfort of the radio preacher's stringent, furious voice speaking—shouting—into the blackness of night, out of a barely glowing dashboard, about something so universal or generic it probably applied to what they both were feeling.

**D**AY TURNED at the old Sunoco, saw again the thick, imposing Africanesque flora of home—the Snakefoot—a yellow faded sign advertising five-dollar palm readings in red writing, the distant thick tapestry of loblolly and longleaf pines and wide bald cypresses, the little house in the trees like a part of the landscape her daddy used to trap for beaver.

Granny could feel Day's approach like a storm glittering across a clear sky. In the spirit air she could see the waves around her moving like snakes. As a little girl, the old woman did not want to have the gift of soothsaying, but it had come down through some of that blood, running back in a vein like a creek from her great-grandmother, whom she knew little about save that she was revered as a witch in the Snakefoot in those years after emancipation, on to her grandmother, whom she could remember collecting roots and mushrooms and herbs and nothings and reading from them some secret understanding, and on to her mother, who had taught her to cherish it as a gift from God, this ability, a responsibility and a blessing, like being a woman. Her mother had once explained that most women had something in them that made soothsaying possible, they just didn't know enough to make use of it. It took teaching to understand it was there and wisdom to embrace it, and teachers were scarce and wisdom hard to come by.

It was late, and bullfrogs belched like slingshots their brief tuneless rhythm, and cicadas ebbed and billowed out their piercing incestuous bagpipe drone. The woman could see again that sad little girl she used to watch, that little innocent girl with all that darkness around her, spitting watermelon seeds, catching fireflies in her daddy's used 'shine jars, living on fast food and swamp squirrel and beaver and coon and groundhog and possum and catfish.

Without greeting, Granny turned in, leaving the door open. Day sat in one of two chairs before a table. The house scared most women—not that many came out this way anymore—as did the old palm reader, but to Day, this was a home up the swamp from where she'd grown up. This was her mother and father and grandmother and grandfather, teacher and priest, sister. The inside of the shack was strung with strange dried vegetables like fingers and spices and bouquets of plants like dead hair, and the floor seemed to move with animals. Day saw a turtle lurch under an old table. A rat the size of a grapefruit scurried without a sound, a shadow within a shadow. Cockroaches glistened darkly in the seams of the floorboards like eyes of dead animals. The old woman came out from a dark room, lit a candle, wore an antique pair of what had once been white veal-skin gloves that would have been worn by a debutante or a woman of high breeding. Day handed Granny a pack of the Swisher Sweets the old woman coveted. From the candle then, still without a word, the woman lit one of the thin cigarillos, drawing deeply from it, the room filling out with a fragrant sugary cloud.

Granny leaned forward, blew out a thin stream and smiled, mismatched teeth protruding from vacant gums so that the woman looked to have the teeth of some fanged creature. Her face was so black Day could see her own reflection in it.

"I could feel you coming back," the old woman said. "All day it got stronger and stronger, till I cramped up terrible. Girl, what you all dressed up for?"

Day ignored the question. "I need to know. Who was Tom cheatin' with?"

"You got bigger problems."

"Please, Granny."

"You know I love you, girl," the old woman said, though you would not have been able to see any semblance of love in her gaze. "Watched you grow up, took you for my own. I'm your people, and you're mine. I always been here for you. But I can't tell you what you want me to. Don't need more misery."

Cigar in her mouth, the woman reached for the purse and withdrew Day's driver's license, releasing the purse, and produced from her shirt a pair of glasses that were far too big, and leaned forward to study the card. She then took up a weathered photograph from the bureau of a little white girl with freckles, scowling at the camera, barefoot and in a white dress, muddy at the knees.

"Yes," the old woman said. "You ain't that girl no more. It's done happened, that thing that always happens to a woman. Innocence gone. Yes. You sure grown out now."

Day said, "I want to know."

"Wanting too much can be a bad thing. You got to control yourself."

The old woman reached forward and lifted an earring, still attached to Day's ear, glittering, real or fake, shining like the wind on water in the sun. "This ain't everyday. Your whole life ahead of you. Give me them earrings."

Day said, "Why?"

"He gave them to you. We got to return something to him, see if it'll satisfy him."

The old woman took them, examining them closely, said some words, and dropped the earrings into a jar filled with an amber liquid. Day could see a swirl like a rainbow emerge, like oil on a hot tar road. The woman watched it closely, shaking her head impatiently.

"You dream something often enough, girl, it going to come real," the old woman said. "You could live that bright light dream. But all your sins going to be accounted for. Dreams is dangerous. You never know the real you gonna wake to. Ain't no hiding from it neither. These earrings ain't gonna be enough. You got to figure out another way to get him off'n your back."

"I bet I know," Day said. "I bet it was Cherry McDaniels, skank ho."

"Let me see your hand."

She leaned over, humming to herself, massaging Day's hand with intensity. Suddenly, she looked up at the young woman, a look of formless terror in her dark face. She dropped the hand as if it had shocked her, then rose and stepped back. Day knew this look.

"I cannot read this. I cannot read your hand no more. Girl, you got to leave."

"You know who," Day said. "And you won't help me. You're the only one can help me."

"You can help yourself."

Day stood, not knowing what to do. So, Granny was leaving her too. That was what Day could see in her face. She'd lost everyone but the old woman, the woman Day believed would never die, never leave her, would always be a kindred being back home in the swamp. She could take it from anyone else, but not her.

"Let me touch you," Granny hissed. "I got to know."

The old woman removed one of her white gloves. Suddenly, she reached under Day's dress and felt the tuft of Day's hair and then the dry wattle of her clitoris becoming moist. Day's eyes glazed. Granny moved her fingers in figure eights until Day moaned; though the woman's hand was bony and cold and calloused, it knew her. Suddenly, the old woman stopped and went to the damp light of the kerosene lantern and studied her own naked hand, something she never allowed of herself.

The woman shook her head, the lines in her own hand plain and disconcerting.

"In your belly exists another life, the child of your sin, your death child, the legacy that condemns you. You have no choice. There is no rest on earth or in death unless you can make your peace with Tom. I can't help you no more."

"What about forgiveness? Could he forgive me?"

"Forgiveness don't mean there ain't a price for what you done. There's a price for everything, girl. Listen here." She grabbed Day's young face. "You listening to me?"

"Yes, Granny."

"It's time for you to walk a different path and be smart. Get out of town. Try something new. Listen to your mind, not your tee-tee."

"Yes, Granny."

"Don't sulk, now."

"Granny? Do you still love me?"

"Yes, I do. I love my little one."

"But you ain't gonna help me."

"I can't. You got to make your own way now." Day was crying, a little girl again, that same little girl who used to run to Granny, who always knew how to make her better, take away the pain. The old woman's eyes glittered, and her strong voice wavered. "You can't never come back here. You got no one here; that's for your own good. I can only see danger for you here. Go on, my sweet little girl. Go on and make a life somewhere else. That's what you want, and that's what you need. Forget about this business. Forget about Tom and Cherry . . ."

She stopped then, watched as Day began to understand.

"So it was her."

"Forget what I just said. Let me give you something to forget it. You go after her, and you'll never get away."

Day's face had transformed. Still the tears, but the girl no more. The woman standing before Granny stood shaking, said, through a kind of lockjaw, "I got things to tend to," and turned and walked out into the dark.

The old woman later walked feebly to a small series of antique fruit crates that served as a bookshelf, pulled down an old volume of the spiritual arts her great-grandmother had acquired, though she'd never learned to read, and looked through it for some guidance. She had seen what would happen, and it had happened—was happening—despite her best efforts. She cried and prayed. She tried to take comfort in the old books that had been her inheritance, futile because she had no daughters, and she knew how alone she was now. That fellowship of women she had cherished had deserted her through the auspices of death, and there was no blood to allow her to continue believing. She felt now, with Day's departure, that she herself was only a memory, remembering all that could never be.

LATE NIGHT, Cherokee McDaniels—better known as "Cherry"—watched as Day Pace pulled open the door and walked up to the bar in a skimpy dress and a little black alligator-skin purse she put on the bar. She was looking right at Cherry, and Cherry thought, *Bitch.*

The Lounge looked like a sad Christmas. Pool balls lay in their silent unfinished arrangements on rough faded tables, the perpetual private poker game going on in the back. Behind that, the lot where men had killed and died for cheating and winning both. Day had heard the stories all her life. No band or DJ tonight. The jukebox had some old Beyoncé going right now, preposterous in its juxtaposition to tonight's sleepy clientele. It was an off night.

Cherry watched her take a seat at the bar, and Arnie, who'd just come from the back, approached in what seemed to be disbelief.

"Day? That you?" She cocked her head, letting him know she was listening. "I'm sorry to hear . . ."

"To lose his business?"

"To lose a friend."

"How sorry?"

"I'm just goddamn sorry as shit. What do you want me to say?"

"Don't say it if you don't mean it. You made money off him."

"He cleaned us out that night. He did good."

"I wouldn't know it," she said.

"I don't know what to say. Tom was a good man. You want a drink or something?"

"I just lost Tom, and I got that baby girl to care for. I don't need a drink. I need money."

"Well, shit."

"Wouldn't you help one of your old girls out?"

"I'd like to, but I ain't too flush. I held that game for Tom as a favor. You can ask anyone. I brought the money in, lost a good bit too."

She began to cry for the second time that night, this time sounding like a train braking in the distance.

"You mean to say that money went up in the fire?" Arnie said. "Shit."

"I knew you wouldn't help me. Just like the rest. I knew it."

Arnie looked shy all of a sudden. "I don't know that I can help," he said, rubbing the back of his neck.

"I got to make my own way now."

"I'm sorry, Day."

"What good does that do me?"

He walked into the back, leaving the door to his office slightly ajar. She followed him, and on her way, winked at Cherry. Twenty minutes later, Day walked out slowly, with straight-backed, saunter-ing authority, wiping her mouth and scratching her nose. She made her way toward Cherry, who stood by the pool table.

"What you lookin' at, bitch?" Day said.

"Get out my fuckin' face," Cherry said.

"Bitch," Day said.

"Ho."

"Funeral's Thursday," Day said, a smile startling her face.

"I'll be there."

"It's on you like a hex, you little bitch, the blame. Thursday, I dare you. Show up, cry, pretend you care. But we both know it's because of you he's where he is now."

Cherry looked hard at Day. "He told me about you," she said.

"Well, he won't be saying no more."

"You fuckin' Snakefoot skank."

"Say that again." Day was up in Cherry's face, her breathing harsh and wet. Cherry said nothing. "You show up," Day hissed, "and I'll have to bury you too."

"What you say to me?" Cherry said, stepping back.

"You heard, you triflin' bitch."

Arnie came out from the back, a new bleary-eyed tranquility about him.

"Now, girls," he said, "let's stay polite in here. Day, here's a little something to help you out."

Cherry put her hands on her hips, stared at Arnie.

Day said, "This only two hundred dollars."

"It's all I can do right now, I swear."

"Then gimme a bottle of that Wild Turkey to go."

As she left, Day thought how good she felt. The anger was good. It helped and felt better than any drink or drug and filled her with dreams. So what if Granny dropped her. Fuck it. Sitting in her Accord out in the lot, she saw the occasional headlights in the distance, down by the turnoff, down the gradual slope. She could feel the control, that wonderous buzz, and watched it all beneath her, spread out like a map. She raised the bottle to something,

Tom maybe, or her daddy or mama, or whatever, took a long drink, cringed and cursed and giggled a little, wiping her glossed lips with the back of her hand. Granny was just trying to scare her. But Day had control of the situation. She had a bottle with her, a ghost to appease, but the world by the hand. On the way to town, she passed the church on one side of the road, the creek on the other where an old pickup had been parked, dew blurring the windshield as if someone's ghost sat behind the wheel.

CLAUDETTE HEARD the porch door slap shut, the thin music beating through the warm house. So then little Destinee started squealing, and Claudette had to count to ten, which she didn't reach as she got up and went to the child and then to the living room to see Day drunk as a hoot owl, humming along with the beat coming from her phone, which she had placed on the counter, and rooting through the refrigerator.

Claudette stood there with the baby. Day slammed the fridge shut and jumped.

"Hey, Claudette!" Day said.

"What you think you doing, waking me, the baby, coming home lit up like a Mexican holiday? Girl, the funeral is Thursday. Put that food away. It's for the reception. Where's your respect? What people gonna say?"

"Life goes on."

"Turn that off," Claudette said. "Where you been? Look at you."

Day was all dressed up, but her eyes were half-closed, and her hair had been mussed.

"Well, I just had to get out. Remind myself I'm still alive."

She was eating cold macaroni and cheese out of the tin now in that dress and kicked off her shoes.

"Claudette," she said. "You won't believe this, but I'll tell you anyway. I went out tonight for Tom. Yes, I did. So don't you be telling me how to grieve. I don't give a shit what people say."

"Watch your mouth in this house."

Day started laughing, a sleepy, drunk, childish laugh.

"Tom did this every damn night of the week. What a woman get to do when her man is out on the town? And you talk about once. And you talk about language."

"But you mourning my son."

"So let me do it how I please. Ain't no use stopping breathing just because someone else did."

Claudette approached the young woman and slapped her. A heavy pause followed, filled yet with the driving beat from Day's phone. Claudette rubbed her hand. She'd hit the young woman with all the force she had, but Day stood unfazed, quiet. Claudette realized she'd hit the cheek that already had a bruise.

"Turn that crap off," Claudette said. "Now. I said, now."

Day did it with a shrug, and the silence was like a fever.

"Ain't got no respect. Coming in the house at all hours. Leaving your baby to get drunk. I better not catch you drinking again, not with that little one on the way."

"What you say?"

"You can't tell me you ain't with child. You got the glow."

Day turned away, rested her hands on the counter, bowed her head.

"It's all right," Claudette said. "It's a joy. See how the Lord takes care of us? When one leaves the earth, another comes. But to behave like this . . ."

"Naw," Day said. "Naw. This ain't no joy. This is a curse."

"You ungrateful woman," Claudette said, still rubbing her hand. But scolding obviously wouldn't work, so she changed her approach. "I know you in pain. That much is plain to see. So am I. Which means I know you loved him. That makes two of us. We family, girl, and I won't let you destroy yourself and that child because of grief. It's time for us to be together, let ourselves be strengthened by God, move forward in peace knowing Tom is in a better place."

"I don't believe he is. I can hear him, feel him, howling out right now."

Claudette stiffened. "You saying he in the bad place? How would you know? Don't say he in the bad place."

"I didn't," Day said, backing away at the look in Claudette's eyes. "But he ain't at peace."

"You don't know anything, girl, but disrespect and YouTube. Well, no matter what it seems to be, the Lord gonna know. Give it to Him. And you best be ready for Thursday, girl, because my one and only boy deserves the best funeral this town ever had."

Day left the macaroni out on the counter for Claudette to put away and went to her room. She could be heard unzipping her dress.

"Girl, you go in that kitchen and put that food away," Claudette said from the hallway. "Or I'll slap you so hard . . ."

Day opened the door. "Touch me again."

They approached each other, but Claudette saw something in Day's eyes that stayed her.

"I don't know why," Claudette said, to herself or to the baby, "and it ain't fair, but the Lord's got a hand in anything that happens, so I suppose He must have arranged it this way. I suppose we ain't destined to like each other. But we here for a reason. We here together. Can't you help me in these times?"

Claudette waited for Day to say something, anything. When she didn't, Claudette set her jaw and said, "Put the food away and go to bed. That, or go find some other place to sleep."

After staring at Tom's mother for a moment, Day obeyed.

She went to her room afterward and looked at her clothes, her cosmetics in their little fraying kit, her two pairs of shoes, Tom's revolver, which she'd taken from his bedside table. She picked it up with her free hand, held it by the light and considered it from different angles as one might a diamond. She pressed the release and tilted it so that the cylinder dropped, and saw again the virgin brass cartridges, all the potential. The baby moved, yawned, fell back asleep. Day then slapped the cylinder back into the frame of the gun. She felt her heart pumping blood into her own body like a flood of oxygen, held the muzzle against Destinee's soft head, felt that rush in her heart, that erratic thrumming, a quickening exhilaration, a buzz she'd experienced when she'd felt herself, furious and weak, stab him to death. She could save this girl from life, take her while she was still innocent. She squeezed the trigger, felt the resistance of the mechanism, watched the hammer lift, wondering just how much she'd have to pull before the hammer fell.

"You doing this, ain't you?" Day said. "I can feel it. You shouting and screaming from the grave. You want me to suffer. Well, leave me alone. I ain't gonna fall for your tricks. Leave me alone."

Day released the tension, eased the hammer back, almost blacking out. She then put the gun on the bed like a dead rat, embraced the baby.

"Not today," she said.

She could feel that sick wetness again, and, eyes closed, baby in one arm, she reached down to release herself.

When she had finished, she put her things away, hiding the gun beneath them, and before falling into whatever dreamworld, said, "We got to work this out. You got to leave me alone. I had enough of you. You can't be hanging around no more. It's over. Now go. Git away from here."

Silence was the answer.

WILL DROVE SLOWLY back to Promised Land at sunrise, after the new summer light had already poured itself out shiny along the roads and on the heavy leaves of the tobacco rows, and got out of his truck, seeing Bennico on the front porch with Sam, coffee mugs steaming on the table between them. He scratched the back of his head.

"Morning," Will said.

Bennico said, "Your breakfast is in the oven, and there should be some coffee. You look like you could use it."

He stumbled inside, poured some coffee, and came back out.

"Well, isn't this fucking domestic," he said, leaning against one of the posts.

"Boy, I'm about to smack you. Say thank you before I light you up."

"Thanks," he said, looking down. "I just talk shit when I don't know what to say. You sleep all right?"

"I didn't sleep at all. Waste of my time."

Sam said, "What were y'all fighting about?"

"We were due for our monthly fight," Bennico said, winking at Will. "It wasn't over anything, really."

"Man," Sam said. "Y'all *are* serious. *Monthly.* Shit."

"You better get ready for work," Bennico said.

"You're right," Will said, bending and kissing her on the cheek and retreating into the house. He showered and dressed for work, then came back out to the porch.

He said to Bennico, "You going to be okay here all day?"

"Sam and me are getting along fine. Might go out, see the area." She held up her hand to keep Will from butting in. "I know, I know. I got to leave Sam here."

"Well, okay," Will said. "Call me if you need anything."

"Baby?" she said. "Let's go out for dinner tonight."

Will smiled. "I get off around four thirty or so. I'll come home, and we'll go out."

One thing was certain: Bennico knew how to play along with a cover. By suggesting dinner, Sam wouldn't question where they were later.

Will left Bennico and Sam on the porch. On the way into Dawn, he was torn between relief that things seemed to be going so well with Bennico and worry over what she might say to Sam, what Sam might find out through even the smallest slip. He hadn't considered they might spend the day together. But he made his peace with it. It was the way it had to be. He found himself smiling with a kind of admiration. Bennico had this contagious energy about her, something that stuck. He'd come home from a night of hard sleep to what had the semblance not of a vacant house but a home.

He parked and ran up the steps to the courthouse and turned left to go into the sheriff's department.

"Hey, Tania," he said, but before he could get a response, Mills called out to him.

"What in the hell is that out there?"

Will stood at the threshold like he might not come in.

"What the hell are you doing back in my office?"

"I'd like my badge back, sir. I'd like to come back to work."

"Well I'd like a nickel for every time my dog craps on my front lawn. Let me tell you something. When you put on this badge, this gun, this uniform, you represent the county. This county. Your home. I know how to run it. Been doing it since you were a kid. You want your badge back?"

"Yessir."

"You can go ahead and pay the fine."

"For what?"

"Speeding. And that's money you know is going to a good cause. Don't you gimme that look, goddamnit. You got to abide by the rules just like anybody else. And you got to learn that we're a team. What you do is what I do. I've been training you for this. When things get tough, we gotta get together."

"Yessir."

"You pay that fine and give me a top-shelf apology."

Will looked over at Tania's desk, the office quiet.

"I'm sorry for the way I talked the other day. It was disrespectful, and it won't happen again. I'd appreciate it if you could see your way to letting me wear a badge and gun again. It would be an honor to continue serving Euphoria County."

"See?" Sheriff Mills said. "That wasn't so hard now, was it? Couldn't have been prettier. Tania, baby, go ahead and give Deputy Will Seems his accoutrements. I got to go out for a while."

With that, Sheriff Mills grabbed his hat and left. Will went over to Tania's desk.

"What are you up to, Will?" she said, looking at him funny.

"What?"

"Don't play me too. You think I believe you come in here to apologize, or to get your badge, for no reason?"

"Why not?"

"Come on. What are you doing?"

"I don't exactly know."

"That kind of talk worries me."

"I got this feeling that no matter what I do, I won't be able to change the outcome."

"What's the point of anything if you think like that?"

"Yeah, I know."

"Let me tell you something," she said, leaning across her desk so that he could see the dimple at the top of her chest. "When he took Miss Pace to identify the body, they were gone six hours. Takes one hour to get there, one hour to get back."

"That could mean anything."

"Will, ain't you gonna tell me nothing? You may need me."

"How can I tell you what I don't know?"

"I see how it is," she sighed. "You're just like him. I'm just Tania on dispatch. I'll get your lunch. I'll be at your beck and call."

"I never said that."

"Not saying it doesn't mean anything. Things that don't get said are just as true as those that do."

BENNICO HAD ALREADY LEARNED from Will where Day Pace worked, over in South Boston at that Vietnamese nail and hair salon, and she planned to go and find out something about the woman before she tried to meet her. She and Sam were getting along just fine, but she wasn't comfortable around him, and the more she thought about her situation—staying here at Promised Land—the less she liked it. She couldn't tell Floressa she didn't like it, because then she'd have to explain Sam was there, but she would have preferred to be based where she didn't have to navigate someone else's secrets.

She'd seen quite a few addicts over the years, and there was something different about Sam that bothered her. Many users had once been intelligent but had devolved, acquiring a numb stupidity that seemed flat, final. Sam had a curiosity about him in the way he looked at her, the way his eyes seemed to narrow, and he'd tilt his head as if listening intently for something in particular she couldn't figure out. How much did he suspect about her? What did he know? Was he going to corner her and ask her something she couldn't answer? Something about Will that only someone close would know? She wasn't willing to spend her time and energy lying for Will. She remained curious but wary—cautious around Sam.

She wanted to talk to him to learn what he knew but couldn't risk him asking her too much.

It was safest that she got away from him before that could happen, before she could slip up. Her talents involved persistence, not deceit. If she'd been a better liar, she could have been a better police detective because she would have been able to play the game she was now free of. Deception: the one ability all cops needed, and the one they could not be trained to perfect.

"Where you going?" Sam said.

She turned at the car. He was coming in from the garden.

Bennico said, "I thought I'd get a bite to eat."

"It ain't but ten in the morning."

"Well, I was going to take Will something for lunch."

"That's funny. Will always skips lunch. Says it slows him down."

She turned and opened her car door. When she got in and put her purse over on the passenger's seat and looked up again, Sam was standing there a few feet from her window, head tilted, looking at her.

"What you looking at?" she said.

"I'm looking at you, woman. Wondering why you really come here."

"I told you already."

"Yeah, I know. Tell me again."

"I'm visiting Will. We're together. What else is there?"

"And how long you been with him?"

"You want to say something, say it."

"I don't know what's going on," Sam said, "but I know it ain't what you been saying. Something ain't right here."

She was about to say something, lie, but something in Sam's face told her to wait. He was looking off—a tremble of cheek below one eye probably meant some emotional reaction—and she didn't want to fight him. They needed to get along. Maybe she would convince him, even bribe him, to keep quiet. But no. She had promised Will she wouldn't talk. But Sam was not an idiot, and he obviously knew something, and she thought he was bound to find out the whole truth sooner or later.

Sam cleared his throat. "What I got to say is this: That man is all I got right now. And he won't tell you, maybe, but he need me too. Don't take him from me. Not now. Don't you be coming between us."

Before she could say anything, he turned toward the porch, head hanging low, and as Bennico rode the ruts of the farm out to the gate under the pecan and walnut trees, full dark with shade underneath, she found herself wiping the side of her cheek and saying, as if in some prayer of resistance to emotion, "Goddamnit. God-fucking-damnit."

WILL TRACKED DOWN the poker players from Charlotte County. He found one owned the supermarket in Charlotte Court House that was called Supermarket, a dirty-looking grocery that seemed to have survived some 1950s apocalypse. The man was Tubby MacLean, and he was also the organist at the Baptist church down the road. He had three fingers on his right hand that looked like brown bananas, and you really noticed the missing fingers when he lifted his hand to take off his straw cowboy hat. Sure, he'd talked some smack after the game. He'd been drinking and had lost his money to that Tom Janders, and he still thought Janders might have been cheating. But after that, he left and came home to a wife who still didn't know where he'd been. But she would say he got in about one a.m., which meant he'd left soon after the game and come straight home. The man appeared to be sorry Tom was dead.

"Let me ask you something, Deputy. Why would I stick a knife in that man's back and burn his house?"

"Why would anybody? You'd lost money against him."

"Well, that would mean I'd have that money now. Search my place up and down, check my bank accounts, see what I care. But don't let my wife know I was playing cards. I get heated sometimes when the gin's running and I'm seeing pretty girls and playing loose with cards. It'll be hell to pay, she finds out."

The other Charlotte man was Mose Rocker, who was a banker in Charlotte Court House. He said he followed Tubby back to town and went home to his wife, who was still up watching TV.

Will was able to leave at four o'clock that afternoon and met Bennico at the house closer to five. She was all done up, obviously ready to go, sitting outside with Sam, who was shelling black-eyed peas. Will felt as if he'd stumbled into something, out of place in his own home.

Will said to Bennico, "You look great. I'll be just a minute."

Sam followed him upstairs and waited in the hallway while Will changed.

"No," Will said as he walked out of his room, before Sam could ask. "We said every other day. You need to wait till tomorrow."

He pushed past Sam and went downstairs, where he argued with Bennico over whose car to take. Will lost to Bennico, who made the practical point that no one would recognize her car. Then, having won the argument, Bennico said, "If you're going to argue, argue, damnit. I hate a man who accepts defeat as an option."

They drove a little over an hour, passing a large building outside which stood a woodcutter's stumps and totems, carved into figures and animals and Indian chiefs, a sign on the warehouse proclaiming "JESUS IS LORD" for all to read. They could hear, beyond the roar of wind through the open windows, the life buzzing and skittering out over the wide openness of the fields, ending in trees and vines thick and tall over the road, the sound of cicadas and other insects ebbing and searing, subsiding again when the land opened up to new fields where tall trees like explosions broke the sky. The grass smelled burnt, and the bugs slapped against the windshield, leaving strange neon streaks.

Emporia was a big hollow ugly stretch of strip malls and truck stops and young cotton growing in the fields around them and I-95 carrying drugs from Miami to New York. Will's grandparents lived there, and he'd grown up hunting ducks, deer, quail, and turkey in the flat fields and flooded timber, in tree stands with the hunt club, and in blinds with his dad, granddad, and cousins.

Will said, "Where'd you get all done up?"

"South Boston," Bennico said.

"Ah."

"Hey, nobody said work couldn't also be fun."

"You find anything out?"

"Wouldn't you like to know."

"What's that supposed to mean?"

Bennico laughed. "Never mind," she said. "I talked to the boss, Vietnamese woman. She did me up. I said I used to babysit Day when she was little. About all I found out is she takes the baby in with her to work, does the best nails around. She's taking some time off because of Tom. The salon's collecting money for her. I threw in a few bucks."

Will nodded, like he was trying to determine whether anything she'd said could mean something.

"So what's the deal with this morgue?" she said. "I know a forensics tech in Richmond who might could do us a favor."

"Troy St. Pierre did the autopsy himself."

"That's who we're seeing today?"

"Yep."

"Sheriff and Troy good buddies?"

"More like Mills and Sheriff Edgars here. But I know what you're thinking," he said, "because I've already thought it. Maybe there is some good ol' boy in this system, but that doesn't mean they're doing anything wrong. It's just how things are."

"Sounds a lot like something only a straight white Southern male could get away with saying."

"Don't you talk to me about white privilege or any of that other shit some academic has thought up from the safety of a classroom."

"Woah. Easy. At any point, did y'all call on State to investigate?"

"Sheriff said that we'd caught a suspect red-handed, so there wasn't a need."

"You're going along with that shit? You're the one been saying the suspect is innocent."

They arrived at the morgue. Parking in the broken lot of what looked like an old strip mall, Will said, "Stay here."

"Nah-ah. I'm going in."

"What am I going to tell him? That I'm helping a private investigator Sheriff Mills doesn't know about?"

"Tell him I'm Tom's sister or something. Bennico Janders. I'd have a right to look at the body. You can't just leave me out here. What if he looks out and sees a stranger is sitting in the car?"

"I don't like this. He's never heard of Tom's sister because Tom didn't have a sister."

"Come on," she said, her eyes winking. "You're overlooking the virtue of the Black family: People are never surprised to hear about an unknown sibling. Now grab some of that white privilege and let's find out what we can. I want to meet this guy anyway."

"I swear, if you fucking . . ."

She outright laughed now, reached over and touched his face, looked into his eyes.

"I'm just messing with you, boy."

They walked into the lobby, and Will asked to see Tom Janders's body, showing his badge. Bennico seemed to have transformed into a sober, grieving woman, so that Will was almost convinced he was escorting the bereaved sister of Tom Janders into the morgue.

He was asked to wait. Eventually, Troy St. Pierre came out to shake Will's hand.

"Deputy, what are you doing here?"

"Troy, this is Bennico Janders, Tom's sister."

Troy was surprised but went with it. "I'm sorry for your loss, miss."

Will said, "I wonder if we could talk about your report."

"Come on back," Troy said, looking back and forth between them.

As they walked down the white halls, chilly with icy corpses latent behind their doors, Troy turned around and said, "I thought you'd have seen it."

"I have, but I wanted to be able to talk it through."

"Well, someone broke in. There was a disagreement, a struggle, and Tom was overpowered, stabbed, and the house was burned to make it look like an accident."

Will said, "I didn't see signs of a struggle."

Troy cocked his eye at Will, looked at him a moment. "How could there be no struggle? Tom was a big man, a football—"

"I know who he was, but what evidence was there? If he was taken by surprise, there might not have been a fight."

"There were scratch marks and cuts all over him. A bruise on his scalp. Not to mention the deep lacerations in his back from the knife."

"I want to see the body," Bennico said.

"How could I let you see it if it isn't here? I thought you'd have known that. Especially you, miss. It's being embalmed."

Troy spun around in his chair to retrieve the printed report. "Sheriff Mills brought Miss Pace on Thursday, and she identified the body. I was ordered to release it for the funeral this Thursday. I thought you—both of you—would know."

Will said, "Did you process all the lab work yourself? Has anything been sent out?"

"I got some quick results here—a murder weapon with Zeke Hathom's prints on it—but I sent samples out to DFS in Richmond. They're going to take at least two months, likely more."

"Anything else you can tell us?"

"We'll just have to be patient and wait for the results. Again, my condolences, miss."

Will touched the small of Bennico's back and opened the door for her. They walked out without looking back, and Troy reclined profoundly in his cushioned swivel chair, smelling the sterility around him, feeling the strange companionship and purpose of his work.

His office was at the rear of the building, and he could see out into what looked more like a field than a lot but had in fact once been paved. It was actually impressive how nature had broken back through, shattering the finality of concrete. He could hear the soulless hum of I-95. He watched Will and Bennico get into a car—a shiny black Escalade—and, on a whim, leaned forward, jotting something down.

After they drove off, he picked up the phone and dialed Sheriff Edgars and said, "Sheriff? I thought you might want to know who came to see me just now."

"Yeah?"

"Will Seems and some woman. Black woman. Says she's Tom Janders's sister, Bennico. They were asking about the corpse, and I told them it's not here. She didn't even know the body was released for embalming. Thought you'd want to know."

"Good on you."

"Should I call Sheriff Mills?"

"I'll do it, Troy. I want to hear old Jefferson's reaction."

"They're driving a black Escalade," Troy said. "And I got the license plate right here. Might be you could see who it belongs to."

"Good man."

S HERIFF MILLS WAS about to go home when he got the call from Sheriff Edgars.

"You know where your deputy's at?" Edgars led.

Mills chuckled. "I don't care a damn. He does what he wants on his time off. You all worked up, buddy."

"Well, Troy just called me."

"Yeah?"

"Guess who paid Troy a visit. Your deputy and Bennico Janders."

"Who?"

"Tom's sister."

Sheriff Mills, watching the ceiling fan, sat up. "What now?"

"I thought that might interest you. Your deputy is going around with Tom's sister, asking questions and such."

"Well, Weenie, that's pretty damn strange, being that he never had a sister."

"Troy got a license plate number for the car they were driving."

"Let me get a pen. Okay. Give it here."

Sheriff Mills took that home with him and forgot about supper and sat on his porch until it was too dark to see. The house sat on blocks, and you could see through to the backyard from the front if you looked under the porch. He had an English setter he let run the yard all day, chasing squirrels, and he liked to come home and let the dog sit at his feet while he drank a Co-Cola and thought things over, listening to that searing of cicadas and frogs, all the little sounds like the incessant creaking of a bed. Though he no longer hunted quail, now that there weren't many wild birds left, he kept the dog as a reminder of a time in his life he felt was pure, and also because he had no family anymore but his cousin Buddy, who did have a family. That was something he thought about sometimes. A redneck like Buddy had got him a wife and had a little army of squirts—four or five of them—and Mills had held out. He felt he could have been a good daddy, a decent husband, but it had never happened. It made him a little sad to think on it. For two reasons. Idiots like Buddy seemed to breed quick and easy, without a hard thought, and those kids would grow up without much of a thought too. But more important was the fact that the only woman he had loved had been taken from him. His own daddy had been lucky to have raised a son who respected what he'd done enough to do it too. It wasn't only that Will had gone behind his back that bothered him; it was that it threatened the one legacy he possessed. Professionally, Will was a son. Mills's legacy as sheriff was like a bloodline he could pass down, but it had to be to someone worthy of it.

"Daddy," he said aloud. "What would you do just now?"

He felt a surge of physical power, like a drug, rolled a cigarette, smoked it as he did sometimes, only when he had to think. He grabbed his dog by the scruff of the neck and heard him whine. Mills held the scruff tight in his hand, knowing that he would not hurt the dog but knowing that he could and that the dog knew he could. He eased his hand up and petted the animal, who slunk back down to his feet and closed his eyes, resting his head on Mills's scuffed boot.

He thought about the call he'd gotten the other day from Miss Gale, Will's grandmother, asking after Will, saying she was worried about him.

"What about?" Mills had asked.

"Just generally," she said. "Have you noticed any odd behavior?"

"No, ma'am," Mills had lied (everything about Will had been strange). "Not in particular. What kind of behavior?"

"I'm just worried. You'll watch out for him, won't you? Make sure he's okay?"

He could tell she thought she was being clever, that she was worried about something in particular, and he tried to work out what it could be. As far as he knew, Will didn't keep any "company." He was only seen alone when he was seen at all.

"You called the right place, Miss Gale. Of course I will. As always, it's just a breath of fresh air talking with you."

Mills decided to pay a visit to Miss Claudette's house to see Day and stood up from his chair. He drove over, put a peppermint in his cheek (a bit more gentlemanly, he thought, than chewing gum), and knocked on the door.

Claudette said, "You shouldn't be here, Mr. Sheriff. It's late, and she ain't had no warning."

"Let me have just five minutes of her time," he said. "Oh, Miss Claudette." She turned back. "Did Tom have a sister?"

"No, sir. I think I'd know about that."

Day was hungover still from the night before. She quickly applied makeup, covering the bruise on her cheek. The last person she wanted to see unprepared was the sheriff. She came to the door clutching herself, wearing an old high school sweatshirt of Tom's that went down almost to her knees, a sweatshirt the sheriff had seen the man wear. Sheriff Mills attempted to avert his gaze as he talked.

"Miss Pace," he said. "I hate to disturb you at this hour, but I'm following up on Tom's death, the details surrounding it."

"I don't know anything else," she said, adjusting the sweatshirt and wiping her cheek with the back of a hand, turning.

"Now, wait a minute," he said, his hand against the doorjamb, resting against it in a casual pose of assertion, lean and athletic. Something in his eyes, Day noticed. Something about him was coiled, ready, hungry. "I need to know if you had any connection with Sam Hathom. Zeke's boy."

"No," she said, surprised at the question.

"But Tom did, didn't he? You ever hear anything around the house about him? I mean lately, past couple months?"

She looked lost, tired, empty. "Why is it you want to know?"

"Well, see, he's a wanted man. We have a warrant out for him, but nobody's seen him. Like to've disappeared, which I don't believe. You sure you ain't heard nothing at all?"

"I've heard a rumor, here or there."

"What rumor?"

"That he's been staying out in the country. That's old talk."

He stared through her at nothing. Usually, he was looking at her, into her. He appeared now to be searching a distant horizon.

"In this country? In my country?"

"That's what I heard. Something about a Promised Land? I didn't never know what they meant."

"Thank you, darlin'," the sheriff said, touching the brim of his hat. "Good night."

Sheriff Mills drove out to Promised Land. Sitting outside the gate he called Will under some pretense, a summons Will had issued. Learning what he'd really wanted to know—that Will wasn't at home, lending credence to what Edgars had told him—Mills grabbed his Maglite and pulled back the slide of his Glock 17 enough to make sure he had a round in the chamber. Among the loud cicada sounds swarming like radio signals around him, picking wildflowers as he walked, Sheriff Mills could barely hear his boots on the brick walkway against the night sounds, amid fireflies like electrical inconsistencies, like thoughts unbroken or some meaningless code, glad to be able to blend with the night like a secret within a secret.

T HEY STOPPED at a restaurant for a quick bite. Tania called from her cell while they were eating.

"Are you at the office?" Will said, before she could say what she was calling about.

"I'm just leaving. Why?"

"The sheriff just called me a few minutes ago about a summons. Usually I'd be talking to you about that."

"Well," Tania said. "I don't know anything about that. He must be working from home, because he's been gone most of the afternoon."

"So what's up?" Will said.

"A Cherry McDaniels came looking for you today."

"What about?"

"She wouldn't say. I asked did she want to speak to the sheriff, because I could call him, and she said it had to be you she spoke to. She wouldn't say anything else."

"She going to call back?"

"She said if you want to talk to her, go to the Lounge out Possum Creek alone. She's there every day, and if she's not there, whoever is can find her."

Will closed his phone and looked off.

"That's good," Bennico said after Will had told her. "That's a lead."

Will shrugged. "Could well be nothing."

"That's a fucking lead, no matter how you look at it. People don't go by a sheriff's office on a whim. Come on now, Will."

Will asked for the check and paid and they walked out into the parking lot. A couple of streetlights were on. On the road, the land seemed to descend, giving the sky the illusion of having expanded like a firework all around them. Bugs stung the windshield and bats swirled over top of the Escalade. Cypress, ash, and tupelo trees grew as if from out of skulls, distorted silhouettes against the shimmer of low, still waters. They rode, skirting the dead-looking region of the Snakefoot to the south. Will had heard of slaves escaping into the swamps and surviving where no white man would go without desperation. The landscape always seemed more imagined than real.

They reached the Rebel Inn, and Will pulled out the receipt Day had given him and verified the date on it.

"We asked Miss Pace where she'd been the night of the murder, and she produced this receipt. So we know she checked in. The owner confirmed that over the phone, but he doesn't speak very good English, and I think we'll find out more in person."

They went into a little room that served as a kind of lobby. It smelled like years of cigarette ash covered by years of cleaning solutions, and the red rug was faded and visibly dirty, worn in the middle from foot traffic and suitcases dragged or wheeled.

Bennico rang the bell at the front desk twice and called out. A little middle-aged man named Chim came out, his hair combed over a bald spot and a shirt unbuttoned over a wifebeater.

Will showed his badge and said, "We're with the sheriff's department."

"I didn't do nothing."

"We were hoping you could help us with something," Bennico said.

Chim patted his forehead with a tissue.

"Do you remember a woman coming here to stay last Tuesday, July nineteenth?"

"I think I maybe had a few people. This is a motel for the many people. I can have sixty-five," he said, pointing at a plaque announcing the maximum capacity.

"I already called," Will said, pulling out the receipt. "We know she was here."

"Why do you want to ask me, then?"

"We need to know if she stayed here all night."

"This was a young woman, twenty-eight, with strawberry-blond hair cut like this," Bennico said, showing him the picture. "She had a baby with her. Do you have a guest book?"

"Of course," he said, getting out a black pleather volume few guests had signed. Will flipped through and quickly found her name, written there with deliberation. It might as well have said "I WAS HERE" like some kid vandalizing a bathroom stall or carving initials on a tree.

"Remember her?" Will said.

"Yes," the man said, patting his forehead again.

"And?"

"Lots of the people come to here. I can say I remember, but what else can I say? I don't go to the room with them. I don't watch them."

"What time did she get here?"

"It was dark. I was eating a dinner. Maybe nine or something like that."

"What else?" Will said.

"Nothing else," Chim said, visibly sweating now and losing his patience. "Do you have a warrant?"

"We're not arresting you," Bennico said. "What room was she in?"

"Eleven."

"Who cleans the rooms?"

"My daughter, Sarun."

"Where is she?"

"Wait me one moment," he said, walking back into an area behind the desk. They heard his voice begin something quietly, then rise with anger in a language neither Bennico nor Will could discern. Soon after, a girl of about sixteen years old, hair pulled back, came out, looking down. Her father said something to calm her, but she already looked calm.

"Last Wednesday," Bennico said. "Do you remember cleaning room eleven?"

"Yes, ma'am," she said, in a relaxed Southside drawl.

"When did you clean it?"

"Nine or ten in the mornin'."

"Do you remember anything about the room? Anything unusual?"

"She didn't stay the night. I know, because the bed was still made and the bathroom wasn't used. There was still a paper cover on the toilet from when I'd cleaned the day before."

Chim said, "People come here all the time for just a little while. They think I don't know, but they come to do things. Then they leave. This is America. You can do what you want."

"Did either of you see what she was driving or when she left?"

"She drove a green Honda, I think," Chim said. "The car was old. I remember this one because it had a big dent in the side."

"When did she leave?"

"I seen her drive away, maybe down the street or something, that night. She was dressed up. I remember, yes, because she was only here maybe one hour before she left."

"Did you see her come back?"

"I didn't see that car again. Sometimes people do that," he said. "Sometimes they drive to the club in town, over at the old mall, then they get a cab, pick up their car in the morning."

"Did you see her again in the morning? This is important."

"I don't remember seeing her again."

"Thanks for your time, Mr. Chim," Bennico said.

They had made it just outside when they heard Chim say, "I remember something. I remember her also because she asked to sign the guest book. I liked her. Not many people care to do that. I sure hope she didn't do nothing bad."

They drove, the sun long gone, the glowing headlights scanning the cowled land for whatever might emerge, the gradual highway undulating in serpentine curves and straightaways where you could see, far ahead, the gleaming road like a blade under the moon.

S AM FELT HIS HEART idle rough like an old motor. He was breathing heavily, talking to himself, shivering. Thinking Will was home, he waited, but Will never used the front door, and even if he did, the doorknob rattled too long. Sam ran out the kitchen door and out back and tripped over something out into the tobacco. It was dark, and he could see the stars like a net over him. He heard someone rooting through the house. He was safest here, on the property, out where no one would look, in this vacant vastness dispossessed of extant human soul.

At length, when he was almost ready to head back to the house, he perceived something faint and new, the outline of a figure black at the black wall of the graveyard.

He heard the soft hum of true words like a current in the air but not the words themselves. Someone was standing over Miss Hannah's grave.

I T WAS LATE. The door opened heavily, and in walked Will Seems and Bennico Watts toward the bar in the hallway, just before the stairs. Will didn't recognize the woman leaning forward on the counter. She was heavyset and wore a black skullcap and spoke with a lisp because of the gap in the top row of her teeth.

"Is Cherry working?" he asked.

"After tonight? You better leave while you can."

"What happened?" Bennico said.

Not acknowledging her, the bartender continued staring at Will. "You better leave, son."

The place looked terrible, chairs all over the place, cans and bottles too. It was entirely empty of clientele. The jukebox was playing something that sounded wrong—something from the '90s with all its unbridled enthusiasm—and next to it an old Marlboro dispenser glowed. Will turned around to leave.

He was already outside, smelling the humid summer night, and then she took his hand, and they turned to see her there by the door.

"Cherry?"

"Who this?" she said, looking at Bennico.

"She's my partner. Miss Floressa and Miss Claudette hired her."

"I called for you," Cherry said. "You're the only one I know about."

"Listen here," Bennico said, but Will held up his hand. For once, she followed his lead.

Will said, "If you can trust me, you can trust her. I'm going to tell her anyway."

Cherry turned, and they followed her back in and sat down at a corner table.

She went up to the bar and came back with a couple of Coors tallboys, handed them to Will and Bennico, and sat across from them.

"Did you know?" she said to Will.

"Know what?"

"Sheriff was in here tonight."

"First I'm hearing of it."

"Well, he flipped this place upside down. Broke up the game. Yelled everyone out. Went back there, jacked Arnie up against his office door. He ain't never done that, and he ain't exactly a stranger."

"He didn't tell me anything."

"She probably put him up to it."

"She?"

Cherry looked at Will now straight in the eyes. He found her so attractive that it was awkward looking at her.

"You people always playing," she said. "Or you're the last to learn something. Why is it cops are that way?"

"I'm a deputy, not a cop."

"I'm talking about D—. I don't even want to say that white bitch name. You know who."

"She can't tell the sheriff what to do."

"She got her way, and they got a history. I'm telling you. He used to come in here all the time, not drinking or nothing, just standing at the bar, watching her move around. Everybody knows it. He would come here for her."

"Is this what you wanted to see me about?"

"People been talking, Mr. Seems. They been saying things, about you, about the sheriff, about other things. I heard you got suspended. That you go out and sit in your truck or drive around off duty, looking for something."

He glanced at Bennico out of the corner of his eye. "I should never have come back to a place where gossip is news," he said.

"Been hearing a rumor recently about you and Sam Hathom. That maybe you came back because of him. That he's wanted in two counties, that he dropped off the face of the earth. That you hiding him."

"Thanks for the beer," Will said, standing up.

"Tom said you're honest. He told me about all that, about you and Sam and what happened. He told me how your daddy moved you away after—"

"I know what happened."

"Well, so do I. And I know a few other things you'll want to know, if you want to do anything about the murder."

Will sat back down. Bennico watched the two of them, always watching.

"Mr. Seems, Tom and I were together. He was going to leave her. The night he died he was going home with that money to offer something to her. I tried to get him to leave her earlier, but he wouldn't on account of his baby girl. He was too good to up and walk out on someone, no matter how bad they was. You see what I'm getting at? He was afraid of her. He never would have told me, but I could see that. Thought she'd found out about us. He loved me, and I loved him." She looked into Bennico's eyes now for the first time. "I'm gonna have his baby."

"Does she know?" Will said.

"I don't know. But she came in here the other day and dared me to go to his funeral. Threatened me if I did. Said I'd end up like Tom. She also got Arnie to pay her two hundred dollars."

"For what?"

"For nothing. She put on her sad face, went in the back with him. She was wiping her mouth and rubbing her nose when she come out. I know what that means."

"What else do you know about that night?"

"I was here when Tom won that money, playing with the cash Zeke had paid back."

"For Sam's rehab?"

She nodded. "He'd been at it for a few nights, maybe a week, making some, losing some with his work money, and when he got Zeke to pay him, he played with that. You know how Tom was," she said, a warm sentimentality breaking in. "All or nothing. Arnie was trying to help him out, brought in some rich dudes from Charlotte County."

"I know. I talked to them already."

"Tom said she would be waiting up for him. He said that money was going to be an offering. That's as much as I know."

"How do you know Zeke paid him back? Day said he still owed Tom."

"Well, that bitch lying, ain't she? He paid him back here, out in the parking lot, and then they came in and had a drink together."

"When was this?"

"The night before he was killed."

"We found his body last Wednesday, July twentieth. Do you mean Zeke paid him back July nineteenth, the day of the game, or the day before that?"

"Would have been July eighteenth."

"Did Tom and Zeke seem to be friendly about it?"

"Oh yeah. Ask Arnie. He was here too. You think this will do any good for Zeke?"

"I hope so," Will said, looking at Bennico.

"There's something else," Cherry said, pulling out something in a plastic Piggly Wiggly bag and setting it down on the table. "She must have slipped this shit to me when she was here. She had got in my face, threatened me. Later, when I was leaving, I found them in my bag over at the bar. Who else would know where we keep our shit?"

Bennico said, "Are you sure she slipped these to you?"

"I didn't have 'em before. I remember Tom showing me something on his phone the night he died, putting it in his pocket, leaving, so I didn't have it. Skank wants me to be a suspect. But that's proof she did it. Right?"

Will opened the wallet while Bennico began searching through Tom's phone.

"There's no money here," he said. "Is everything here the way she left it to you? Have you taken anything?"

Bennico added, "Or gone through his phone? Deleted anything?"

"I did look at his wallet, just to see. But all that money he won wouldn't have fit in there. And I didn't even touch the phone. I put these in this bag and made up my mind it was time to tell you. Would I have done that if I had something to hide?"

"Do you know how much he won?" Bennico said.

"It was a pile of money," Cherry said. "Six grand plus."

Will spoke, more to himself than to her, "We still need to find that money, if we can. Zeke never had it."

"You know Day's got it," Bennico said. "She has to."

"Damn straight," Cherry said.

Bennico said, "Did you have a history at all with Day before? My understanding is she worked here too."

"No history," she said, her hackles up a bit. "When I started here, she was still working. Pretty soon after, she was with Tom and quit. Went to work over in South Boston at some salon or some bullshit. Thought she was better than us then."

"Did you and Tom have a history?" Bennico said. "Maybe while he and Day were starting out?"

"Am I in trouble?"

"I want to understand her possible motives."

"Yeah," she said. "Tom and me, we always had a thing. It stopped for a while, when he got with her, but he came back eventually. She'd tricked him, you know. Everybody know that. But he already had a taste of this, couldn't stay away long."

"Do you think Day knew you were cheating with Tom?"

"I don't know about that. All Tom said was he was afraid she knew something. When she came in two nights ago, Sunday, she definitely knew it was me."

"Are you willing to testify?" Will asked Cherry.

"If it put that bitch away, I will. I'd do it for Tom." She paused and said to Will, "Can we talk alone? I got something else for you, from Tom."

Bennico stood up. "I'll be outside."

Cherry removed something from her bra and handed it to him. "This is a list Tom gave me, the night he died, slipped it to me with some money he'd won, and I didn't see it until later. But I knew what it was. He'd told me about everything before. Meeting you, what you asked him for. He would have wanted me to say it's never too late. He said you were a good man. You can use that badge now. People would understand."

The paper trembled in his shaking hands. He knew what it was as he opened it, his eyesight blurring over the names that meant everything to him, even though he had not known them before. A weight came over him like water. He had not known what he would do if he'd ever found them, any of them. Looking through files and driving around or sitting in his truck nights had seemed to him enough of an effort to assuage the guilt of the past yet innocent enough that he did not have to feel more guilt than he already did. Now, he would have to choose to act or to deny, to seek justice or ignore it. He could no longer remain neutral. He could no longer live the illusion that had given him that purposeless purpose that was as comfortable as lukewarm summer water.

"He said you'd want it, that you'd understand."

THINGS WERE COMING together, and Will felt a kind of frenetic optimism. He and Bennico had done good work, and there was plenty more of it to do. They seemed to be getting closer to the truth about Tom's murder, and Will felt certain they would be able to prove Zeke's innocence. But eclipsing all of that for Will was the fact that he now possessed the list of names that he had needed, and this alone gave him a feeling of approaching the breathless finish of a long race.

The morning after he and Bennico talked with Cherry, Will came in through the front doors to the sheriff's department. He was plugged in, a part of unfolding events, existing in the moment.

"Morning, Tania."

"He wants to see you."

"Something wrong?"

"Buddy's in there too."

"Shit," Will said.

He knocked. Sheriff Mills hollered, "Seems! Get in here!"

Buddy was sitting there in the ill-fitting spare uniform he wore as needed, between—and probably during—stints of manufacturing illicit substances. Those zoned out, vacant eyes and that pale unhealthy skin and his dull, sullen, melancholy demeanor indicated he was at it again, if he hadn't been all along.

"Sit down," Mills said.

Will said, "Sir, I checked with the motel. Miss Pace didn't stay there all night. It's likely she was at home, left only to return after we'd shown up."

"I'm right put out with you, Deputy, going behind my back like you done."

"You told me to check on it."

"Way you gone behind my back and teamed up with this PI from Richmond."

"Sheriff," Will said. "I found a motive."

"That again."

Buddy grinned, looking at his shoe, where the sole was beginning to separate.

"Tom Janders was involved with another woman," Will said. "Miss Pace knew it. That supplies a motive."

"I suppose your girlfriend told you that, huh?"

"Plus, she had Tom's wallet and phone."

"Bullshit. Prove it."

Will brought out the evidence.

"I told you to leave that poor woman alone," the sheriff said. "Where'd you get these?"

"Day slipped them to Cherry McDaniels at the Lounge when she went there to threaten her."

"So we check for prints, and they're gonna be Cherry's. How do you know we shouldn't suspect her?"

"Day was at the Lounge Sunday night. As soon as Cherry knew she'd been slipped Tom's personals, she reached out to me. I've already questioned her, and she's willing to take the stand."

"Let me ask you something, hotshot. Did you know your girlfriend was fired from the Richmond police? Conducting illegal searches, breaking and entering, tampering with crime scenes, that type of crap? She's been trying to make it as a private detective for a few months now. She's washed up, just like you."

"How do you know?"

"I'm the sheriff of Euphoria County. Conducting an investigation is what I know how to do. She ain't got a right to be looking into nothin' down here. This murder investigation ain't anywhere close to being in whatever you might call her territory. This is my territory. It's mine, and if and when I need help, I'll find it. In the meantime I'm taking you off the case. Don't roll your eyes at me, son."

"I didn't roll my eyes."

"You don't want to go down this road."

Will said, "I didn't fucking roll my eyes."

"Son, what in hell have you been smoking?"

"You can't take me off Tom's case."

"Can and did. I been running this county since before . . ."

"Yeah, and just fucking look at it."

"Give me your badge and your sidearm. You're finished. Won't work for me again."

Will slammed them on the sheriff's desk and walked out, and Mills shut his door so the shade rattled against the glass.

As Will was leaving, Tania stood and whispered his name. "You could have told me," she said.

"I didn't want to get you in any trouble. Anyway, it wasn't my idea, and it was a mistake from the beginning."

"I mean, if you trusted me I would have helped. I know who hired her."

"I do trust you, Tania."

"Well, why don't you ever let me in on anything?"

"I'm sorry."

"It's like you're either half-asleep or you're studying files for who the hell knows why, and I'm here the whole time, and you don't even know it."

"How did y'all find out about her being fired anyway? I searched for information online and didn't see that."

"RPD kept it quiet."

"Well, how did y'all find out?"

"Sheriff knows a couple people who work for RPD. They knew right away who she was. Said she's trouble."

"And I got stuck with her. Of course. Well, it's too late now."

"We need you, Will," she said. "Don't you know that? We needed Grady too."

"Well, I'm not quitting. I'm getting canned. There's a difference."

"You think Grady quit? Well, I guess you could say he did, but you could also say he was encouraged to resign."

"No shit."

IN HIS OFFICE, Sheriff Mills again contemplated the syringe he had found in the wastebasket in the Seems house. He had thought of bringing it out and presenting it to Will, a kind of dramatic point that could be made only with a visual of the incriminating evidence, but then he would have shown his cards. After all, Mills had not seen Sam. He considered going back and arresting Sam, but something held him back. It was odd, this hesitation. After all, the law was clear: Sam Hathom was wanted for breaking and entering and larceny in Euphoria County, and the sheriff knew where he was. But he did hesitate, the way a hunter, upon seeing a buck emerge, within shooting distance maybe, waits anyway for the buck that does not yet detect the threat to come forward, loving that intimate secrecy. The challenge was knowing when to shoot, not waiting so long that the deer might scent you.

He thought of the way it used to be, back when they'd hunt the fields all over this country, back when the wild birds flew. He remembered Blind James, the dog trainer descended from swamp maroons who said he spoke to dogs in their own tongue. Once he broke a setter or a pointer, that dog would stand like a statue, even if you couldn't find him for a week, starve to death if needed, all to stand a covey of quail or even a single bird.

The irony was not lost on Mills that he, like Mrs. Watts, had conducted an illegal search by breaking into Promised Land without a warrant. But this was his county. And since he had done it once . . .

"Buddy," he said, "I've got an assignment for you."

BENNICO HAD SLEPT in and woke up feeling good, well rested, fresh. She saw there was coffee on the stove that Sam must have made and poured some and took it out to the porch. She looked out at Sam in the garden tying up the tomato plants. The sun was bright and hot and warming, and she sat out on the back porch of the house in the late morning, loving the distances of Southside, broken by dreamy copses of trees draped with kudzu, the hazy sun gathering up the world in its embrace.

Through the polite opening and shutting of doors she'd heard Will leave early in the morning. She smiled at the thought of Will. She felt she understood him. He'd been so haunted by what had happened to Sam those years ago that he'd come back as a deputy. He'd been on the job, in his mind, for years. There was something about his intimate and personal frustration that moved her, made her feel they had known each other a long time.

Sam finished tying up the tomato plants and gathering tomatoes and black-eyed peas and beans and picked up the garden tools. He gave Bennico a cheerful wave and loaded the tools in the wheelbarrow and pushed it over to the old cabin where they stored them. She saw a red cloud rising along the rutted drive and Will's truck coming up the slope from the main road toward her. It was like a little dreamworld, living out there, like living in the dust of a past that looked so soft from a distance, like some kind of effect in one of Will's photographs.

He was driving fast and slid to a stop in the red dirt patch out behind the house. She started to get a bad feeling. Something was wrong.

Will slammed his truck door and Bennico watched as he bounded toward the porch and seemed to freeze midair, startled to find her there.

"Will," Bennico said, standing. "What's wrong?"

"Why did you leave the police force?"

"I can explain."

"After all your talk of trust. After I told you about Sam, opened up to you. I knew this was a fucking mistake."

"I thought you of all people would understand."

"What's that supposed to mean?"

"Oh, come on! What, like you aren't harboring a wanted criminal in your house? Like you aren't wearing that badge just to carry out a personal vendetta you haven't had the courage to complete?"

It was harsher than she'd intended.

Will said, "Difference is, I never lied to you. We were supposed to work this together. And now, I lost my job because I didn't know, didn't see it coming."

She reached out to touch him—to connect—but Will backed away as if she'd tried to hit him. Well, it was clear now how much they understood each other.

"Haven't these past couple days been a success?" she said. "Who cares if you have the badge or not? We've got information now. Real evidence. We should be able to get Zeke acquitted and put Day in jail."

"This is over. Get off my property."

"You know what, fuck you. I thought you were different. A white man who really cared."

She went inside and tossed her things together, acutely aware of the absurd and sudden change in energy and emotion, and though she was angry, she felt that they were both acting a certain way because of a technicality, that neither wanted this to happen. But clearly there was no going back.

"You're going to regret this," she said, storming past him on the porch.

She turned at the Escalade, hands full.

"You know what I think? You want me gone because you're afraid I might figure out you got your eye on the person we think killed Tom."

"You crazy fucking bitch. You wouldn't know the truth if—"

"I see where you focus your camera."

"Get out."

"And for the record, you didn't hire me," she yelled. "So I'm still working. And I'm going to blow this whole thing up."

"Well," he said, a hoarse furious lump in his throat. "Do it quick, because if the sheriff or I see you again, we're going to haul you in."

W ILL WATCHED HER diminish into the cloud of his own approach and then the vacancy, the hollow he knew all too well, the hole that needed to be filled. The sadness was immediate. So that was it. There, in the silence, he sat in the chair she had just abandoned—that he'd forced her to abandon—feeling the slight warmth of her body, detecting her faint fading scent. This air she had breathed so recently, this air of heady walnuts in the yard, of wild blossoms in the uncut grass. This world she had inhabited. The dust seemed to hang from the sky above the tobacco like a decision. It was as if he'd pressed play on a film of the moments of his life that kept playing, a film that made sense only to him. He was eighteen again. The sound of his mother's singing as he went to bed, the look in her eyes toward the end, the image of her reconstructed face in that coffin. Then sixteen. Sam lying, glowing like pain in the dark grass, barely alive. And now Bennico's lies and the sheriff not wanting the truth and Will being here—for what? His anger wanted their pain. He wanted to absorb it. He could endure anything, administer any kind of suffering. "Fuck you," he said to nothing, everything. "Fuck you." To himself, to his mother, to his father, to Bennico, to his ancestors for paving this existence of pain and loss. Always the loss. He'd been born of losers, born to lose.

Sam approached from somewhere, healthy-looking, sweating with the work.

"What was that about?" he said.

Will barely heard him. "Nothing."

"You all right? She coming back?"

He almost didn't notice that suddenly Sam was gone, back in the house, whatever conversation there had been forgotten.

As the sun rose, his spirits fell. He went in for his camera, loaded with black-and-white film, moved across the ground, golden and hot and bright, close to noon. He photographed the stark trees exploding through one of the old wood-frame buildings on the property, the glare of the sun pouring over everything in a kind of halo. The pond, where the trees grew like bones, the mud becoming water covered in a skin of bright green algae, water still and thick as coffee. Capturing, trying to capture, the raw blazing glow of midday. He saw the possibilities, had visions, ecstasies. Always it was this way. Sometimes this could be a source of peace, catching things as they were, as they would always be. A KFC box upturned in a swale of grass. Not far off, a broken forty-ounce bottle of Colt 45. How did this trash even get out here? Thinking of her again, Hannah, his mother, of Sam, he raised the camera, realized that even focused he couldn't see clearly. Nothing seemed to be able to help.

He could taste it now, in the back of his nose. He saw something move by the edge of the swamp, a possum, hideous and matted and gray as a Confederate ghost. He unholstered his pistol and shot the animal at twenty-five yards. It hissed and squealed, and Will walked closer, as if his life depended on the completion of this one thing, and shot it again, watching the animal's taut convulsions. He couldn't even seem to control the life of one thing, his own or another's.

Those years in Richmond, Will had believed returning to Southside would be heroic, that home could be an elixir for whatever he lacked. Well, now he had it. He was here. And where was that? He'd arrested Zeke, lied to Sam, gotten fired, and accomplished nothing of any substance. He thought of all the times his father had tried to dissuade him from returning.

"Believe me, son," he'd said. "You're better off letting it stay the way you want it to in your mind."

"I'm going back."

"There's nothing there."

"There's my history."

"History can be an escape, a mirage. It's real, but it can't be changed."

It seemed now that he'd walked into a trap. He thought back to his mother and Sam, the two tragedies of his life. Why had he returned, really? To accomplish what? His dad had said he was running away, his grandfather that he was facing up to a challenge that meant nothing. He thought of their faces, a phalanx of shadows, that pained hoarse voice, deep as the angry word of God, ready to hurt Sam or him—either would do. The hate in their blank faces that he felt and understood here and now, since he also hated. The fear it had caused him, and more hate. The fact now that their hate, as a result of older hatred, had dictated his life, that Will had surrendered to it. He'd never be free because he'd always be guilty, no end in sight.

Will took a photograph of his bloody work, a glisten of guts, something to regret later, something unchanged and unchangeable. The last picture in the roll of film, the camera whirring like an engine, a flushed covey of quail, and Will wiped his face and buried the possum tenderly in the new bright soil of home as if it were his own kin, his own ugliness, the true self only he knew and only he could know, the nature beneath his intentions like an unbudging stump just beneath the opaque water of some still unmoving pond. He could see her now, them, hating them all as he hated himself.

**B**ENNICO PULLED OFF to the side of the lane into the driveway of a house she presumed was abandoned. The roof had partly disintegrated, exposing wooden beams underneath. Sections of pine two-by-fours had been nailed across the door, a child's bright tricycle in the yard. It made her nervous, what Will had said, offhand, that in Southside you couldn't ever tell if a house was really abandoned. Quite often, even if it was, someone found their way to its shelter.

*Fuck Will.* Just when things were starting to make sense. She'd been betrayed by all men in her life. She needed something, some breakthrough. Rain clouds slipped along the eastern horizon as she dried furious tears, hating herself for allowing them. She thought of calling Floressa. She even thought of calling Custis, her girls, and took out her phone, but she dialed a different number: Lewis Ayres, her ex-partner. Everything was ex now. Husband, partner, friend. He had been able to salvage his job but had moved to forensics, out of the detective squad. She had to call twice before he picked up.

"What, Bennico."

"Did you hear about that murder down in Euphoria?"

Lewis sighed. "I may have seen something about it. House arson as a cover-up? That one? Real original."

"They released the body for burial, but they've got the wrong guy."

"Bennico. Stop trying to be a cop."

"Listen to me, Lewis. I've been hired privately to work this, and I need you."

"I don't even know what you want me to do, but I know I can't do it."

"The sheriff here isn't even looking into it. He knows the local coroner. It's all good ol' boy connections."

"This is smelling a lot like that rape investigation. You remember what happened. Why can't you ever learn?"

"Wife of the accused hired me, and I'm not going to give up. All we got here is the body and a weapon I can't get my hands on. I need to get this body seen by an unbiased forensic technician. I need you."

"No way. I can't get down there. No way. You don't even know what you'd be looking for."

"Anything. I'm telling you it's all being overlooked. Think of what this could do for you." She had paused to control the tears in her voice. "Lewis. You're all I've got in the world right now."

A long pause gave her hope.

"I'm sorry," Lewis said. "But I don't want to lose my job too."

"You know what? Fuck you."

"You never know when to stop. And things have been going along okay here. I can't fuck that up."

"Fucking white men. What if I could get the body to you? Just give it a quick look over. I took the hit on that investigation. You knew what I was doing. I never asked you to jump in, and you didn't. I wouldn't ask you for help if I didn't need it. Now grab a sack. You owe me this much."

The line was silent for a minute, long enough. He sighed into the phone, and she thought about that police routine, a lot of nothing, the boredom, and all the pent-up jitters, just trying to get somewhere, stay awake, stay alive, do something, anything, make an intangible difference in the transient dark world. That was why she'd broken in to steal evidence. She just couldn't wait any longer for the law to do nothing.

"You'd better be on to something," Lewis said. "I can't risk my job for a maybe."

"All we got are maybes. You know that. But this is better than what you get up to on an average day. I got a feeling."

"You always do," he said. He sighed into his phone, and she waited. She didn't want to push too hard now.

Finally, he said, "You're going to have to figure out a way to get the body here."

"Thanks, Lewis. I knew you'd back me on this."

He forced a laugh. "If I know you, you'll figure out a way. Anyway, you can't get fired twice. Give me a shout when you get here."

He hung up, wondering why it was that he could never say no to that woman, an ex-partner who even as an ex had a strange power over him. But he knew he was lucky. She was as real as someone could be and always had the heart of the matter in focus.

Now, sitting here in this vacant driveway, Bennico had something to prove, and this rushed through her veins and into her head, and her heart quickened, but she forced herself to wait here. She could see Will's back gate through a gap in the trees. Eventually, she saw his truck drive out and past the driveway where she had parked. She pulled out and drove the back way to Promised Land, found Sam upstairs in his room.

Sam said, "What's up, Bennico?"

"Did Will tell you anything?"

"I heard y'all shouting. Tried talking to him, but it was like he was off somewhere else. I know better than to mess with him when he gets like that. What the fuck did you do?"

"I'm gonna have to tell you something—a couple things—that aren't going to be easy to hear."

"Everything okay?"

"I'm a private investigator. Your mom hired me to investigate Tom's death."

He shook his head, smiling. "I didn't believe it at first," he said. "Y'all had me going, though. Shit."

"That's not all. Are you gonna be okay if I tell you something bad?"

"How am I supposed to say yes to that?"

"Your dad has been arrested. He's suspected of Tom's murder."

"You're fucking with me," Sam said, but his face told her that he knew it was true. "My dad? How could they . . ."

"He was there at the scene. They've found a murder weapon, and his prints match those on the weapon."

"Ain't no fuckin' way that's true!"

"I know. Will knows. We've been looking for evidence . . ."

"Fuck that mo'fuck! He didn't tell me any of this. Fuck him. And you too. Why didn't you tell me?"

"I promised Will. He was worried for your safety. Thought you might leave or relapse. I told him he should tell you, but I swear he thought he was doing right."

She wondered why she was standing up for Will just now.

"Right, my ass," he said, starting to get his things together.

"Where are you going?" Bennico said.

"Going to prove that mo'fuck right. Getting the hell away from here."

"Come with me, Sam. I've got a plan to help your dad. It's going to be risky, but I could really use your help."

"Why the fuck should I trust you?"

"Your mom does. She hired me, Sam. I swear, this is all for your dad. Forget me. Forget Will. Let's do what we can for him."

"What do you want?"

She moved forward, held Sam's hand.

"Just come with me. We don't have much time. I can't do it alone. We can get your dad acquitted if we get the right evidence. And there's only one piece of evidence I can think of that will work."

"What's that?"

"Tom's body."

W ILL DROVE OUT to Willie Pie's store along a curving road overhung by tired, drooping summer trees and turned at an old, abandoned school broken through with green wild grasses and vines. A hedge of honeysuckle lined a road gone gravel, and when the hedge ended he could see the wheeling rows of tobacco and a distant storefront in a yard of pecan and walnut trees.

It was still called Willie Pie's store—that was the official address—even though Seth Grady had never sold any wares. Still, its general-store display windows were a prominent feature, its late nineteenth-century construction lending it a kind of dormant anachronistic authenticity. The high shelves inside centered on a woodstove and housed books, with rolling ladders on either side of the store to reach them. Will could remember whole-hog pit barbecues for his dad's high school friends and playing out in the yard or watching movies with the kids upstairs. He didn't know what he'd find; he hadn't seen Mr. Grady—Deputy Grady—in years.

Cicadas buzzed in an eddy of sound, and Will walked in through the front only to see an empty store. He went around back, passing the woodpile, the smokehouse, the pit Grady used to barbecue, and he heard now, faint against the wall of cicada sound in that wall of trees, the thin sound of a radio—angular jazz, Thelonious Monk—one puny layer in a great collage of melodies, harmonies, rhythms. A man stood, stooped, in denim overalls so faded they almost matched the white T-shirt he wore underneath. An old, smudged Richmond Braves cap sat backward on his head. Paint gobs had landed in the dust and on his bare feet, and he was cursing steadily under his breath: "Come on, goddamn you. Oh, it's like that is it? See if I fucking . . ." Will regretted coming.

Suddenly, just as Will was backing out of the yard, Grady exploded and threw his paintbrush to the ground, produced from somewhere an old side-by-side twelve gauge and fired two broadsides, then picked up the shredded canvas and threw it into a heap of other such paintings in the yard.

He turned, a look of horror on his face, frozen, staring, breathless. "How the fuck long you been standing there?"

"Long enough, I reckon."

"I reckon so. Don't be concerned," he said, waving his hand in a vague oratorial gesture. "I'm retired."

"Will Seems," Will said, extending his hand.

"I know who you are. I been wondering when you'd come see me. Put 'er there."

They shook hands.

"Damn, Judy will get a kick out of seeing you. You remember her?"

"Of course. We used to run around all the time."

"She's inside. Let's say hey. JUDY!"

She came down the steps in an old sweatshirt, a little heavily built, and said, "Will Seems? How you been?"

"Hey, Judy. How you doing? Seems you got your work cut out for you."

"Daddy? He does need some looking after."

She apparently had never left home, but Will didn't want to ask her too much. She was obviously unmarried, and in Virginia, marriage by a certain age becomes the gauge by which most people determine whether you're all right. After a certain point, a single adult or a woman without children will be seen as something strange, uncomfortable, even foreign—not to be trusted.

"Judy, honey. We got any beer?"

"I don't think so, Daddy."

"Want a beer?"

"Is my last name Seems?"

"Well said. Come on."

They drove out to a filling station about two miles away where Will could remember a late night, years back, when he and his father were leaving Grady's, and they hit a deer and had to pull in here, his dad's truck dripping blood and antifreeze. He remembered in particular a man getting out of his parked car barefoot, trash and beer cans tumbling out in a conspicuous clatter, a wet spot on his sweatpants, going inside to the restroom. It was the first time he'd seen a grown man who'd pissed himself.

Now they pulled in and parked in front of the ice machine, and a Black man in jeans, do-rag, and oversize shirt came out with three full cases of Coors Light stacked in his hands.

"Mr. Grady," he said.

"Need a hand, TJ?"

"Hell no," he said, shaking his head, laughing.

Inside, men were buying bait and tackle and beer.

Grady said, "What you want?" to Will.

"Anything."

Grady picked out a case of Yuengling, paid for it while making fun of someone he apparently knew who was buying tackle. "Don't matter what you get, Jimmy. You're so ugly the fish won't bite. My advice is, wear a mask or fish at night."

Back at the house, they sat out in antique dining chairs in the yard, trees backlit by the long western sun, snicking open beers.

Mr. Grady said, "This what you were expecting?"

"Not sure. I remember coming out here, seeing your art. I think that's why I got into it."

"You doing it now?"

"Mostly photography. I've made the basement into a darkroom and process everything there."

"Show me your stuff sometime. How's your daddy and sister?"

"All right, I guess."

"Oh, I see. Not talking?"

"Look, I'm hoping you don't think I was trying to take your job."

"Shit. You didn't. I was done with it. It's a young man's game, anyway."

"Tania let slip something that made me think you were forced to leave the position."

"Sweet Tania."

"She wrong?"

"No," he said. "No. Things had run their course. I couldn't work for Mills anymore, and he couldn't stand me. My hat's off to you in this whole fiasco now. I don't believe Zeke did what he's been accused of. Poor son of a bitch."

"The sheriff is convinced he's guilty. The evidence is damning—murder weapon with his prints, he was seen running away from the crime scene, that kind of stuff—but you don't have to look too hard to see that Zeke is innocent. I think Tom's girlfriend should be a suspect, and I told Mills that, but he wouldn't hear about it."

"That doesn't surprise me."

"Because of the upcoming election?"

"Well, that's probably part of it."

"What else?"

"You really don't know anything, do you? He ain't told you nothing."

"Who?"

"Your dad."

"He ran away. I came home. I do know that."

Grady waved his hand through the air, clearing the bullshit. He sat up, picked at something on one of his boots, and took a deep breath.

"I reckon he's got his own reasons for not telling. None of that—leaving Dawn, your poor mama's death, nothing—was his fault. Can't go around blaming a man for doing what he has to do to protect his own. Your daddy left town because that was the only way."

"I find that hard to believe."

"Doesn't make a difference what you believe."

From his overalls, Grady brought out a pouch and some papers and rolled a cigarette.

"It's all tied up together, in a way," Grady said. "I've been sort of hoping he'd come along and represent Zeke . . ."

"I asked him to."

" . . . but of course he can't."

"Why the fuck not?"

"Well, I reckon it's up to me to set you straight. Your daddy is not one to cut and run like maybe you're thinking. I guess I can see now that I'm the only one who understands how this all matters in the case at hand. Well. Back in the summer of, I think it was 1995, how old would you have been?"

"Thirteen."

"Your daddy had just passed the bar and was tying one on with some buddies. I don't know if you remember how big a deal it was, him getting out of tobacco, which your family had raised for generations, to become a lawyer. Anyway, he'd been out with some people down at Shining Rock, and somehow he ended up getting separated, going out to Arnie's Lounge to play cards. He was friends with Skip Malone—who's dead of course—had run into him at a liquor store or something, switched cars, and gone with Skip. We were all pretty wild back then. Mills had recently become sheriff (after his daddy's retirement), and I was a deputy, and we were known to have some fun on occasion.

"Well, I had shown up at Shining Rock in plain clothes, seen your daddy earlier. He was on a streak that night. Anyway, according to Skip and other witnesses, there was some character there at the Lounge who showed up with some woman. Nobody knew him well, but he'd been around. Ex-army, but in a piece-of-shit way, been in jail all over since, real trash. Your daddy went back to this card game, and soon after someone ran into the back room, said this dude was beating on his woman. Your daddy happened to be the only other white person there, and he ran out with the others to the lot to see this trash, sure enough, beating on the woman the way he'd go after a man. Her nose was busted, and he had her on the ground, was kicking at her ribs. I can attest to this, because I seen her later. Anyway, your daddy stepped in. Said something to him to get him to stop. The guy charged him with some roundhouse karate bullshit, and your daddy caught his leg and flipped him on his back. Well, that dumb shit fucked everything up by hitting his head—in a dirt parking lot—on the edge of a bottle, part buried in the ground. Your daddy called it in from the bar—even then, the law didn't usually go to the Lounge—and by the time Mills and I got there, the man was dead, bled out. I remember well that terrible scene. That poor woman unconscious, and more blood than you could believe making that red dirt even redder. Your daddy was beside himself with grief. It didn't take much time at all; Jeff and I knew what to do. Mills made the call then and there that we had to dump the body. I still don't know if we did right, but I'd do it again. That whole thing could have destroyed Bill's life, as well as yours and your sister's and Hannah's. You know that line between voluntary manslaughter and second-degree murder is pretty thin, and both carry jail time. The dead should be allowed to serve some purpose, though they rarely do.

"Well, that body we disposed of belonged to a guy name of Ricky Pace, a man from the Snakefoot who'd done nothing but cause a heap of trouble everywhere he went, including his home whenever he saw fit to return.

"This is the part I don't believe your daddy knows. Say what you will about Jeff Mills, he felt guilty about what we done to that man's body. Mills found out Pace had a little girl, and he took an interest in her. He helped that little girl and her mama as much as he could until that poor ol' gal killed herself. It's ironic that little Day, when she was of age, worked where others in the Snakefoot look to work when they don't want to go too far and want to get cash under the table."

"Arnie's Lounge," Will said.

"I don't believe she ever knew her daddy had anything to do with the place let alone died there."

"So that's the reason Mills is set on Zeke as a suspect?"

"All I know is he's been looking out for that girl since her daddy died. The fact that she was the mother of Tom's child, and Mills is latched on to Zeke as the suspect, makes me think he's trying to protect her or himself for what we did those years ago."

"You think she knows what happened to her daddy?"

"Mills will go to the grave without spilling that to her. We haven't spoken of it since we dumped the body that morning."

Mr. Grady stopped talking. He seemed tired, run-down.

Eventually he said, "You got to find some way to protect Zeke."

"I told you my dad refused."

"Well, of course he did," Grady said.

"Because Mills is holding it over him?"

"Exactly. I told your daddy, 'Bill. He's not going to forget you owe him. The only way you can leave that past is to leave this place.' That's what he did. Changes your thoughts about your daddy, doesn't it?"

Will stood up, looked off through the trees into the fields.

He turned to Grady. "You should come back, run for sheriff."

Grady choked on his beer, cleared his voice like a truck without a muffler. "I'm too old for that, kid. But *you* should."

"Fuck no."

"Why not? You been on the job a year or so. By the election it'll be almost two years probably. They'd let you run."

"No. I'm not here for that."

"What the hell are you here for then?"

Will squinted at Grady. He knew he was about to share too much, but this was Mr. Grady. He might be able to help.

"Do you remember Sam Hathom?"

"Been missing some while, ain't he?"

"Did you ever find out any of the boys who hurt him? Why did nothing come of that?"

"Your dad wanted to help the Hathoms but couldn't. Nobody could or would identify them."

"I find it hard to believe someone couldn't have been found with blood on their knuckles."

"Over there in Turkey Creek, man, it's hard to track people down. Harder than you think. I'll expect you know that by now. You never know whose house is whose, whose is nobody's."

Will pulled out the list Cherry had given him. "Any of these names seem familiar?"

"Where'd you get this list?"

"Tom."

"These people have moved on. Some have families. Some of them have learned to live with it; some weren't very involved. Where do you draw the line?"

"I don't know yet. I'm trying to find out."

"I know what it's like to break the law for a reason. It doesn't make things right. You want so badly to do it that you forget what you might feel afterward. Either way, there's guilt. Either way, you're in the wrong. It's not something you want to live with. But this—if you're thinking what I think you are—would be a whole new level of guilt, not to mention a life of regret. I've seen men break down after winning fights. Because there's no way you can win. No matter how a fight turns out, or what side you're on, you lose. Your daddy'd tell you that."

"They need to know the damage they've caused."

"To Sam or to you? My guess is Sam has learned better to live with it than you. And ain't nothing going to make him like he was. Damage has been done, and it don't need more to help it out. Take it from me—your daddy would say this, I'm sure—violence is not the best way. It brings a pain that brings more pain. You've already seen that. You'll always have too much of it but never enough. You have to ask yourself if you really want to solve a problem or if you've learned to use it as a crutch. Sometimes, we learn to savor our pain. Look at this place as an example. Never got over the War, and why? Because the South lost. We think we hate the hurt, but we can't part with it. Ask yourself if this is more about some guilt you feel than it is about bringing them to justice. No act undoes the past."

"Fuck. You sound just like him."

"I'll take that as a compliment."

THURSDAY WAS THE DAY of Tom's funeral and the ninth day since Tom's body had been found. Day sat on her bed in the little room at Claudette's house, looking down at Destinee like some creature brought out of the reservoir and wiped dry. Because of the baby, Tom was present. What did it take to leave a place, start again? Destinee was her and not her, Tom and not Tom. Instead of hope, she felt sick to her stomach and remembered what Granny said. Another baby on the way. How could she have been so stupid?

She told herself that after today she'd be free to leave town. She could leave the baby with Claudette and go. She could tell the sheriff she needed to get away. Just until the trial. He'd understand. She remembered the way he used to come in to the Lounge, about the time she and Tom were getting started, the way he'd come late, making the rounds, would stand there and watch, and sometimes, when she was little, he'd come by their house in the Snakefoot with cans of food. She knew, and she'd enjoyed the tingling that moved through her like a warm blush from head to toe. There was a quality about him that was like a landmark you see every day or a window that frames your world. That gray face both paternal and independent of paternity, as American as the deep red dirt beneath them, timeless as a void. Something about him calmed her. She remembered how he'd stand at the bar, not even drinking, watching only her in that wise calming way of his, as if to say, "You go on dancing forever, and I'll want nothing. I'll starve and parch for you. The wanting is all I want." She began to consider staying in town. Folks wouldn't suspect her now that she had stayed through the investigation, assisting the sheriff whenever needed. Today was the day that would release her. It was not the cessation of life but the disposal of a body that put one to independent solitary rest. They would bury Tom, and that would be enough. The future was opening up like a road. The thought of what lay ahead brought her to song, and she crooned to Destinee, kicking and squealing in her mama's arms. Day felt that warmth tingling through her from head to toe. This brightness was so different from her usual character that Claudette knocked on the door.

"Day, sugar, is that you?"

"I'm just singing to the baby. We should celebrate Tom's life today."

Claudette turned away. She had run herself ragged trying to prepare for the funeral. She was beside herself with grief, which dawned on her now like the realization that she must step onto a stage, but in her deepest heart, the thought that the mother of Tom's daughter could have been the slightest bit happy filled her with foreboding of the day's coming events, and with a deep, uncomfortable sensation. She began to understand, praying furiously over her grandmother's Bible, that what she was feeling was hate.

AROUND NOON, DAY could hear Claudette moaning, alternating between crying and praying, rising high periodically with a *Lord*

*Jesus, Lord Jesus, have mercy on us.* Day went to the kitchen for one of Destinee's bottles and saw, through the half-open bedroom door, Tom's mother sitting on the edge of her bed, all dressed up for the service, looking at the picture of Tom, kneeling in his football uniform, on the corner of her bedside table, dabbing her eyes with a handkerchief.

Day felt something she had been free of until now that reminded her of the sounds her mother used to make when her daddy was home or when he was away. Always the pain, with or without. Happiness depended on a man, but misery always came about because of one. Day got up and went to Claudette, some semblance of empathy welling in her heart.

"You okay, Mama?" she asked.

"I miss my boy."

"I know you do. I do too. I'm sorry."

"What are you sorry for?"

For her mother and all women. For herself.

"I was hoping to grow close with you," Claudette said. "We lost the same man. But you push me away every step."

Claudette closed her eyes and held her hand over her face.

"I keep feeling Tom is here," Claudette said. "In my dreams, in this room. I try to talk to him, pray at him, because I know he wants to tell me something. I just know that. He never had a chance to say good-bye." She looked up at Day, standing over her, tears in her eyes so that Day looked like something you might see underwater. "That's what hurts," she said. "It's not just that someone took his life, it's that I never got to say good-bye. You took him from me."

Day stepped back.

Claudette said, "Ever since you moved in with him, ever since there was Destinee, he didn't never come see me. I never got to say good-bye."

"Mama, I'm sorry. I didn't mean to."

"Call me that again."

"Mama. Mama."

The old woman reached out for Day's hand, clutching it with great power. "I need to feel I got a family. I need to hold that straight line to Tom."

The doorbell rang.

S AM STAYED IN the car as Bennico opened the gate and walked through the flat little yard at Walker Court onto the porch. She took her finger off the doorbell and waited. Claudette answered the door, holding Tom's baby.

Bennico said, "Is this the Janders residence?"

"Yes," Claudette said, not understanding, since the two women had already met.

"Is Miss Pace in?"

Claudette closed the door, her heart racing, wondering why in the world Bennico would come here before the funeral.

"It's for you, Day."

"Who is it?" Day said.

Claudette ignored the question. "She at the door."

Day opened the door, and Bennico thought she had the face of a little girl, as innocent-looking as any doe. Bennico offered flowers, a gesture that seemed to soften Day just a little. She accepted the bouquet, looking down.

"I'm sorry for your loss," Bennico said, taking note of the heavy makeup over Day's cheekbone, something hidden there. "I'm Bennico Watts, a private detective, and I want to help you."

"Help me?"

"They haven't caught Tom's killer, have they?"

"Zeke Hathom's in the jail," Day said.

On the surface, she was polished but not refined. Her accent was hard to pin down. Definitely Southern, but if you closed your eyes, you'd be unable to tell if she was Black or white. Bennico quickly formed the opinion that Day had learned to adapt for survival. She seemed a girl in a woman's body, a girl playing woman. A lithe woman not much different from an animal; a girl who knew how to survive.

"That's what I mean," Bennico said. "We both know he didn't do it. Everybody knows. It's going to get thrown out in court because there won't be enough evidence, and they'll have to start over."

"I already spoke to the sheriff's department," Day said, and that survival instinct crossed her demeanor in the form of distrust. She watched Bennico carefully. Something wasn't right. "They want to talk to me again, they can come and find me. You got a badge?"

"I'm a private detective."

"Who hired you then?"

"Don't you want to find who did this?"

"I know who it was. That bitch Cherry McDaniels. Well, go on. Get out of here. Ain't got nothing else to say to you."

Day watched Bennico walk through the yard and out the chain-link fence. She turned to go inside, where Claudette stood, the baby in her arms, a look of suspicion and pain on her face. "What that woman want?"

"Nothing."

"Why you so upset, girl?"

"I don't want to talk about it."

"What you got going on? You know something about Tom that I don't?"

"No."

"She was right," Claudette said. "Zeke didn't do anything. How can you not want to know who did this?"

Day stepped back, clutching herself as if exposed, naked. "So you were listening."

"Why don't you want to know what happened to Tom, Day? Or do you already know?"

Claudette wasn't even speaking angrily. She was filled strangely with a feeling of love, of pity, with a sudden perspective she credited God for that there was nothing really to hide from because nothing could be hidden from the Almighty.

She approached Day and put her arm on the back of the woman she was thinking of as a girl now, a daughter of God, a lamb fully lost in a black wilderness.

"Oh God," Day said. She thought then about running, and she knew that she always could, but now, Tom's mother's hand on her back, she felt trapped. She wanted to be deserving of such sympathy. She sobbed.

"There, there, child," Claudette said, stroking the young woman's neck.

Day felt a strange desire inside her where she had once carried little Destinee, and she felt the hands of the woman who had given birth to Tom. She wept, unable to act any longer. They never would understand. No one would or could. She was a girl who never should have left the swamp. Either that or she should have gone far away.

"I been wondering how come you didn't want to learn more," Claudette said. "But I kept it to myself."

"That woman," Day said. "You said you were going to hire someone. Was that her?"

"Yes, it was."

"Oh God," Day said. "How could you do this to me?"

"I didn't ask her to come here. She must have had a reason."

"It ain't fair."

"You're in the darkness, girl. You need the power of the one true God; you need the healing power of Jesus Christ, who died for our sins."

"Yes," Day said. "I know."

"Do you want to be healed? Do you want to let that love into your heart?"

"Yes."

"Do you want the light of God's truth to take your troubles away?"

"Yes." Day began to cry, pleading with Tom's mother, who held her hand tight.

And looking at the two women, the grandmother holding the infant, through the front door, one would have seen a lovely family in mourning—a touching scene—until Claudette reached under Day's chin and turned the young mother's face up to hers.

"You little bitch. It's too late for God's mercy."

"What?"

"Now we are going to forget about this. For now. We are going to go to the funeral and honor Tom's life. You will have to act, but you already acting. Then, you are coming back with me, right here, and we are going to get to the bottom of this. You and me. You're gonna tell me the truth. What really happened. That is the only way. And if you don't—Lord God have mercy on me—I'll kill you dead myself."

WILL RETURNED TO Promised Land after another night sleeping in his truck—only last night had been different. He'd made up his mind to tell Sam his dad was suspected of Tom's murder. No more secrets, no more lies. This was the right thing to do.

Will looked around, called out. No answer.

He moved through the house with increasing fervor, a panic beginning to settle in. He rushed out to the porch and scanned the fields. Nothing but soulless crops. He ran to the barn. No one there.

So it was like that. He had gone to all this trouble to take in Sam, give him work. Hadn't Will provided him the safety of this place? Hadn't he protected him?

*Ah*, Will thought. Sam must have found out somehow about the funeral and decided to go on his own. Maybe Bennico had told him. That was it. He had found out somehow, maybe actually ventured to town and found that today was the funeral. After all that consideration, deciding he would tell Sam that Mr. Hathom was their suspect, Sam had left on his own. Will became simultaneously furious that Sam would do such a thing and afraid of what would happen to him. He had to get to him as soon as possible to avoid arrest or whatever else might come. His fears had come true; he had to save Sam from himself again. Will changed for the funeral and rushed out the door, cursing or praying or both under his breath.

**F**LORESSA KEPT CALLING and calling until Mills threatened to arrest her.

"What for!" she demanded.

"Obstruction. Annoyance. Bullying."

"You the sheriff, I reckon. Can do what you want. But let that man to the funeral."

"Well, damnit. I can't do that."

"You can't seem to do much of anything."

"Mrs. Hathom, you're downright uncivilized."

"We'll see how this next election turns out. People really going to vote this time. People want results, not a cracker on a throne he's made himself."

"I have protected you and this county for more than thirty years."

"I been here for all of 'em. And I ain't satisfied."

"You gonna need to watch yourself, ma'am."

"I want Zeke to come with me to the funeral today. He deserves it."

"Well, hell, Mrs. Hathom, I want my mama to come back from the graveyard and fix me a Christmas dinner."

He had already decided to take Zeke to the funeral and wished Floressa would stop pestering him so it wouldn't look as though he'd capitulated to her demands. He figured it could only work in his favor to let him go. Blacks would see Mills had treated Zeke well, which might help in the November election. But he thought it would be a good idea for Zeke to have to see Tom lowered. Zeke had the worst poker face around. Mills wanted to see Zeke's face at the funeral. He had learned from his daddy that a man's face will tell you almost everything you need to know about him.

"I can't let him go with you, but I am going to take him. Now leave me alone."

"You doing the right thing."

She hung up. "Goddamn," Mills said to Buddy. "If I was married to that crazy woman I'd of killed someone too."

He put Buddy on dispatch and went and took Zeke out to the cruiser. He thought he perceived a growing fear on Zeke's face.

"I'll bet you thought I was going to keep you here," he said to the prisoner. "And I'll bet you wish you could stay. But you're going to go and witness the pain you've caused everyone. You're going to have to feel the pain."

B ENNICO AND SAM passed the Philip Morris plant and wound into the city on I-95 north, curving down into Shockoe around the old train station with its clock tower high above the tall-stilted highway. Via one-way city streets in Church Hill they wove crookedly through the area. The cigarette factories had become apartments, and Broad Street, not far away, had been cleaned up. Five, ten, twenty, thirty years ago, Richmond had been a city of shadows cast by old, slanted buildings where, come dusk, it was wise to get off the street.

She and Sam found a back entrance to the old train station and moved across the wide lot, overgrown at the edges of the chain-link fence surrounding it, and backed up to a loading dock at an old nondescript brick building beneath the overpass that looked like a longhouse. Lewis came out, a look of performative disgust on his face that Bennico had anticipated, with two others who grabbed Tom's corpse from the back of the Cadillac.

Lewis said, "I'll call you when I need you."

FLORESSA SURVEYED the graveyard as if it were a field planted with a peculiar crop. Beyond it, she could see the swimming hole where Sam had been baptized and on the bank of which he had been senselessly beaten almost to death, and in a moment of whimsy, wished her son might emerge whole out of a nightmare that had lasted thirteen years. She scolded herself for her dreaming, but she had no one to put her hopes on now. She knew Sam thought she'd abandoned him because she'd refused him shelter. But he wasn't her son when he was using. Even so, you never really gave up on a child of yours, not even if you said you did.

She saw Will Seems walking toward her from the church, out of the ragged horizon, pale worry in his pale face. The way he looked now reminded her of taking Sam to the hospital that awful night. Bruises ripening on his cheek, blooming black, so you could see the sickness clear. Why had God chosen Sam to be hurt so bad, and they hadn't even broken Will's skin? But she knew she shouldn't compare, shouldn't doubt God's will. Will Seems was here now, here to serve some purpose.

Along the edge of the field, folks were beginning to park their cars.

"Mrs. Hathom," Will said.

"Hello, baby."

They hugged deeply for a long moment.

Will said, "Did Sam come with you?"

"You playing with me?"

He looked sick. "I thought it was you. I thought you'd come and got him."

"So all this time he been at your place. You know damn well I ain't seen or talked to him since he went into rehab almost a year ago."

Will felt like something had opened him up and hollowed out his guts. He'd be arrested. Both of them would be if he couldn't find Sam. But he couldn't miss Tom's funeral. He had to be here. As the procession arrived, Will kept checking his phone. Nothing.

Floressa said, "All this time you keeping him there, thinking you're helping him, and now he's gone? You need to find him, get him back before something happens."

"Have you talked to Bennico today?" he said.

"She's *your* partner."

"Not anymore," he said, trying to laugh.

"Boy," she said. Floressa's eyes were grief-red and her face swollen with all that she could say. "You *trying* to lose everybody? I had more faith in you. But I was wrong. God, was I wrong."

"She lied to me about her record as a cop. She got fired because she conducted an illegal search."

"Son, that's why I want her. She'll do anything to get justice."

"So you lied too."

"I needed you. I couldn't tell you about her record."

"See, I don't even care about that record. I care about the lying."

"So you want to quit. Listen here. Can't you see the bigger picture? Illegal don't always mean wrong. And here you sit, without that job you was telling me you had to keep to protect Zeke—oh, yeah, I heard about you getting fired—thinking you stand for something, that you're doing something for this county you want to call home again. I hired that woman, went out of my way to do it too, because Zeke's life is at stake."

"What do you expect me to do?"

"Do what I guarantee that woman is doing behind your back. You think you got rid of her, but I'll bet you anything she working. You just gave her the freedom to do it her way, alone. And frankly, son, I'm satisfied to let that girl run. She way out ahead of you."

The sheriff's truck pulled along the road and pointed its nose into the field and parked. Sheriff Mills hauled himself out of the driver's side and opened up the back, from which he helped out Zeke who was wearing a suit Floressa had left at the courthouse. She put her hands to her face, observing that in such a short time Zeke appeared grayer, thinner, not himself, and vowing to herself that she would send over a basket of food later. He had chains around his hands and ankles, a ridiculous measure, Floressa thought, because she could tell he was too weak to run anyway, and where would he have gone? She cried, "Zeke! Zeke!" and Sheriff Mills stopped her before she got too close, saying, "No touching, or I swear I'll arrest you too. I'm taking enough of a risk letting him out as it is."

Sheriff Mills stood close by Zeke.

"They treating you okay?" Floressa said, tears along her face. "Everything all right?"

Zeke began to cry alongside her.

Then the hearse emerged and somewhere in the procession had come Miss Claudette and Miss Day, all made up and holding the made-up baby girl. The wind stirred across the graveyard. One could see plastic flower bouquets adorning the graves of those better loved or better remembered.

Many had turned out for the service. All the men who had worked down at the sawmill with Tom, a bunch of his old high school football buddies—T-Man, Herbie, Arnie, Maurice, all the boys. Will noticed Tania. He continued scanning the audience, hoping he might see someone else he could recognize in some way from all those years ago—anything that might spark recognition—though he knew he could not have identified anyone by sight alone. He had the list in his pocket. He met Tania's eyes and glanced away.

The service began, and Will saw Cherry McDaniels walking toward them from the parking lot across the road, dressed up in a black dress and a hat with a black veil, so that she looked to Will like a shadow, a silhouette. He watched Day's face painted all up, vulnerable and impassive both, watching the casket unwaveringly with bright, wet, burning eyes. Before they lowered the simple casket, Day stepped forward, clutching Destinee, and said, "Open it."

"Miss?" Pastor Marcus said.

"Day!" Claudette said.

That sick wet feeling was spreading.

"I want to see the father of my little girl one last time. I want to know."

Pastor Marcus looked at Troy St. Pierre, the funeral director.

Troy said, "Miss Pace, the body wasn't prepared for a viewing."

"Is there something wrong with his appearance?"

"No, ma'am. But . . ."

"Then I want to see him," she said. "Is that too much to ask?"

Troy nodded to one of his assistants, and they opened the upper portion of the coffin and jumped back as if a snake had been inside. What happened then was akin to lighting a string of Black Cats and watching them writhe and pop. The pallbearers stepped away from the coffin, and Pastor Marcus held his hands high, the thick black Bible in his hand, and said, "Hallelujah! Deliver him from evil! God has raised him up!" Claudette and Day stepped forward. Claudette was crying, lifting her hands. "It's a miracle," she yelled. "He done been raised up! Oh, Jesus. Oh, Jesus!" She fell to her knees in the dark grass, chanting, "Praise Him! Oh, praise Him!" Day stood, clutching Destinee, Destinee screaming, Day staring all around at the ground, at the sky.

Troy was yelling at someone. Floressa moaned and clenched her fists with joy. Sheriff Mills shook Zeke, saying, "Was this your doing?" And for a minute, aside from the coffin, this all looked like it had been some kind of field party. A helicopter would have seen the attendants scattering in various speeds out from the epicenter, all except two people who stood across from each other on either side of the opened casket, there by the freshly dug pit, one clutching an infant, staring not at the other woman but all around her. Behind the thick lurid makeup on her face, her teeth ground hard together, and she hissed, trying to control herself the way she used to, hearing her daddy come home, withdrawing into herself, into her own body. She looked on at nothing, but she saw and felt many things all around her, the texture of another realm. The other figure stood still and silent, her hands resting against her tiny stomach, covering the secret there. Destinee howled now, as if she understood, and a soft, depleted cursing could be heard from the young woman holding her, who became aware of Cherry's presence.

"What are you looking at," Day said. "You . . ."

"I know what you done."

"Coming from the bitch who caused it."

"You see?" said Cherry. "Tom's after you. He won't stop neither, not until the truth done come out. You: guilty."

"Baby," Day whispered. "Oh, baby, baby."

Sheriff Mills approached Will, wild-faced and pale, appearing to be blind, holding on to the arm of Zeke's suit and pulling him like a dog, saying, "Seems, what do you know about this?"

"Nothing."

"You find out what this is all about."

"You fired me."

"Don't think you can get off so easy. You're working for me again, goddamnit, until I get what you owe me. Time. Loyalty. Pain."

Will began to depart with a sensation of floating, as if none of this were happening, until Floressa caught him by the shoulder, a triumphant look in her exhilarated face.

"You know who's behind this," she said. "God sent her to us. Don't you forget that. Let them think it's a miracle. But you and I know. Now you got to choose. What side you on. Good, or evil. There ain't no more in-between. It's one or the other. Oh yes. You got all the prayers you need to see the light. Now, go and do the work God brought you to do!"

Mills yelled back, "Seems. You're on duty, goddamnit."

Floressa got in her car, and Will, sprinting, caught up with Troy.

"What the fuck happened here?"

Troy stood there, waifish, lifting his fragile arms in a shrug like a scarecrow.

Will spun around and caught the driver of the hearse, who held up his hands in surrender.

"What about you? Don't walk away from me. How did an empty casket make it here without you knowing?"

He was looking away, anywhere but at Will.

"Come on," Will said, shaking him. "Tell me what you know."

"She said if I did, she was going to have that man kill me."

"What man?"

"I'm going to be sick."

"How much did she pay you?"

The driver looked down, shuffled his feet, took out his wallet, whispered, and tried to hide behind his car so that Troy couldn't see him. "Don't tell my boss. Promise me."

Troy was not far off, but he seemed oblivious, disheveled.

"Give it to me," Will said.

"This here's mine."

"You don't want that dishonest money. I take it, it's honest."

"What'll happen to it?"

"Sheriff's department will decide."

The man pulled out three $100 bills and gave them to Will.

Will said, "Now get the hell out of here."

As Will reached his truck, the scene he took in was bare, and only the gravediggers were still there, standing with their shovels as if, of all the things they had seen in this life, this was something new: red clay on their shovels, nothing to cover, nothing to do, the voided earth like a space of sorrow to be filled where something could have grown.

Will sped down the road toward town, heading for Miss Claudette's house.

NEARING SUNSET, the peach-colored sky curdled with deep dark clouds and the sun flashed red over the worn pale streets and cobblestone one-ways of downtown Richmond. Bennico and Sam had been waiting in the chilly lab, taking breaks from the icy air-conditioning by stepping out and feeling the evening air. Walking out the door felt like lifting the top off a rice cooker.

They walked to a gas station down Broad Street to stretch their legs and grab Sam a pack of cigarettes. The light from the sky had shifted suddenly to a dim, hazy darkness, and the streetlights began to buzz and sparkle. They were underneath I-95, and the cars and trucks roared overhead, shaking the winding highway as it descended from south to north. It wasn't too far to where B's corner was, less than a mile as the crow flies. Sam was confident he could shake Bennico and make it. He could disappear. But just then, Lewis called Bennico—a timely distraction—and they hurried back to the lab.

Fluorescent lights above the autopsy table shone down on the body of Tom Janders. With a gloved hand, Lewis pointed toward the back of the body, up behind the left shoulder of the deceased.

"The wounds in his back are two inches long and were made by an ordinary butcher's knife, which is no surprise given that the body was discovered in the kitchen. But the angle of these gashes indicates they were inflicted by someone facing him. In his face. There wasn't much of a struggle, even."

"Stabbed in the back by someone facing him?" Bennico said. "How do you figure that?"

"My best guess is they were embracing. She would have picked up a knife without him seeing and hugged it into his back with both hands twice."

"How did you know it was a woman?"

Lewis indicated the chest, then lifted the shoulder to offer a better view of the incisions.

"Do you see these scratches?" he said. "They show up here—close to the wounds—but also around his genitalia and indicate that someone with fairly long fingernails wearing a coat of glitter polish killed him."

"But you said there was no struggle. Wouldn't he have reacted?"

"See this discoloration on his forehead? That's a bruise." Lewis pointed to an area that looked like a stain at the hairline, about the size of a quarter. "At first I thought she hit him, or that he hit something when he fell, but it seems to me the most logical explanation is that his killer was still close to him, in front of him, pinning his arms. He would have had to use his head to attack and free himself. For that moment, it would have been his only choice."

"So he could have hit someone's cheek?"

"Absolutely. The head or face of his killer would have been a likely target."

"There's still something I don't get," Bennico said. "With all those scratches he endured, how could he have allowed her near enough to stab him? Wouldn't he have found a way to get rid of her or leave?"

"I'm afraid I haven't made the nature or chronology of this act very clear. This was a sexual crime. Tom was raped, postmortem it seems. He was stabbed first. I am basing this on the fact that these scratches around his genitalia would have inflicted significant pain, yet there was completion."

"Is that possible?" Bennico said. "For a man, after death?"

"Well, it seems so. As the body shuts down, certain senses and nerves can be conflated, can still work, for a very short time. I've just talked with a few others about this—even called a medical expert at UNC who specializes in this kind of thing—and, though none of us had ever seen it before, it appears to be possible."

They—none of them—could look at each other anymore. Instead, they stared down at Tom's corpse as if their only solace now might be found there.

"She was very assertive and obeyed her instincts," Lewis said. "I don't see any other way this could have happened. Zeke Hathom's fingerprints may have been on the belt, as you said, but what he said about the victim's pants being down when he found him was not a lie. My guess is he was trying to cover his friend, and when he realized he had left evidence, he decided in a panic that he should let him burn, the evidence with him. Unfortunately, it made him look guilty. But these ridiculous fingernails. This woman. I almost wish I could meet her. Is there a suspect who might meet this description?"

**D**AY CLUTCHED DESTINEE all the way home, staring at the infant's pinched, worn-out face with fear and dismay. "Do you think . . . ," she said to Claudette. "Do you think he . . ."

"You saw it, girl. You saw it, same as me."

Day muttered, "That woman. That woman who came to me earlier." She turned to Claudette. "What if Tom's watching us? What if he's here?"

"Ain't it a comfort to think about. Lord, I hope he is, praise Jesus. I needed a sign. No, I wanted a sign. I don't believe in tempting God. But He sent us a sign."

Day gripped Destinee, in whose face lived on that version of Tom, until the baby squealed. Granny had told her how things would be, that she had to make her peace with Tom. Now she held the baby like a charm against him.

Day felt herself grow dizzy, time or something like it swirling around her. She had taken for granted she would feel free, but free wasn't this. She closed her eyes and tried to look at the shapes behind her eyelids until that was all she could see, but she could only picture Tom coming home that night, the unmistakable rustling motor of his truck, followed by the door shutting like a heavy thought. The way he'd approached her with that drunk postgame high school swagger, asking her how much she needed to finally end it. They stood face to face. She could remember first seeing a particular handle in the knife block the way you fixate on something when receiving bad news, noticing something as if it had never existed before your awareness of it. Day thought about that furious light-headed feeling and clutching that knife and, regardless of Tom's athleticism and strength, hugging the knife into his back, that curt little tearing sound and knowing she had to commit now, then quickly driving it in a second time, realizing only then that such force as she had mustered had been unnecessary—the result of fear—and that she could have tempered the act with tenderness and killed him just the same. And the numbness that came as he drove his head down, catching her cheek. Then a blankness she had known before. Then she was looking down at him as his eyes tried to run all around, finally ending on her in a question even she couldn't answer. Tom spoke in tongues, and she smiled a little, a surprise she remembered like love at first sight, felt something growing in her, continued unbuttoning her dress, let him see her again, the last image to carry to the grave the body of the woman sending him there. She watched his eyes until they no longer blinked and knew somehow the world that opened beyond him, closed.

But his death was the beginning of something she'd never felt before. She could see that he was hard—some reflex, perhaps—and unbuckled and slid his slacks to his ankles and felt him with both hands. He hardened and grew. She didn't have much time. His black blood trickled along the slanted floor of fake curling tile like used motor oil. He seemed still to be sweating, a sheen across his face and his stomach. His arm twitched, startling her. Though the moment had passed, he seemed still to be alive by fleeting degrees. Life was such a mystery. Where did it begin and end really?

She was sick with wet, like the swamp brimming after a rain, and sat him, rode him one last time, his eyes open and hers closed, the knife handle attached to his back hammering the floor, a little sound coming from his mouth as if he were protesting whatever dream this was. She tensed and shivered, grieving this even as it occurred, this last of his body. "Oh, baby," she said, closing her eyes tight to see all the eyes of all the angels holding their useless tongues. "Oh, baby, baby." She felt her face wet too and rode him harder, a punishment for one or the other, trying and trying and trying, and then she could smell it like spring, knowing it was really over now, and there in her ragged nakedness she embraced herself, wept.

"Day!" Claudette said in the car. "Calm yourself. You're hurting Destinee!"

Day released her grip. "He's here, isn't he? He's here. You're here."

"It's good news. It's a sign. In the end, all truth shall be revealed." Claudette's eyes narrowed. "And you and I need to have that talk."

Day would have to act quickly. Either way, her situation was dire. If Tom had been raised up, he would keep coming for her. If he hadn't, and someone had removed his body, what other purpose could there be than finding out more about what she had done?

They pulled up to the house, and Day stepped out of the car with Destinee tight in her arms, and Claudette said, "We got a conversation to finish." Day stared at Tom's mother, at the yellow house, then moved toward it with a purpose, grabbing her belongings and the folded-up stroller and hauling the baby out the door in one cyclone of activity.

"What are you doing?" Claudette said.

Day merely gathered, one-handed, the fragments, her possessions, forcing them into an old school bag, deciding last minute to leave the stroller, then quickstepped out to her car with Destinee in one arm, bag over her shoulder, key in the other hand.

Claudette called out. "Where you going? Come back here! We got to talk! You need to eat something, and we got to talk!"

"I got to go now. I got to go."

"At least leave me Destinee. Whatever you doing, wherever you going, you don't need her."

Claudette rushed toward the car, opened the back door to get the baby.

Day said, "Get away from her," coming around the back of the car. She pulled Claudette so hard by her dress that the older woman fell backward against the chain-link fence. Claudette looked into Day's eyes, full of wonder at first, narrowing quickly by degrees as if focusing on something small and clear.

"You did it, didn't you? That's why that woman was here. To find out just what you'd say."

Claudette made another move for the back seat, but Day was between her and the car and shoved her hard with a strength that defied her size.

"Stay the fuck away from my baby."

"Leave her, please!" Claudette cried, beginning to panic. "Leave her to a good life with me. They gonna find out. It'll mix her up. I don't hate you. I don't. But why'd you do it? Why do that to him?"

Day seemed dazed, like the little girl she used to be, like some animal, sleek, observant, bewildered by the world of women and men.

Claudette saw an opportunity. She lunged once more for Destinee, but Day in one motion stepped to block her and swiped at Claudette's face. The old woman tumbled back against the fence and into the yard. The tall pine tops swirled in a quiet distant breeze, clouds unstopping above. Claudette touched her face, wept.

"I need her more," Claudette said, pleading, pawing in Destinee's direction, looking up at the crazed silhouette of her son's killer, lover. She pushed these words through her broken lip. "She's all I got left."

Day stood over her, fists clenched, her lips curled back in a snarl.

"No, she ain't," she said. "You ain't got her."

Day climbed back in the car. Destinee was crying from all the commotion. "Shut the fuck up!" Day yelled. The door closed, muffling the radio, and the car rattled away.

Claudette knelt in the grass, held her hands to her face, cried out, "Lord God! Oh, Lord Jesus! Oh!" and wept alone in her yard.

Will had been watching, sitting in his pickup down the street. He would have gone to Miss Claudette's aid, but he had to follow Day's Accord. Some neighbors had come out. One walked over to help the old woman up, but before he reached her, she rose and composed herself and went inside for her phone.

D AY SWERVED WIDE and swung with such velocity, braked with such force, that the tires screeched and the car shook, and her own seat belt locked against her body. The car rested aslant, out of the parking lines in front of the court-house. Day left the baby and hustled into the sheriff's department.

Will waited off the square in the Dollar General parking lot, where he could see the courthouse. Why the hell would Day have gone into the office? He was about to get out of the truck when his phone rang. It was Bennico.

"What the fuck," Will answered.

"It was her. Lewis found traces of glitter nail polish on the body. It was her."

"How the fuck could you have done this to me? You know how many laws you've broken?"

"I told you I was gonna blow this shit up."

"Sam's with you, isn't he. Put him on."

"He doesn't want to talk to you."

"Big help you are."

"You know what? I just called out of courtesy to say we're on our way back. Sam told me not to, but I did anyway."

"Wow. That makes everything cool."

"Never mind," she said. "Fuck you. Everything I've done—" But Will hung up when he saw Day pushing out of the sheriff's department, looking around from the top step, then rushing to her car.

The sheriff's department number called him.

"Will," Tania said. "Day Pace was just in here looking for the sheriff."

"He's not there?"

"I don't know where he is. Miss Claudette just called too. Said she got in a fight with Day. She's real worried about the baby Day took with her. She said Day killed Tom."

"Lock up the office and meet me outside the front door now. Make sure you're packing. Oh, hey," he said. "Get my badge and gun, will you?"

He drove out of the lot and saw the lights of the green Honda ahead in the distance in front of the water tower. He pulled up in front of the Confederate memorial and watched Tania turning the key and running down the stairs, still in the dress she'd worn at the funeral. Then the truck door opened, and she climbed into the cab, and Will could smell her full like marshmallows and mint as he swung a U-turn in the middle of the street and sped toward the water tower.

Will said, "She say anything about where she was heading?"

"She just came in, looking for the sheriff. Wanted to know when he'd be back. I asked her to sit there and wait, but when Miss Claudette called, she bolted."

"You know Bennico Watts, that PI who got me fired? She stole the body and took it to a forensics specialist."

"No, she didn't."

"Oh yeah," he said, unable to suppress a sideways smile. "Sure flushed Day out, though, didn't it."

"You think Day is skipping town?"

"Something's about to happen. And we'll be there when it does."

"Why didn't you tell me? You know I wanted to help."

"You still maybe can."

They came to the main road, a highway that cut through the county east to west. There was a gravel road on the other side of it, which she wouldn't have taken. They didn't see any sign of her car. If she wanted to get out of town, she could have gone either way. East an hour and a half would get her to Virginia Beach, or to Richmond if she took 85; west would take her deeper into the boonies, and the myriad options of places for her to lose herself meant vanishing was a real possibility. He turned east, searching for another road, remembering what Cherry had said about the sheriff going out there to the Lounge, watching Day, and then he thought beyond that.

"We're taking the Old Swamp Highway," he said as he made the turn.

It was a Hail Mary.

"The Snakefoot?" Tania said.

"Grady said she grew up out there and that the sheriff has looked out for her like his own since her own daddy died. I'm not sure what's going on, but I got a feeling."

The highway appeared spectral in the headlights. Frogs jumped in the road. They saw the ghostly eyes of deer illuminated and hollow in the fields to either side, one bounding across the road. Then the trees closed in around them, a beautiful drive during the day but dark as black could be now. Freckles of moonlight could be seen through the distant treetops hanging with poison ivy and kudzu. His father's headlights had gone out one night on this road, and they'd driven by scant moonlight, seeing no one on the road the entire time, no one to guide their way or shine them on.

It seemed a sacrilege to speak as they proceeded. Something in the overgrowth of night sequestered their words.

The road turned and twisted gradually in large winding swoops, a snake writhing. Then it dipped slightly, flattened, and a warm stale air smothered them like a pillow. The trees, even at night, seemed to envelop them more closely, and then the landscape opened out and the sky grew wide and the trees jagged and broken and leafless as headstones. They were now in the Snakefoot Swamp.

The trees they saw now seemed grown to die, honed for some miserable end. The occasional building—house, church, trailer—lay unbelievably ravaged by vine and dark growth against the wan green moonlight glinting off the uneven road. They passed a shroud of Bubble Wrap tangled against a tree.

A light glowed in the distance, giving off an anachronistic radiance, lantern light of a previous time. A copse of trees around a bend gave way to the artificial light of the sign for a Sunoco. Behind the station, a horse eating at weeds.

Just past the Sunoco, they saw brake lights turning down a little road off to the right, leading into thick overgrowth. He slowed and turned left at the highway median and drifted over toward the Sunoco, next to which was a large vacant stretch on which some old moon-colored general store had been boarded up, broken by angry vegetation. He parked by it, directly across from the road Day had taken. A dark billboard a couple hundred yards to their left advertised a salon miles away, over in South Boston, and it made sense now that this sign had been a dream like a friend to a child with nothing. Seeing it gave Will the sense that he knew something intimate about Day.

They sat and watched to see if anyone else would come. The night sounds hovered eerie and strange around them, and lightning bugs buzzed and sparkled, and the air felt thick and warm, as if they were moving through some kind of viscous and surreal substance.

Tania pulled out her phone. No service. Minutes passed: nothing. Will pulled the release, and his door hung ajar, beeping until he took the keys.

"Will," Tania said, and Will saw the sheriff's truck slowing, turning.

They could see the headlights behind the wall of growth traveling parallel with the highway, then taillights red as hell, then nothing.

"Lock and load," Will said.

**D**AY HAD PARKED in front of the old clapboard house where she'd grown up. The door was unlocked, had been for the seven years since her mother had passed. Her daddy had been first, a few years before that, not that he was around all that much anyway. Day remembered that feeling anytime he came home from wherever—bingeing or trapping—her excitement and disappointment every time. He'd kick her out to sit on the stoop or draw with chalk on the broken walk out into nothing. She remembered her daddy's beaver traps hanging on the clothesline when he'd dye and wax them, or stowed away in cheap bins by the stoop where she'd sit, and beaver pelts stretching on the side porch, red of blood and brown and black, disks of fur: that strange coin of that strange currency for whatever deep backwoods life he lived away from them. And his muddied waders, and his hands always smelling like the raw meat her mama would slow-cook down or cut up and flour and fry. All she'd wanted to do was go somewhere bright and new. And she'd come back home to this place, to the nothing of herself.

She left the baby in the car and walked up to the front door and opened it, tried the light, which didn't work. She brought out her phone flashlight and looked through it all, hearing her own steps with magnified weight. She could still smell them. There, the room where she would sleep with her mama when Daddy was away, Mama telling her how hard he was working. There was the bed, and she touched the real thing. She sat on it, heard the same creaking. There, on the wood-paneled wall, she saw the framed picture of Jesus, rays of light spreading out from his face. On another wall, a picture of a nice brick house in the snow with a holly bush out front. Day could remember: it was the top of a box containing a shirt for Daddy one Christmas. Her mama liked the box top so much that she cut it out and framed it.

Day reached under the bed and pulled out a pair of her daddy's boots, scuffed and covered in white mold. She began to cry, then stood up, looking down on the bed that took up most of the room. "It ain't my fault," she said. "It ain't my fault I'm still chasing you, even after all you done to me."

She took her car key and slid it under the right bootheel. It popped off easily without a sound. A small key fell onto the floor. She took it up and walked into the living room. She grabbed a thin fire poker from beside the old quiet hearth and dug at one of the floorboards as she'd seen him do at night, when he'd be drunk on whatever it was that looked like water, smelled like death, peeking out from her door when he thought no one was watching. She took out an old ammunition box with a lock on it, crouched and opened it, pouring the contents onto the old floor: a piece of notebook paper folded, a picture of the three of them, a map showing where he'd been in Vietnam, a pocket watch that was his only heirloom piece, and a knife he'd made from a file and two slats of walnut. She remembered him showing her the knife, holding it to her.

"Scare you?"

*"I ain't scared."*

The paper, she knew (she'd looked before, years ago, after he'd disappeared), was two columns, two lists of names: one women, one men. In many cases, they were not names at all because he didn't know them, and so a brief description would be given, jotted hurriedly, trailing into the margin, scratched out like an animal trying to claw free. Such descriptions read, "woman from the Phu Dac cafe" or "girl with the yellow teeth, yellow everything, from the border" or "son of a bitch who walked by tree I was hiding behind, didn't know what hit him" or "father of the girl from the border." She opened it up again and scanned the women, seeing her own first name there, repeated as if to pretend it was a last name or a name to be brooded or tripped over, "Ferriday Ferriday," toward the bottom of the list, her mother's first and maiden name higher up: Katrina Vinson. Strangely enough, she liked seeing her own name. There was a kind of comfort in the knowledge that her father had put her name down on a piece of paper (with her mother) and found it important enough to bury. That was how she knew she'd meant something to him. She remembered how he'd hurt her, how she glared at him in that defiant, furious surrender, how he'd closed his eyes like he was praying, how the names of the Vietnamese women or girls made her wonder if she was part Vietnamese. She took the knife and held it, feeling sick, put it in her bag, and remembered the baby and went outside to get her.

She sat with Destinee on the stoop, looking out at the Sunoco lights through woods held in a net of wild muscadine and poison ivy. The yard was overgrown, but the tall sign rose and shone its strange, ethereal light over the Snakefoot. She'd always been something of an outcast, even here, being a white girl whose family was not descended from slaves and whose only virtue was that they were traceless: no past and no future.

"Let me tell you something. Mommy used to sit out here, look out at those lights—see?—coming out of the filling station, waiting for Daddy to come home or listening to him and Mama inside. Those lights never went out. Night or day. Daddy came and went, Mama slept and cried, always was afraid. I was afraid too, but I made up my mind early on to make it seem like I wasn't. Maybe that was Mama's weakness: she just seemed scared, so he'd stay on her. When he did to me, I made him think maybe I liked it. I had to bluff him like that, scare him. She could have been so pretty. He wouldn't let her feel it, the special that she was. She never wore nothing to better herself. I guess I don't know what I ever wanted. I guess I never want you to feel that way. I grew up rough, girl, without nobody much speaking for me except Granny, and now she can't no more. I'm past hope. But I still miss it, some. Shit. I don't know why. Wasn't but hard luck here in the Snakefoot, and I thought I wanted to run away to some place that draws the pretty to it, but here I am, bringing you to the home I never called home, bringing you into this world of ugly. I'll tell you the truth, right now. I killed your daddy. I'm worried he's coming for me. And the other thing I got to say is, you're all I got now. I didn't want you much, but to give me him. But now, sitting here, it's just love. And I know hate's love too, because you have to love if you're going to hate. And if it's all the same thing, what difference does anything make? You hate a place all your life, and then you miss it. You miss a man because he ain't here, even though you know if he was you'd wish him gone. I think I did love Daddy, even after I promised to hate him and every other man. I think he loved me, and Mama. It don't make a lot of sense. All we knew was us and here.

It wasn't nice, none of it was, but here I am, back and feeling like I want it back, just because I know it and don't know what's ahead. Shit, girl. Don't you start that bullshit again. Good girl. He should be here soon. You're going to hear some bad things about me, and I guess that can't be helped. I don't know what Mommy's gonna do. But I am feeling maybe it is the right thing to do. Maybe you'll have to live with your grandma (she don't like me either), but that's okay. You got a place, and I never did have much to give or share or hide behind. Been bluffing all my life. Never did know my people. As far as I know, I don't have any. Unless you count this fucked-up list as a kind of family. Shit. I know you're gonna grow up strong, stronger without me."

She heard a vehicle slowing, gravel popping from the shoulder, lights swinging around, then turning off the road and into the soft ground, and saw the white of the sheriff's truck parking under the trees. Mills got out, sauntered over to her, looking both ways at nothing, as if crossing a busy street.

"I don't like this, Day. I don't like coming out here. Didn't think you would either."

"The funeral got me to thinking."

"Thinking what?"

"Tom wasn't there today. He was either took, or he's been raised up from the dead and is watching me. Either way, there ain't no running from the truth."

"What are you driving at?" Mills said, his thumbs hooked into his belt, watching her with one eye narrowed, aiming hard.

"I guess I just can't talk around it anymore. I got to confess. I was the one killed Tom Janders."

Mills's expression lightened a little. He spat in the broke yard.

"That ain't funny," he said, but it looked like he might smile.

"I ain't joking, goddamnit."

"Bullshit."

"It's true."

"I'm not gonna let you do this, Day."

"Ain't you got a form I can sign?"

"Sign anything you want, and I'll tear it up."

"That don't change the truth. Tom knows it. He's raised up, restless, and I got to come clean. He wanted to quit me, and I killed him for it. Just because. I killed him, took his money. And now he's watching me."

"That kind of crap don't stand up in court. You say you got his money. Where's it at?"

She took it out of her bag. He looked through it, whistled.

"How the hell could anybody trace this?" he said. "You been saving it up. A working woman is all."

"The day a man listens to me . . ."

"Goddamnit, Day. The evidence is on someone else. The nail is in his coffin. After all I done for you, you want to do me this-a-way?"

She began to feel weak, a little faint. She thought about that little one on the way. The curse of it all. She wanted to feel clean, but something dark moved inside her.

"It was self-defense," Mills said, dropping everything and walking toward Day. "Tom beat you. You'd had enough."

"You'd never find a mark on me from Tom."

"What about that bruise?"

"Tom was as different as he could be to my . . . And I killed him just the same, and just because he was a man. A daddy to my little one."

"You were hurt. That bruise on your cheek. You can't tell me Tom didn't hit you. He'd been drinking, playing cards, and he went for you."

In the light from the Sunoco, Mills looked bright and ill, like a plastic figure glowing in the dark. That light of her childhood. She could almost feel something pure, deeper than all this, that wild animal innocence she'd once had. But it was gone now. She wanted it, but it was too late.

Mills said, "I told your mama I'd always look after you. That means protecting you against yourself."

"But I don't want to carry this no more."

"You don't know what you want."

She put the baby on the stoop in her secondhand car seat and took the sheriff's hand.

"You'd do anything for me," she said.

She touched his face, and the sheriff stopped chewing. His chin was sandy with the day's growth, the way her daddy's had been. There was only one way. She led him into the house, looking back at him with youth in her eyes, then glancing at the baby, squirming on the stoop. She shut the door.

She went into the bedroom, the Sunoco lights flooding the little room, torn curtains like a gauze against the wound of light, tree shadows projected against the wall, moving in a slight breeze.

She put her purse on the floor next to the bed and said, "I want you to do something for me."

Mills swallowed. "What."

"Look in this here bag. Take that there knife out. Bring it here."

"I won't."

"Hold it to my throat."

"No."

"Do as I say."

He held the knife a few inches from her neck.

"Closer, goddamnit. Like you mean to use it."

She was writhing on the bed and began to touch herself. She reached her hand for his shirt, pulled him toward her. She began to moan like a car passing.

"Tell me," she said, "why you always looked out for me."

"Your daddy died."

"Lots of daddies die."

"Yours went missing."

"Where?"

"I don't know."

"You can't protect me no more."

He stared down at her, then closed his eyes, deep in a kind of prayer. He had been a distant guardian for most of Day's life. He had thought himself the protector of a girl who needed protecting. He had watched her grow into what she was now, and though he had dreamed, a dream could not be prosecuted.

"Day, honey. It can't be like this. Not here."

"It has to be here."

"I'm old enough to be . . ."

"Daddy," she said. "Daddy."

He slid her panties off and pushed himself into her all at once, just as he heard the baby crying, and it was as if his life had not even begun, and he knew that now it was all over too. After those times of coming to this house, the mother killing herself just like Hannah had done. Hannah. He rubbed his hand across Day's face, brushed his thumb against her lips, smearing her lipstick. Her face was a running darkness of tears. Plain-faced, there was a resemblance, undecorated, raw. Everything he touched . . . Nothing mattered now. The grief would always be there. This was fleeting. Like making love to a ghost. But he had to consummate this—something. He had to live now. He'd waited so long. But the fear.

"The baby," he said.

"Shut up. Keep that knife on me. He used to bring me in here. Kicked Mama out after years of kicking me out. Held that same knife to me."

"I don't want to hear it."

"Tell me what happened to him. I deserve to know. He ain't really dead and gone unless I know."

"Killed in a fight."

"Where?"

"Does it fucking matter?"

"Where is he now?"

"Deep in the reservoir."

A tremor in her voice. "Kill me. I've confessed. Don't stop until you kill me, and don't stop then. It's what we deserve."

He took the knife away from her, withdrew, his face wet and shaking, and she reached for Tom's gun in her purse and aimed it at him and said, "It's you or me."

"Day. Goddamn, woman. Too much death."

"It's you or me."

Sheriff Mills said, "Let's talk this through. Listen—"

By the time Mills hit the back wall, a second shot had ripped through his abdomen, and the smell of hot brass and burnt gunpowder and sweat and Day filled the room. Day dropped Tom's revolver onto the bed, a silent weight softly absorbed. She moved toward the sheriff, touched herself and let a moan escape, knelt and held him, said, "Daddy," watched him stiffen again, climbed him, said, "Daddy" again.

His eyes moved quickly, childishly, and blood came from his mouth, and the ringing in his ears flooded his consciousness, and when he saw the knife raised in her hand, he also saw the gun in his own, the black blood slipping out of her stomach in two tears, the head where his third shot had thrown her back, a dark whip of spray against the wall, all the while the footsteps on the stoop, the baby crying full on now, somewhere in the ether, Will Seems's voice saying, "Euphoria County Sheriff's Department," a thick swamp warmth and tadpoles swimming in his head, and then nothing.

"**Z**EKE," FLORESSA CALLED out when she heard the front door creak open, shut soft as only one could do who'd heard her bellow whenever someone let it slap the doorjamb. "Zeke, baby, is that you?"

Every day she dreamed Zeke might walk through the front door. That Will would have convinced the prosecutor, or the judge, or whoever, to drop all charges.

He could hear her at the sink still, washing dishes. The sounds, all heightened into a climax of pleasure and pain—evening birds, the running water fizzing like a soda, and then the small smell of the house, so distant a memory colliding suddenly now here in a sober musty smell of carpet and window cleaner, of old cigarettes and summer, of the honeysuckle and pine coming through the screen of the front door. It was the smell of home, a dream he'd forgotten to dream.

"Zeke, honey."

And then her steps rocked the groaning floorboards underneath the shag carpet, and there she stood.

"Mama."

She lifted her hands to her chest. She seemed older, the same woman but transformed by fatigue and age and grief, and he couldn't look at her at first.

The place looked good, well maintained, and she had been doing chores in a T-shirt and some jeans, a bandanna over her head. Some things did not change. She was a woman who never let time idle; she worked as if work was all a person had to stay sane.

"Baby," she said, looking up. "Lord. Lord, thank you." And she smothered him in her warm embrace, the two of them unable to keep from tears.

She wept on his shoulder. Pulled herself away to look at him. "Sam, honey. You looking so good. You looking like you got a little bit of hope now."

CLUTCHING FLASHLIGHTS to handguns, they canvased the scene: grotesque, one of blood-strewn nakedness. Will took a few quick pictures with his phone but could barely look at her, the lightning of the flash illuminating a display better left forgotten: both bodies leaning away from each other, both indecent from the waist down, the air in the room thick and rank, warm with summer and recent breath and sweat. The distant Sunoco lights radiated through the kudzu and muscadine growing up the treeline and the sagging chain-link fence that at one time had been a barrier of some kind between this and that. In the artificial glow, the bodies looked green, as if underwater. The night surrounded them, outnumbered them in sound. Frogs and crickets and cicadas and other insects scratching through the walls of night. Blood pumped out of wounds like some distillation of darkness.

"Goddamnit," Will said, holstering his pistol. "We're too late."

"You better check," Tania said.

Will knelt, checked for pulses. Miss Pace, dead, a corner of her head missing. Will had to look away from her, had to fight something inside him. Sheriff Mills . . .

"Go to the gas station and call an ambulance," Will said. "Quick!"

He could hear Tania's steps diminishing across the broken yard.

"Jesus Christ," he said to himself, covering his eyes.

He tried to snap out of it, think through what he knew. They'd heard five shots: two heavy loads followed by three pops that would have been the sheriff's nine-millimeter. They were lying all over each other, one barely dead, one barely living. Will found a home-made knife on the floor. Double-edged. Made from a file. A knife for killing. A rind of blood appeared along one edge. Upon close inspection, he could see several nicks and cuts on Miss Pace's neck. Had Mills pulled a knife on her? Had she shot him in self-defense?

Then he saw the money in her open bag, a softball-size wad on the bed with a rubber band around it. It had to be the money Tom had won.

Will knelt again and felt for a pulse and heard a gurgling sound escape the sheriff's lips. He bent so that his ear nearly touched the man's mouth, glossed with a lipstick of blood.

"Self-defense, son," Mills said. "Self- . . ."

Will recoiled. For a moment he considered finishing what had been started. Then he decided to leave the scene and let it take care of itself. But instead he peeled off his undershirt and tied it around the sheriff's stomach, the blood quickly seeping through. Somehow, Will was guilty too. He did his best to hoist the sheriff's britches back on, his hands slick with blood by the time he'd succeeded. He eased the sheriff onto his back, his own knees wet through. A strange euphoria crept through Will, and like a buzz or high, a dimension seemed to open like a trapdoor of air, and he cared only that the sheriff stayed alive. And it seemed years passed between breaths—that he was breathing years, his sacrifice, his life, his regrets—years passed, and he himself was an old man shot and dying, embarrassed at the mess he had made, leaving a life like a dumpster. And the darkness of the room brightened at the corners of his vision, and then he was blind, staring at nothing but the flash of night. But he could feel it all, everything like skin. And Will saw that his skin was blacker than any blood, a deep bruise like a swamp. And visions came to him as he blew his white breath into the sheriff's mouth and pinched his nose and pumped the heels of his hands into the old man's chest. And this was his father. And this was his brother. And he was one of them. And Will had identified their faces and was trying to forgive them. He had it all back, and it all went the same. But he felt every blow, loving that pain of his brother's as he would a dog or child. And his mother, sad and proud, smoking one of her Sunday cigars and reading the paper, a bandanna around her head, and something in him knew that she would die and wanted to kill her for it. Something in him wanted to break her spirit and always had. And he could not forgive them because he could not forgive himself. And he said, *Guilty.* He had long forgotten her voice. And he said, *I said guilty. Are you listening?* And like a judge she said nothing. And he said, *Listen to me.* And he heard his name.

Tania stood in the doorway. "Will. The ambulance is here."

The medics pushed in, and he stood like a man who had forgotten how to stand. He leaned on her, blood against his knees, and they stepped outside into the one world, and his sight found the baby on the stoop struggling against the air. The baby cried upward, angry at sky or whatever sky held, and Will wanted to hold her, but his hands were bloody.

"He said it was self-defense," he said to Tania.

"You believe him?"

Will looked up at her. "He's one of us."

"I called Sheriff Edgars. He'll be here within the hour."

"Let's check the sheriff's truck for some bags and gloves."

The medics hustled Mills out on a stretcher.

Will said, "Will he be all right?"

One of the medics shouted something Will couldn't understand, and they shut the ambulance doors and peeled out of the
yard and up the hedge and out onto the road, and he could hear the
siren like a shooting star.

"I'm going to go make a call," Will said, and stepped out for
the Sunoco. "Rope this off, will you? I'll be back shortly."

"Are you all right?" Tania said.

At the Sunoco, out of breath and light-headed, Will had to
show his badge to convince the woman to let him use the phone.
He stepped behind the counter, like a jail cell with bars along it. The
aisles were sparsely stocked, and the linoleum floor was all torn up
with holes and scuffs. The woman working the counter had a face
like a pan-seared steak and seemed oblivious to his bloodstained
clothes.

Will looked through his phone for Bennico's number and
dialed it on the landline.

"Where are you?" he said.

"I'm on the square. I've been trying to reach you."

"I need you to haul ass on over here." He gave her directions
to the Sunoco.

Bennico said, "What's going on?"

He looked at the steak-faced woman who had not taken a hint
to step out.

"Just hurry."

After he hung up, the woman said, more to herself than to Will, "I heard them. Yes I did. Heard 'em, *boom boom, pa pa pa.*"

Faster than he expected—thirty minutes maybe—Bennico pulled up, and Will got in her Escalade. They jounced over the median, up the way a little, and turned through the wall of growth and back a little way to the scrawny yard. Tania was talking to an ancient yet ageless woman, so black her eyes glowed, who was holding Destinee.

"Tania," Will said. "This is a crime scene."

"This woman knew Day. She said—"

"We don't have time for that right now. This here's Bennico Watts. She's going to look everything over before Troy and Sheriff Edgars arrive."

Bennico got some gloves out from her car, and she and Will walked into the house, flashlights out. She stepped carefully through the room ahead of him.

"Mills was here? Against this wall?"

"That's right."

"Her legs over his?"

"That's right."

She inspected Day's head, her body where the rounds had penetrated. There was the revolver she'd dropped on the bed. Bennico considered the angles of the room. She looked closely at the knife on the floor, not far from Mills's pistol.

Bennico stood up, turned off her flashlight, wiped her forehead with the back of her arm, holding her hands apart from her body then, as if in some stance of complete readiness.

"What do you want from me?" she said.

"What do you think happened?"

"Mills and Day made an arrangement to meet here. They obviously had a history, and this was a place they both knew. His pants were down, you said?"

"Mills said it was self-defense before he passed out. You think we should arrest him?"

"We don't even know if he's going to make it."

"What do you make of the knife? You saw those marks on her neck?"

"I saw 'em. I don't know what to make of them."

"So, what, she pulls a gun on him? And he can't draw the weapon at his side and has to grab this knife?"

"She must have shot him first," Bennico said, "thought he was dead, put the gun down on the bed. Approached where he fell against the wall. And if I learned anything today, tried to rape him."

"Say that again?"

"My contact in forensics said it appeared Tom was killed and raped after. By a woman with glitter-coated fingernails. Almost certainly after his death. Something about the conflation of senses. It's been a weird fucking day."

"Jesus."

"Maybe she picked up the knife here—maybe this was a sexual crime too—Mills draws his weapon, shoots her dead. How many shots did you hear?"

"Five."

"Two in him, you said? And we can see three in her." She dropped the magazine from the sheriff's Glock and saw that there were three missing rounds. "No misses."

"So, it could have been self-defense."

"Sure. Yeah. But no one here is innocent."

"You think the sheriff would be prosecuted if things went down the way you said?"

"Not if he claims self-defense. That's if this thing even goes to court."

On the way back out, Bennico said, "Hold on," and walked into the living room, cavernous though it was not large. There she saw a hole in the floor where a board had been removed. Will followed her and watched as she lifted out an old ammunition box from underneath the floor.

EVENTUALLY, A BLACK SUBURBAN and a white minivan bounced across the uneven ground toward them. Troy St. Pierre and Sheriff Edgars and a couple of detectives. Will came out onto the stoop, where the old woman sat, rocking and talking to Destinee.

Edgars said, "Is Jeff okay?"

Will said, "I don't know."

"I'm guessing this is Miss Bennico *Janders*," Edgars said, looking at Troy. "You sure keep the integrity of your crime scenes," he said to Will. "Anything we need to know about here?"

"You're the detectives."

Edgars nodded, and the men headed up the stoop and into the house.

Sheriff Edgars said, "Better for you that we do the investigating. Whatever happens, the judge is going to want to see that this has been looked into by an impartial agency."

"That supposed to mean you?"

"I'm just trying to help you out, kid. No need to talk like that."

With trembling hands, Will signed over custody of Day's body to Troy and said, "When will you have the results?"

"I'll have something for you tomorrow," Troy said.

Will stepped out, nodded at Tania. Tania apologetically took the baby from the old woman.

"Troy," Bennico said. "Got room for another body?"

Troy looked at them both, wary.

"This a joke?"

"No. *Dead* serious. *That's* a joke."

Will said, "Jesus."

"Where's it at?"

"In my car."

He grumbled, looked at her and Will, and said, "Is it Tom? It's Tom, isn't it. I should have goddamn known."

They walked over to Bennico's Escalade.

"Tania and I better get this baby back to her grandmother," Will said to Bennico. "You can go on back to the house. I'll see you later."

Will went across the road and brought his truck back for Tania and Destinee.

Tania broke the hum of the ride: "She said something to me, that old woman."

"About what?"

"Day. How she was more a mother to Day than her own mother was. How her daddy used to come home and . . ."

"We found a list of people, presumably her father's. She's on that list."

"List of what?"

He fought a sudden and surprising impulse, clenching his jaw to suppress it. "It's a list. Of men killed and women, girls . . ."

Tania held the baby, plain-faced and glaring out the window. Will could hear that she was crying when she spoke again. He could no longer hold back.

"That bastard," he forced through his own tears. "That fucking bastard."

Will looked away, wanting to hide. He wondered if everything a person experiences stays there, like a kind of sediment, as much a part of them as their own skin. Then he turned to face Tania and Destinee.

The child had calmed as Tania began to sing something plaintive and tender, holding the baby against her chest, and Will felt something he'd never felt before, as if looking into another person's life. He suddenly remembered something from a great distance of time and existence, a familiar voice, deep and hoarse, knew that he had come back for this too. A solitary car passed them on the old road, and in the light it cast out like a shadow before it, Will glanced at Tania, who was looking at him, the child at her. That moment: something like family.

WILL GOT BACK to the house and found some comfort in the fact that Bennico was already there. They sat out on the porch, moths floating around the porch light.

"Where's Sam?" he said.

"I took him home."

"You told him, didn't you?"

"He had to know to do what I needed him to do."

"I was out all night last night and made up my mind to tell him." Will ran his hand through his hair, looked off. "Now it's too fucking late. You know, I could arrest y'all."

"You're not that stupid," Bennico said, "to bite the hand that feeds you."

"You're up on your high horse."

"I think you got that the wrong way around. If it wasn't for me—for Sam and me—you'd still be chasing your tail. Now, you're acting sheriff, you know Day killed Tom, and Zeke should be acquitted." She looked at Will. "But I owe you an apology."

"Forget it. We were both talking shit. Wanted to hurt each other."

"I thought you had a thing for her, but it was your instinct. She was guilty. Your instinct was right, and I should have given you more credit."

Will changed the subject. "I'm afraid the sheriff is going to get away with everything."

"Then why'd you try and save him?"

"I don't know. I don't know if I did the right thing or not."

"I wish we could have kept her alive. All we'll have is your and Tania's statements, but he can say whatever he wants about what happened. It'll be his word. It's hard to put a sheriff on the stand. You got any idea about how to discredit him?"

"Yeah," Will said. "But I can't use it."

"What do you mean?"

He told her what Grady had explained to him: that it was his father who had killed Day's daddy in a fight. That Sheriff Mills had held that over his head for years. That that was why his father had moved to Richmond.

Will said, "Just a little something added to the pile. So I don't know how we'd use that against Mills without causing more trouble than we want."

"So the sheriff doesn't know you know," Bennico said. "We might be able to use that to our advantage."

"How?"

"He told you she confessed. So he knew she was a suspect, at that point."

"Right."

"Well, if he knew, and he got involved with her anyway, that's grounds for some serious allegations."

"I guess we need to see what Sheriff Edgars finds, or chooses to find. Then we can see how to play it. I don't like it being out of our hands, but it's just the way it has to be."

They sat awhile, looking out into the dark fields.

"The irony's not lost on me," Will said eventually. "That Sam's dad is locked up for a murder he never committed, and my dad killed a man and walked away."

"You should have told him, Will."

"I thought I could fix everything."

She reached out and held his hand. "That's your problem. You're so busy trying to fix shit you can't fix that nobody, not even you, knows you need help. Except maybe for me."

I T WAS A LONG NIGHT. Will couldn't sleep in the house, and for some reason—he couldn't be sure why—he went to the office instead of his habit of hunting the back roads and sleeping out by the creek. It was strange being there alone. He was waiting for eight o'clock, when Tania would come in. He couldn't get certain images out of his head. She was dead. She was dead.

He eventually fell asleep at his desk only to be woken by a phone call on his cell. Sheriff Edgars told him Sheriff Mills had been taken to Richmond, where he was now recovering in a white sterile room from an operation on his vitals, where a bullet had passed.

"When will he be released?" Will said.

"I don't know. They want to watch him. A couple days, maybe."

"Is he okay?"

"I don't reckon I'd be if I was shot through the guts by that piece of Snakefoot trash."

The call ended. Will didn't know if he had hung up or if Edgars had, or if they'd been disconnected.

He stood and saw that it was almost five thirty and made some coffee. He grabbed two mugs and filled them, carrying them in one hand, the keys in the other, and walked back down the hallway and into the jail. He knocked on Zeke's door and opened it.

"Will," Zeke said, rising from his cot. "It's early."

"Sorry to wake you, Mr. Hathom."

Zeke was rubbing his face. "Ain't nobody with you?"

"Not today. Here. I brought you some coffee."

"Thank you," Zeke said, taking one of the mugs tenderly with his coarse, gnarled fingers. "What are you doing in here? Everything all right?"

"I wanted to tell you. The sheriff's been shot."

"Dead?"

"He's in the hospital."

"Well, I'll be damned. Did they catch someone?"

"Day Pace was killed. She shot him."

"Damn."

"Now, I don't know what's going to come of all this," Will said. "But I wanted you to know, Sheriff Mills claims she was confessing to Tom's murder. I think it's fair to say you're luck's about to change. There's a light at the end of this tunnel."

"What does it say about this world that my good luck comes with someone getting shot?"

"Either they're going to drop charges, or you're going to be acquitted. I can't see it going any other way."

"That's good, Will. That's real good. Thank you."

"Well, I can't figure out what would be wrong with that."

"I don't know, Will. I don't know if I can face people again."

"Yes, you can."

"That poor girl," Zeke said, shaking his head. "An awful lot of bad must have been done to her to make her do them things."

"There's something else," Will said, looking down. "Sam is back home now."

"He is? Is he okay?"

"He's doing better than I've seen him in a long time. Your family's waiting for you. So keep your head up."

Back in the office, he began to write a report of last night, but the words were slow to come. He couldn't stop worrying about Sam. In front of him lay a folder, the list. He still didn't know where they lived, where he could find them. He still couldn't decide what to do. It seemed he was waiting for a sign that would never come.

He went over and poured some coffee into his mug and turned off the burner. Soon after eight, when they opened, the phone rang. It was Mrs. Hathom.

"Did I hear right?" she said. "It was Day killed Tom?"

"Yes, ma'am."

"Thank God!" She paused. "And you're acting as sheriff now."

"I guess that's true."

"Let Zeke come home."

"I'll have to talk to the prosecution, see if they'll drop the case."

"When?"

"I'll try today."

"And what about Sam? Can we get rid of that warrant?"

"I can't promise anything."

He heard her breathing.

"Well," she said. "What the heck was you thinking, taking Sam in like that?"

"I thought that if I could do something for him, help him get better, that it would all be okay. How is he?"

"You should have told him about his father. All that time, I was wondering why he wouldn't reach out. Wondered if he even cared. If he was even alive."

"I was afraid he'd leave, relapse. You understand that, right? The way you tried to help my mother. And you just couldn't."

"Damnit, Will, I tried. She was a powerful woman, and I loved her, drew strength from her strength, so when I seen how sad she was, her heavy weighed heavy on me. But you know how headstrong she was. Whatever she was going to do, she was going to do it. She'd cut her nose off to spite her face, as they say."

"I know. I remember."

She sighed into the phone. "Upset as I am, I understand why you did it. Someday I hope you'll learn that Sam getting hurt wasn't your fault."

Even she couldn't understand. She was true and loyal, unlike Will, and Will knew that he could not accept this uplift from anyone in the world because he had failed Sam in the original moment. He could not trust her or anyone else to help him, because he could not give them the truth they would have to know to truly help him. He was too dark.

"I'm glad he's with you, finally," Will said. "I'm sorry I never told you where he was."

"I understand," she said. "You were trying to protect him. Give it to God, son. Forgive yourself. He forgives you."

Will didn't say what was on his mind. But if he had, he would have said, "No, He doesn't."

TROY ST. PIERRE CALLED Will to report on the autopsy of Ferriday Pace. She had been killed by a nine-millimeter round to the head. Will already knew that. But he had not known she'd been pregnant. He felt sick.

"What do you make of those cuts on her neck?"

"Hell," Troy said. "I don't want to know."

Will went into the sheriff's office and sat behind his desk, appraising the room, and the main lobby beyond, from this vantage point. He looked at the fish and deer heads on the walls above him, at an old black-and-white photograph of a family standing outside a dogtrot shack. He took in the clutter of a man with a title who never caught up with the demands of the job.

Will fingered the desk, the bookshelf behind him, where a turtle shell sat next to a couple of turkey feathers in a small vase. Awards hung on the walls, and there wasn't much free space at all. One photo, in particular, caught Will's eye. It had that antique coloring of late '70s–early '80s photographs, and he saw Deputy Mills standing next to his father, Sheriff Mills, squinting into the camera, stars above their hearts, wearing silverbelly Stetson Open Roads, thumbs resting casually in their belts. There was a young, simple confidence about the picture. Over a decade later, his own father would kill a man, though the man probably wasn't worth the killing, and the woman defended probably wasn't worth standing up for. He was not as passive as Will had thought, behind his suit and tie, eating bowls of soup for lunch in the white sterile marble business district of Richmond. He had shirked nothing. He had stood for something: the defense of a woman. He had been a man of courage.

As if being guided by some other curious hand, Will began opening drawers, and he found something face down in the third drawer, the felt back of a photograph frame. Will turned it over.

It was a black-and-white high school or college picture of his mother, dressed up and staring directly at him. Then he could see the resemblance, the similarities. Perhaps he had not realized it because his mother never wore makeup, but here he saw her, dolled up for the school picture. He began to feel sick.

He continued to look through the desk drawers with increasing speed and fervor, knowing he would find something, feeling the hand guiding him. And then he did find something, in the file cabinet. An empty file with his own name on it. Something was missing from the file, but what? He wondered if it had been the sheriff who'd broken in that night Sam was there alone. Had it been the sheriff, looking for some dirt to hold over Will? That would explain the mangled wildflowers scattered about her grave, and it made sense why Sheriff Mills had held the old favor over his dad. He had wanted Hannah for himself.

O N HIS WAY BACK into the county, Bill Seems stopped in at Mama Jay's Get 'N' Go for some boiled peanuts, then drove out through woods evenly bisected on either side. He saw a thick snake meander its way, head up, indecisive, across the road, and he went into the wrong lane to pass it. Copperhead. It seemed a small act of kindness in a country fertile with death. All the carcasses lying bloody in the road: possum, coon, deer, dog. Eventually he came to an intersection, turned left at the one-story brick abandoned school with window-high grass all around it, one of many such buildings that never failed to remind him of the sadness and defeat that seemed to exist in the humid and oppressive essence of his home, glad he didn't live here to see the sad of it every day. Not far up an unmarked lane was Willie Pie's store.

There was Grady's old eight-foot-bed Dodge pickup out in the gravel, in the sunshine. The field across the way from the storefront was head-high tobacco, and his car ticked after he cut it off beneath the sounds of a light breeze and a few birds and squirrels barking, chirping, and scuttling around. At the tall, oblique glass panes of the storefront he peeked in—still the books lining ladder-high shelves, a woodstove in the middle of the floor, a counter—but he couldn't tell if anyone was there. Grady had been an odd career deputy in that he was the hungriest reader Bill had ever met. He heard something increasing in volume as he approached the far corner of the old house. A radio.

"Abandon hope all ye who enter here," an old yet energetic voice said as Bill approached through the already open back door and into the puzzling green summer light. "I'll wager that's Bill Seems, old prodigal son of a bitch."

They shook hands, big familiar long-time-no-see grins above their throats.

"How'd you know it was me?"

Grady shrugged. "I guess I can identify my old friend by his ponderous gait."

Grady stood in overalls and a shirt with the cuffs unbuttoned, looking like a scarecrow. He was painting something. A blue bandanna was tied around his head, and he had sweat through it. As if he'd seen Bill yesterday instead of eleven years ago. Rather, he continued to paint and asked Bill to take a seat.

"I'll have Judy bring out the whisky." He called out, and Bill could hear Judy's muffled response from behind some upstairs window caked shut by years of paint.

"She still here?"

"She didn't never seem to want to leave."

When she emerged, it was obvious she had not left the house, showered, or changed her clothes in some time. She brought out some whisky and Jefferson cups, greeted Bill, and left the men to it. All those manners gone to waste, Bill thought.

"It's funny the things that make us feel we belong to a place, or a place belongs to us," Grady said. "I reckon whatever's brought you back must be pretty serious. Tell me, does it have to do with our friend Jefferson Mills? Does it have to do with Tom Janders, by any chance?"

TANIA TRANSFERRED THE CALL from the commonwealth attorney, Michael Sauer. Will had called before the weekend, expecting the prosecutor would drop charges against Zeke after hearing Day had confessed. He'd tried several times with no response, which he thought an inauspicious sign.

"I understand you're the man in charge now," Mr. Sauer said.

"We've found Zeke Hathom is innocent." Will explained the recent events, the evidence that Day murdered Tom. "So, how do we get these charges dropped?"

"How long have you been doing this, Deputy? You seem not to understand how this works. Once you charge someone with a crime, you do not decide whether he or she is guilty. The judge does that."

"You can drop charges without the judge and save us from going to trial."

"No. I couldn't do that. I've got a responsibility, and there's frankly too much against Zeke Hathom to let this all drop. How do you explain the fingerprints? The defendant's presence at the scene? No. I'm afraid we're going to have to press forward to the preliminary hearing. If, at that time, our case doesn't have enough behind it, we'll drop the charges."

"She confessed. The sheriff knows it. We know it. We have forensic evidence."

"You *think* you know. You *think* you have evidence, but evidence must be interpreted in court."

Will hung up and checked his watch. "Shit," he said.

"What's wrong?" Tania said.

"That jackass says the state's going to take Zeke to trial one way or the other."

"Even after all this?"

"That's what he said," Will said. "I gotta run out for a while. I'll see you later."

On his way to Mama Jay's he saw two homemade "Vote Seems for Sheriff" signs.

"I'm gonna have to talk to that woman," he said to himself.

Bennico was waiting for him at a corner table in the fake-wood-paneled section of the Get 'N' Go. The store sat at a crossroads, where a two-lane country road ran across the highway, but there was nothing besides the station there except a kind of industrial lot filled with a warehouse and trailers. Though technically the lot was paved, it was so broken and cracked and filled with dirt that it might as well have been dirt. Otherwise, the towering pines dwarfed this world of men and seemed even to skew the sun. He sat across from her in a metal chair padded with red vinyl.

"Sorry I'm late."

"That's okay," she said cheerfully. "I saw some signs up already. You're really champing at the bit, aren't you?"

"No, I'm not."

"Floressa?"

"That's my guess."

"Think you'll actually campaign?"

"I don't know. I really haven't thought much about it."

He wiped his head, parting his hair, sweaty from wearing his hat.

Bennico smiled. "Well, she knows a good thing when she sees it."

"So you're really going home today?"

"Yeah."

"I can't believe I'm going to say this after you've only been here, what, a week and a half? And you've been a pain in the ass, to put it mildly."

"Awww . . ."

"But I'm gonna miss having you around."

"Well, thank you, Will. Did you get in touch with the prosecution?"

He told her about the commonwealth attorney.

"I was afraid of that," she said. "Once a prosecutor smells blood, there's not much incentive to let a case go."

"You said your husband is an attorney. Do you think he would represent Zeke?"

"He doesn't usually take anything related to what I'm working on. But, actually, that's why I'm going back."

"Really?"

"Don't get your hopes up. Sometimes that man cannot be budged. But I'll let you know."

Eventually, Will went up to the register, nodding at a table of locals next to the big dispenser of sweet tea and two containers of boiled peanuts.

Mama Jay said, "It's been paid, honey."

289

"'Scuse me?"

"It's been paid." She jutted her old chin toward the table in the back.

He turned around, looked at Bennico, scratching his head.

One of the men between them stood up, said, "That sign out there's for you, ain't it? Or did I see your daddy come through here yesterday?"

"I believe that's for me."

"Don't sound too sure, now, does he," someone else said. These were faces he'd grown up seeing, now older, perhaps wiser. They were the real phantoms, the ushers of his upbringing.

"Yessir, it's me."

"Good on you," the man standing said. He reached forward to shake Will's hand. Soon, Will had shaken every hand at the table. "You gonna put that man out of a job."

Will had the sinking feeling that these men were dug in behind Mills, that he didn't have any business challenging the man.

"You got sand, kid. Just remember this: people ready for a change. This ain't the country we're all from."

"And we all know," someone else said, "Zeke ain't done what they say he done."

The first man said, "You and that Hathom boy grew up together. We remember that business. You're gonna look out for Zeke, ain't you?"

"Yes, sir."

The man slapped Will's shoulder. "About time somebody made some sense around here."

"Thank y'all for breakfast."

"Come on and sit with us anytime."

Bennico got up, said hello to them as she passed, pulling her purse over her shoulder, and Will opened the door for her.

"Hey," one of the men called out to Will. It was Mr. Squire. "I believe I did see your daddy yesterday evening. Didn't get a good look, but I'm pretty sure it was him. When you see him, you say hey now, will you?"

"Sure thing," Will said. "Thanks again."

Outside, Bennico said, "I didn't know your dad was in town."

"That makes two of us."

CUSTIS HAD ALREADY OPENED a bottle of wine and was standing in their redone kitchen in an Oxford shirt, the tie loosened and the top button undone. He'd set out some cheese and crackers, and he was listening to *Marketplace* on the radio. The backyard was lush and green, overgrown with summer, and the evening light morphed in hazy and unrefined colors as the sun lowered in its smoldering descent, one more fire burning to coals.

Tater, their bluetick hound, lay at his bare feet, his thin velvet fur soft and warm. Maybe everything would be okay, he thought. He'd dreamed of other women, in particular a lawyer in his firm who looked at him in a way Bennico never did. Bennico wasn't sexy with him. She didn't really flirt, and it made the marriage feel like work. But he cared for her. He remembered thinking kids would solve that. But they hadn't. People didn't change, it seemed. Over the phone, she had sounded cheerful, like she actually wanted to see him. He'd been the one to initiate the divorce, but he'd been hoping for a reason not to go through with it. A reason that would come from her. But she didn't play games. She didn't go for that kind of stuff. He'd said *divorce*, and that had seemed to be the deciding factor. His mother had told him once that you couldn't turn back to safety in a marriage once the D-word was uttered, and he beat himself up sometimes for ever bringing it up. Over the phone, when they were apart, he loved Bennico most.

When she got home, she came in, kissed him briskly, and stood opposite him at the island.

"So," he said. "What is it that you wanted to talk about? Or'd you just want to see me?"

"A little of both," she said, pouring a glass. "Have you heard from the girls?"

"Yeah. Spoke to Chloe yesterday. Mercer the day before."

"I can't get them to return my calls."

"They're going through a phase."

"Some phases don't end," she said. "And you, buying them everything they could want. Just like you've done for me."

"That again. I've given you love too. What more demands can you put on my workdays? It's after seven now, and I'm home early."

"I'm not talking about demands. I'm saying it's us that matters. If we're not a part of this relationship, and it's all about things we can buy, what's the point?"

He lifted one hand, helplessly, took a drink.

She went over to the radio and cut it off. "But speaking of demands. I do have a favor to ask of you. It's about the case I've been working."

Custis had a way of listening that Bennico had found infuriating early on, because it looked as if he weren't paying attention, fiddling with things, looking anywhere else but at her. When he looked like that, though, he was focusing. After she finished telling him about the murder, about Zeke and everything else, he was silent. He untied his tie, withdrew it from his collar, folded it neatly, and placed it in his shirt pocket.

"Do you know how troubling it is for me to know the things you've done? Stealing a corpse is a bit over the top, even for you."

"Don't change the subject."

He looked at her now, knowing he could not refuse, even though he'd convinced himself that by divorcing her he was proving his own independence. She believed so hard in everything she did that even her decisiveness, itself, drew him to her. When she'd been without a steady job, it had been hard to see her because she didn't have that verve that made her who she was. She needed work. He wanted to be fishing, or hunting, or reading a book, but she wanted to be out there, running a scent like Tater, like any good hound. He began to wonder if he'd decided to divorce her because he thought she'd changed, when in fact, she hadn't. She'd only been without a task.

"How much could they offer?" he said, at length.

"It won't be much."

He sighed. "Okay. If this really means all that to you."

F LORESSA WENT to South Hill the next day to pick up some balloons to celebrate Sam's return, then went home and began making a big dinner. She was breading and frying catfish from Jake's and okra from the garden and boiling corn on the cob and simmering turnip greens with onions and bacon in chicken broth.

She had spent the morning putting up campaign signs for Will Seems, even though the election wouldn't be for another couple of months. It was something simple, physical she could do, but she wondered if she was really doing any good at all. Sometimes she thought about the darker mysteries of life, things her mother had admonished her to pray away. *Don't think like that. You go crazy if you can't trust in God. God made things the way they are, and you can't figure them out because people ain't meant to.* But she couldn't help wondering now, what was the point of this, of any of her actions, when you could do everything right, you could try to help a neighbor whose house had caught fire and be arrested in turn for homicide. She'd never felt as defeated as she was now, regardless of what the verdict would be.

She thought back beyond the hurt to two miscarriages and then, after the doctors had said she would never bear a child, the miracle of Samuel Bernard Hathom, in whose wrinkled infant face—soft with wonder—she saw the future, the world, the universe. She stargazed in his black eyes as he looked up at her, his own sky. They'd needed each other then, and she believed they needed each other now. He had grown up with a good family, and what difference had it made? He had a reason to be mad. You had to be mad, crazy, to live here, mad at everything, because you loved it, and it was your home too. That was the poison of it. That you did love it; that it was home. You could leave it, but then what did you have to stand on? No one anywhere else understood it, this love and this hate, so you might as well stay here and live through it.

She was getting lost in it, in that sick feeling of anger, of hate, and she wanted to ask God why there was so much meanness. She wanted to keep praying there in the kitchen, but seemingly in agreement with a higher power, she stopped. She walked outside and glanced out at the undulating world that surrounded her. What good was it? What good had it ever been?

She cut the TV off in the living room, the TV that had been a constant myriad voice for her, a soothing, empty vaguely humanoid presence against the stretched fields when she'd been up crying at night. She had had little appetite, and so she had not prepared any meals in a long time, but here, with Sam again by her side, she was happy to have the excuse to really cook again, nourish her baby, sustain something.

"Thanks, Mama," Sam said when they sat down at the four-person table.

"Everything okay?" she said, reaching out and touching his scarred cheek. "Let me look at you again."

He lifted his head and looked out from the one good eye and all its pain, a history of guilt begetting guilt begetting pain begetting pain. And tears were in them. And she thought that was good. That was good. It was not the cold look that she had last seen when he'd been using, but the gaze of a man sober enough to feel.

"Eat your food, honey," she said.

"Yes, ma'am," Sam said, like he was excited, like he was a kid again, trying to keep her spirits up. Like they could go back in time just to run back through it all again.

S HERIFF EDGARS DROVE Mills back home from the hospital, along with a supply of oxycodone they'd picked up from the pharmacy, and helped him into bed before heading back to Emporia.

It was hard for Sheriff Mills to take any pride in anything, as his mama had taught him to do, while bedridden after being shot by a woman he'd tried to protect half of her life. He knew he'd gone too far, and the shame had brought him to tears several times. In the hospital he'd hoped to fade out. He hoped that if he just kept his eyes closed, he would sleep it off and never have to open his eyes to the harsh white world again. He'd been raised to protect a woman in distress. All those years he watched patiently, magnanimously, paternally, thinking he was in control, and in a single moment he had lowered himself, and he was filled now with a fathomless grief. No matter what happened, what was the point? He had ended the very life he had tried to protect. He the protector had become the victim. He could never have her back. His wounds were badges of shame and would remind him of his actions.

He was trying now to take comfort in little things—the sunlight that came through his bedroom window, the sound of his dog, the simplicity of lying in bed during the daytime—but he could not get away from the truth: he'd lost her. He'd lost.

That afternoon, Mills heard the dog barking, a welcome distraction from his mind.

"It's open!" Mills shouted hoarsely, his call graduating into a nasty coughing bout.

The door opened, and Bill Seems stepped in.

"Bill, you're here."

Bill came in and carried a chair from the dining room into the bedroom.

"Suppose you tell me what happened," Bill said, setting down the chair and taking a seat.

"She came at me. Tried to kill me. She was confessing. I swear."

"Who? Slow down. Tell me everything about that night. Start from the beginning."

Mills told him, squirming in his bed, ashamed, afraid, pleading at times for Bill to understand, at times in tears. Bill's face changed when he heard the last name of the deceased.

"'Pace,' you said? Did you say 'Pace'?"

"You remember her daddy."

Bill stood up. "I can't do this."

"Listen, Bill. Hold on a minute. We got to talk about it. It's not about him, it's about her, but either way you can't ignore the connection." Mills looked away. "Back when all that happened, I found out he had a wife and daughter, and I made my mind up to look after 'em. They were poor as anybody I seen, living out in the Snakefoot, where he'd disappear for days and weeks on benders or trapping beaver, and his own family never knew which it was. It was personal for me. So I looked after 'em."

"I never knew he had any kin at all. Why didn't you tell me? I would have done something."

"I know that, but it was my cross to bear. I had gone against the law protecting you, because you had protected a woman. You'd done the right thing, but what I did . . . I owed it to the family to look out for them. Then her mama passed, and it was just the girl and me."

"Well, what does that have to do with this incident?"

"She wanted to meet me the night of Tom's funeral. When I got there, to that old shitpile of a shack where she grew up, she confessed."

"About what?"

"Said she killed Tom Janders."

They listened as a small wind blew shades through the room.

"What do you think, Bill? What do you think that means for me?"

"It ain't too good of a case. You being . . . involved. She confessed, and you somehow ended up taking advantage of her."

"She took advantage of *me*. I know it looks bad. I feel awful about it. But it was self-defense. She shot me clean through. Isn't that enough?"

He began violently coughing, and Bill helped him ease back.

The sheriff said, "Bill, you owe me this."

"I left because I knew you'd never let it go."

"Then why'd you come back? It's either because you're afraid, or you know you still owe me your life. You know as well as I do the line between manslaughter and second-degree is thinner than a fish fart and you could have been charged with either one."

Bill watched Mills carefully. "Has any move been made to arrest you?"

"Not I know of."

"So this is preemptive."

"You could say that," he said, looking at Bill now with such a look of self-pity, Bill felt sympathy for him. "I don't want to lose what I got. I've lost everything. Everything else."

A moment of silence. A distant car like a snore. Birdsong. A rustle of wind in the limbs of the dogwood outside the window, casting a kaleidoscope of striped light across the bed. In that moment in that silent wind, for both men: Hannah.

"Look, Jeff. No matter what I could do for you, I can't say I can help you keep your job. You did things that I predict will not go well for you in court, and I could only mitigate that a little."

"Self-defense. Ain't nothing sacred no more?"

"Let's just hope you aren't charged."

"You'd better be ready," Mills said. "Because if you ain't on my side, if you don't cover for me, I'm not only going to take you down. I'm going to take down your boy too."

Bill breathed hard. "What does he have to do with this?"

"I've got some dirt on him. If anything happens to me—if this goes to court and spins against me—you and your boy are going down. I've got somebody watching him now, watching his every move."

Sheriff Mills told Bill about Will holding Sam Hathom in the old house, supplying him with heroin.

"How do you know this?"

"Let's just say I always take out insurance. And I've got the evidence. Just you remember what I did for you. We're in this together, the three of us. One big family."

S AM HAD BEEN HOME for several days, cold turkey. But he had felt the sensitivity grow and could even hear his mama leaning over in her bed late at night to listen for any sound he might make. He was under surveillance, and there was no secret about it. With nothing to occupy him during the days and being unable to go out because he couldn't risk being seen, he got to where he even wished he could be back at Promised Land, where he knew he could have his steady supply, where he could go outside without being seen from the road. These days, he slept in until about noon, and was up until two or three in the morning. One morning, when he came to the kitchen for a late breakfast, she noticed him shivering. He looked pale, weak. Other than his eighty-nine-day dry spell in rehab, these past several days had been the longest he'd gone sober.

"Son, you all right?"

"Course I am, Mama."

"You ain't using again, are you?"

"Why you gotta jump on me like that?"

"I'm worried for you, Sam. You all I got right now." Sam was looking out the window. "Son, what's gonna happen?"

"Mama, I don't know. How could I know?"

"Tell me everything is gonna be all right."

"How I can do that with you breathing down my neck, expecting me to do wrong?"

"You don't need to snap at me, baby. I'm here for you now. It's just a mother's way, I guess."

"I know, Mama. But you always watching, waiting. I can hear you listening, waiting for me to disappoint you."

"What else can I do? I love you. I gave birth to you. At one point we were in harmony. My heart taught your heart to beat."

It was like two strangers living in a house they both knew. It got so bad that he knew he was going to steal from her again and hated himself for it. Then he justified it by saying she'd want him to have it, that he needed it. It was for her. He had to leave to protect her. One day, when she was out, he went through her hatbox in the closet and took a hundred dollars. Returning was no good for anyone involved. You couldn't dream in the house where you were raised, where your history kept you down and you couldn't forget it. He thought about Promised Land, but he couldn't go back. Not to Will. It would have been best for him if he could, but he couldn't. He had to go elsewhere, out of the county.

He left late that afternoon, before she got back, deciding to risk being seen in pursuit of escape rather than sit around like a vegetable. He would stick to the fields as much as possible. After stuffing a backpack with a change of clothes, he placed a note on the kitchen counter, writing, in his trembling childish print, "I'm sorry, Mama. I love you."

He set out for Richmond. He was going to get one more good high, feel that bright wet cool spreading horizon dream, and then he'd figure things out. When he buzzed, when he could place his hand on his chest and feel that calm strange flutter, he would think it all through, the job he'd have. He still had it in him, the strength to bust a gut. He'd been working the tobacco and garden at Promised Land and could work every day. He'd focus, hone his mind again, away from here. He'd put money away, enough to get a car. He'd drive back in his own car, and they'd see. He'd go walk the walk instead of returning to rehab, where all he'd do would be to talk about all the things he would do again as if he wouldn't. He could see himself somewhere else. Somewhere else. It didn't matter where. Just not here, where you were stuck decades behind, living imagined previous lives again and again because there was no future, only the lingering of what had already come, and where you were not yourself but the son or daughter of your parents, the descendant of servants or slaves or masters. Where people wore down, tired and hopeless, settling in for a wasted countryside, that red soil that once had promised a future as deep and bright as itself, yet no longer made promises of any kind. He had to go somewhere else, make something of himself. He imagined working—maybe he'd take that job Will had arranged at Dixie Insulation—nothing to do but to sweat and work and get that blue paycheck he said they paid every week. He would save and return in his own car. He'd take his mama for a ride. He'd drive her to South Boston to one of those salons. He'd hand her that hundred bucks he'd taken plus another hundred, like it was nothing. His pops would be home then. Bennico would have taken care of that. It was the only reason he might have convinced himself to stay, but the way she'd talked, it seemed as good as done. He was leaving his mama and regretted it before even doing it. He knew he needed to get high, and he didn't trust anybody here because they would know who he was. So he kept on. He had a peculiar history of doing the very thing he knew he shouldn't be doing simply because he'd assuaged the guilt by thinking about the right thing which he'd decided not to do. The sooner he left and got high and got sober, the sooner he could get that job and make that money and get that car and return proud. There was always next time. There was always the possibility of a glorious return of a man who depended on nothing but himself, in his own car which he had bought and wearing the new clothes he'd bought himself. He'd come back. He'd come back in the future, when he was all better, to this land of the past. He just needed to get away so that he could.

A LONG THE EMPTY, unpainted county road, between the gravel shoulder and the ditch of grass, dry and coarse, a figure—a shadow or silhouette—lurched, so that any passerby would have thought the man recently injured, in need of medical attention. He had cut across long fields, out of sight of houses, until coming to a road. Upon close proximity, discomfort would have set in. The desire to stare in fascination. In fact, one might think some unseen wire pulled this ghost or spirit forward, all joints akimbo. He had walked six miles and approached a country church when a Mack truck slowed in a back-eddy of wind beside him.

The window slid down.

"Hey, brother," a voice called out like something forced through an impossible substance. "Need a ride?"

Sam stared up at the driver.

"A ride. Can I give you a ride?"

Sam clenched his fists.

"Brother, where you going, man?"

The driver looked ahead, down the road at nothing. "I'm on my way to Richmond," he said. "I'll take you as far as you want to go."

Sam climbed into the truck, breathing heavy. The truck moved, all that loud effort just for velocity. They passed fields, trailers tucked into pines or silhouettes of mobile homes on the bare rises, an old plantation house overtaken by poison ivy and honeysuckle and wild privet and wisteria. He saw his country unfold as from above, watched it change and stay the same.

The driver glanced sideways. "You a God-fearing man?" he said in that deep hoarse voice that sounded angry even though it wasn't.

Sam said, "Not that it's done me no good."

"It does a body good, even if you don't know it. If you fear God, you fear sin as well."

Sam did not want to hear this kind of talk.

"You been baptized?"

"Yeah," Sam said.

"Well, all right then. Where you heading?"

"Wherever. Richmond, I guess."

"What you looking for?"

"I don't know."

"You can tell me. You hunting something. I can see it."

"Nah."

"I bet I can guess what it is. See, I know. I can see it all over you."

Sam was sweating, shaking. He didn't want to be so obvious.

The driver said, "You hunting somebody. Revenge. But Jesus right with you, and you don't even know it. You looking for Jesus, and He everywhere. This is God's country. And you found a brother in Christ here."

"Can I get a cigarette?" Sam said.

The man gave him a pack of Marlboro Reds, and Sam took out two, putting one in his mouth and twisting the tip of the second one, tucking it behind his ear for later. He pushed in the lighter and waited for it to pop out, drew in the smoke and blew it out so that it clouded his view momentarily.

The driver said, "You ever been in a rig like this?"

"No."

"Got a bed in the back. This baby's sweet."

"How much you get it for?" Sam said. Anything but this God talk.

"That's between me and the Lord. I'll be paying that off for another ten years."

In Richmond, as the lights began to shine and they passed the Philip Morris plant and wove into town, the man said, "Man, this place sure has changed. Changed since I was here last month. Where you going?"

"Anywhere," Sam said.

"Man, you a real drifter. Trusting people. That's good. You know what I think? It ain't that we got to be all afraid like we is, but that's what everybody think. It's the other way. Trust. Everybody can be a brother or sister in Christ. If you see them that way, and trust that the Lord will work His will through them, then we can trust each other, and all that fear will just melt away. Ain't nothing can't be overcome."

After a pause he said, "I'm talking too much."

They had made it into Richmond like a whale amid drivers slouching in their sedans and SUVs with RVA stickers all over them in personalized absurdity and all kinds of pickups great and small like an assortment of fish and took the exit and pulled up to an Exxon, and the driver parked to refuel.

"It won't take too long to gas up," he said. "I can let you off wherever after this."

Sam stayed in the cab and watched the driver go inside, where he used the ATM and disappeared into the men's room. Sam scoured the cab. He pocketed the cigarettes and found a pistol concealed under the driver's seat. He took it and racked it, holding the receiver and seeing it was loaded. He was about to climb down and leave, but something made him change his mind, and he waited, like a crow, like the shadow of a crow.

RUMOR PERSISTED that Bill Seems had come back to Euphoria for long enough that Will drove out to Mr. Grady's. Grady and his father were sitting outside in the yard, drinking coffee, his father smoking a cigar.

Bill stood up. "Son," he said with a clumsy warmth, approaching Will, who stepped back.

"How come I'm hearing from others you're in town, and I don't even know it?"

"Let me explain."

Grady said, "Go and get a chair."

"Why the hell would I do that?"

"I'm going to explain to you what's going on here," Mr. Grady said. "It's about Zeke and you."

"Don't push him," Bill said. "If he wants to run away again, let him go."

"Run away, like you?"

Bill said, "Son, this is going to seem strange, but—"

"Let me tell him, Bill," Grady said. "Will, you remember what I told you the other day. About Mills holding everything over your daddy. That's what's happening right now."

Will found a seat. "How?"

Grady said, "If your daddy doesn't represent him, Mills will take him down. And me too probably."

"I don't understand," Will said. "If any of that came out, it would incriminate him."

Grady said, "That's the one thing we all had protecting us before: The sheriff had everything to lose. If he's taken to court, he's got nothing to lose. If things go badly for him, one other charge won't mean a damn thing for him. But it will for us. He's already threatened your dad."

"So, you're really going to take his case."

"I'm taking the case not because I owe him," Bill said, "but because I'm protecting you. Mills says he has evidence that you've been holding Sam Hathom in the house, supplying him with drugs, despite the fact that there's a warrant out for his arrest. He's going to take you down and put you in jail if I don't do this. Got someone watching you, he said."

"Goddamnit."

"I think maybe I'm the one who should be a little pissed right now. But let's move beyond that and get at what's important here. We need to do what we can for Zeke while keeping ourselves out of trouble, off of Mills's radar."

"How are we gonna do that?"

WILL WAS NOT EXPECTING Miss Claudette to call. She said it was urgent, that he had to come over as soon as he could, that it was about Sam.

He saw Floressa's car parked out front. He got out and walked up the steps, feeling light-headed, ready to hear bad news.

Floressa had been crying prayers.

"Will," she said. "Sam gone. He run off. He left. You know what that means."

"I haven't seen him."

Claudette said, "We heard from Arnie that Sam hitched a ride with a truck driver to Richmond. Said he took Sam downtown, and Sam took his money and his gun and left."

"How did Arnie know this?"

"Said the truck driver from around here. He came back yesterday, had to go to Richmond, got robbed. His wife talking about it all over. Word is, it was Sam who robbed him."

"I knew I shouldn't never have left the house," Floressa said. "I could tell things weren't right."

"Who's the truck driver?" Will said.

"Da'Shawn Peters."

Will left, or rather floated out of the house, their voices somewhere behind him. He found himself on a familiar road, one of
many going nowhere, the piece of paper from his wallet shaking
in his hands above the steering wheel, reading the first name Tom
had written for him: Da'Shawn Peters.

WILL COULD SMELL hickory burning when he parked his truck down the lane, a hog on chicken wire over some pit. The ghostlike smell filled him with the dream of promised meat. The Mack truck rested beside some trees up ahead. Will had made sure to shake his tail—Buddy Monroe— before coming here.

Da'Shawn Peters was smoking his last cowboy killer, his lucky cig, up against the tractor trailer, appreciating the sudden disquieting stillness after spending so much time on the road. Kendra had freaked out when he'd shown up yesterday with his face all busted, and now he was ashamed to look at her. God had delivered him, he explained. Everything happened for a reason. Even after the first drag of that last cigarette, he found himself fatigued within, bone-tired, hungry, worn thin. He had come to believe in forgiveness, and he hoped, as he rubbed his sore, busted cheek, tasted the iron on his split lip, that he too would be forgiven. Everyone deserved a second chance, some more. The American dream had been built on second chances, though he knew many never had a first. What were the chances he would have run into that kid after so many years? Da'Shawn had thought he was past all that. He was just picking up someone who looked like he needed help. God was behind it, of course. How else could it be explained? He had brought Da'Shawn face to face with his own past sins, and he was grateful for the pain.

Da'Shawn smoked half of the cigarette. He could see it all now, pairing what he'd heard about Sam Hathom's injuries with the man he'd picked up. That's fate, he thought. He heard the screen door. Her hand rested on her hip, and she was looking at him so that he knew he had to go on in.

"Baby," Kendra said. "Got food on the table."

The screen door slapped the house, but she'd left the big door open so that he could hear her walking through it and back to the kitchen, the kids trailing her, cheerful and innocent. He would have to go in but didn't want to be around them right now. He flicked the cigarette into the tall grass, wanting to be on the road, the miles sliding under him like an accumulation of some meaningless currency. He'd been someone else back then. He had not known what he was doing. What else was there to do in a country like this? He remembered how it had changed. He remembered the aimlessness of it, how there had been no plan. There he was, this white boy, glowing against the creek like something artificial, and Da'Shawn couldn't explain it, not even to God, how his heart knew so well how to hate. But the way it had turned against him. He had not seen it coming. The way that Hathom boy had turned on them, stood up for a white boy who let him take a beating. Of course, Da'Shawn and the others hadn't wanted to go for that scrawny Black kid. But the way he'd come up like something rabid, talking shit. They couldn't let that go. Da'Shawn had loved that terrible feeling of finally having a reason to punish someone, only it was the wrong person. He tried to pray about it now, but God had watched over his punishment last night, a pistol-whipped blackness within the blackness. It was like a hangover, this feeling. He hoped he was forgiven now, felt almost relieved in a way for the fact that it had made sense, that he had been punished intentionally, not randomly and for some unknown reason.

Da'Shawn heard something on the gravel at the shoulder of the road, turned to face Will Seems. God's will be done. Da'Shawn stood independent now from the truck and took his left hand out of his pocket, ready.

Through his busted face, Da'Shawn said, "I thought you might be coming." The voice was hoarse, a deep scratching sound from Will's memory, a sound that had dragged Will through life. He knew he had come to the right place.

"What happened?" Will said.

"Saw him crossing a field, offered him a ride to Richmond. Stopped to fill up, and he took my gun and pistol-whipped me cold. Took my cigarettes and a hundred and sixty bucks and both my credit cards and my debit card."

"Did you recognize him?"

"Not at first."

"Did you report it?"

"I'm reporting it now."

"What gas station?"

"Exxon on Belvidere, near Monroe Park."

A sound came from the house. The kids laughing.

Will said, "Come over here, behind your truck."

"Come on, man."

Will wagged his pistol, and Da'Shawn obeyed with his hands instinctively held up above his shoulders.

"Can't you see he already got me? You quiet types. You weak ones are the dangerous ones. You're the ones that never forget."

"What you did to him," Will said. He could feel himself going hoarse himself, and he regripped his pistol, holding it on Da'Shawn. "It was you. It was you. I've been looking for you."

"I don't remember you doing anything to help him," Da'Shawn said. "Matter fact, I can see you now, standing there, watching the whole thing. You chasing me or yourself for what you did or didn't do?"

WILL DID NOT remember everything, but he did know he had not fired his gun. He'd already checked the clip twice while driving. His hand might be broken, and one of his knuckles looked caved in. He couldn't close his hand all the way. He guided the wheel with his left hand while his right lay cradled and aching in his lap. He did not think the man was dead. But he was not moving when Will had left him. Will found he was still talking, talking to himself in the car, a conversation ongoing and one-sided: "I'm your daddy. I'm your fucking daddy, you motherfucker." He was almost certain the man was still alive.

Several miles gone, Will picked up his cell and called Tania. He was going to Richmond and would be back for work tomorrow. Before she had time to argue or comment on the wild tenor of his voice, he hung up. Soon, he merged onto I-85 north and from there onto I-95 north toward Richmond.

W ITHIN THE HEAVY BREATHING of a summer night, there was no relief, no rest. Will started on Belvidere and crossed street after one-way street, circling the area with the same thorough attention of a coyote working a field. He had known all along he would not find Sam. He knew, somehow, that his greatest fear must come true. That he would lose him before he could tell him that he was responsible for it all. Or worse, that Sam already knew. That he had stood that day like a statue, unbudging, unable to move. Da'Shawn's memory, his words, had released it, and now it was out, like a spirit running across the land of causes foregone, lost. He could not catch it now. Even if he could find Sam in some understory of Richmond, what would he do?

Will covered the city with a kind of compulsive hopelessness, trying to conjure him up, nevertheless thinking that around some corner, or in the glimpse up an alley, or in some huddle of men at the corner of some crack house, he would see Sam and take him back again, no matter the cost, and save him. He saw the worst of the city. Richmond's growth and gentrification, the expansion of VCU, and increased funding for the police department, had been credited with making Richmond safer, but its crime had merely become concentrated, adapting to survive. Will talked to Sam like a god he pitied, a god he'd wronged. He watched the corner in Church Hill, drove the one-ways to the shot-out lights, rolled his window down. B stepped out of the huddle.

"What you want, white boy?"

"You seen him?" Will asked.

"The fuck you think I am? Missing persons? I don't rat nobody out. What you want?"

"Nothing."

B lifted his shirt, producing two handguns at a cross-draw, chrome or nickel, shining like his teeth. "Mo'fuck, you better drive on."

The huddle approached the car like a strange amoeba, and Will put his foot down, sped away.

That was only the beginning of a bad night. He saw two grown men who appeared not to know how to fight or not wanting to fight, cheered on by a girl in a driverless car in a sad-looking Taco Bell parking lot with the driver's door hanging open. Then two other actual fights, the second more violent than the first, leaving someone on the ground. Fearing for Sam, he could do nothing. Sam had told him how bad it could be. That he would be willing to steal from anybody to get more. But by morning, when Will found himself parked by the James, the sun rising behind him and over the river and against the buildings and the roads, he knew very well he would not see Sam. He'd known it all along. He had fallen asleep and woken with a crick in his back, and so he got out of the truck and walked to the edge of a bluff overlooking some warehouses. A forlorn city at this hour. A city bright with the rays of a bold apocalypse of sun.

He was going to need to leave for Southside before too long, but he decided to drive out Hull Street. He got there early, fell asleep waiting in his truck, woke up to Caleb knocking on his window. Will went in and had coffee in his plywood cell, a swimsuit calendar on a wall and the smell of wood and that benign sterility of insulation in a warehouse that was a familiar, innocent environment.

Caleb said, "What are you doing out this way?"

"Remember that guy I was telling you about? Needed a job? He come to see you yet?"

"Nope."

"I was hoping he'd come by."

"You look like hell, buddy. What happened to your hand?"

"Nothing. Shouldn't Joe be here by now?"

"I had to fire his ass last week. You know, he just took it one step too far. He stopped calling in, answering, any of it. Left for lunch one day, and took the company truck. That was nothing out of the ordinary, but cops found the truck with Dixie Insulation painted on its side outside Richard's strip joint. That's bad advertising. He knew better. Joe said he was fighting with his wife or something, but I always told him I didn't care what he did on his time off, long as it didn't affect work. You try all you can for these people, and what good does it do them or you? I will say I miss something about him around here. It's not really the same place without a man to make you feel like you're always working hard. Hey."

"What?"

"You tell your boy there's an opening; he can take Joe's spot any day. I could hire a damn middle-school girl and get more out of her."

"I'll tell him if I see him."

"Shit," Caleb said. "Who am I kidding? I didn't want to fire Joe. I had to do it, and he made it that way. You can't teach a guy like that responsibility. But it bothers me; I don't know that he wasn't just trying to get fired. He didn't even seem to care, and him being here sixteen years. I wonder what made him push me like that. You think he was reaching out for help?"

"Who knows what was going on in his head."

"You wouldn't have even recognized him at the end there." Caleb sat back, tried laughing it away. "Sounds like I'm talking about a dead person."

Will left for Southside with a feeling that everything was changing everywhere. Joe getting fired. If he had learned anything, it was that there was no going back to a thing except in your mind. Everything changed, and instead of doing so in cycles, time continued moving through a strange territory, a road that just kept going. Will figured the only way to avoid the change was to quit early so that you could remember it the way you wanted to. Like a poker game, you could leave when and if you were ahead. Maybe Joe had realized that, not that he'd been ahead. But maybe something in his heart just changed, and he wanted it to be over. Joe had been a part of the fabric of the company, as regular as insulation on the racks or the warehouse itself or the trees hanging over the drive. He was as much a part of Richmond for Will as the statues, and now he was gone. And Sam out there, somewhere, and Will unable to find and help him. He should have told him about Zeke's arrest from the beginning, but how could he apologize to Sam if he couldn't find him? He should have done things differently. He should have stood up with him. He should have known what to do.

There should have been a god to tell him. It was only an hour and a half driving back to Dawn through Southern overgrown fields and tired humid heat, but it felt like all the years he'd known and some he didn't. Richmond burning. It felt as if he had lived his whole life looking for someone and ending up where he'd started, only where he'd started had changed, and he had not. There was no place to return.

T HE NEXT DAY, Bill went to see Mills and found Sheriff
Edgars standing over the bed.

"Morning, counselor," said Edgars.

"Look here," Bill said. "I don't want you coming around while we got this investigation going on."

"Well, that's why I'm here. Ol' Jefferson here, I figure he's had enough. He'll be recovering for some time yet. We figure, he did the wrong thing, you know? But he didn't know she was a suspect—not really. And he only fired his piece in self-defense. So, you can go on home, now, Bill. He'll be all right. The government won't be coming after him. No special prosecutors, no arraignment, no humiliation. For either of you."

Edgars had made coffee and offered some to Bill, who felt the warmth through the bone-white mug.

Mills said, "It's pretty lucky, ain't it, Bill?"

Bill felt loose and strange, like he'd been ready for a dangerous action but was never actually put to the test, a pent-up readiness in the ether that would go to waste. So this would continue to hover like a spirit. But the look on Mills was one that bothered him. The gall he had to grin.

"What about his position?" Bill said. "What about the sheriff's department?"

"Far as I'm concerned," Edgars said, raising his mug, "this here is a sheriff wounded on the job. This county's right lucky to have him looking after it."

"Bill," Mills said, glowing with a warm, ruddy relief. "I won't make that kind of mistake again. And when I'm well enough, I'm going right back out there. I'm going to die sheriff of this county."

There was a strange pause. Homemade signs for Will Seems running for sheriff had started appearing around town, and they all knew it. It bothered Bill that his son had been learning to run the county—had embraced the opportunity, it appeared—and now would have to work again for this man. Bill already had suggested Will leave Southside, but Will was the stubbornest boy he knew. Like his mother, that way.

"Well," said Edgars. "I better get on. Congratulations, Jeff. See ya 'round, Bill."

When Edgars had left, Mills said, "Bill, what's got you down?"

"I want you to give me the evidence."

Mills looked out the warped window. "No," he said. "Can't do that."

"Promise me you'll leave that boy alone."

"Your boy?"

"Who else."

"'Course. I'll call off my dogs."

"You said you had evidence against him. Whatever he was doing he was doing for the right reason."

"Take it easy, Bill. Ain't nothing to worry about. Long as I'm sheriff, I won't go for him."

"That means Sam Hathom too."

"You may be forgetting the situation. You aren't in a position to make requests."

"Well then, I'm asking you as a friend."

"After all I done for you."

"How many times do I have to thank you for that?"

"And all those years you had with Hannah. All those years you had her. And you didn't know what you had. You just couldn't have. You were just too lucky to know."

F INALLY, the preliminary hearing in September. Custis Watts represented Zeke Hathom, who had been in police custody almost two months. The facts were clear as a mountain stream somewhere far from the rolling flat of Euphoria County. After witnesses, including Cherokee McDaniels, Mr. Chim and his daughter, Sarun, the Charlotte County gamblers, and the others who'd played with Tom that night, the prosecution withdrew its charges, and Zeke, at long last, was released, the long road of the rest of his life lying ahead of him.

Sheriff Mills, who had recovered but continued use of a cane, was approached by reporters outside the courthouse. He used his cane to clear a path without comment.

OCTOBER WAS A SOFT MONTH of warm days and cool nights, of leaves dying, of the last of the tobacco being harvested from the tops of stalks that were naked, stripped and emaciated looking from the periodic upward harvest like cell bars branding strange shadows across depleted fields. Floressa and Claudette insisted Will campaign for sheriff in earnest, an idea Will had not taken seriously and even rejected at first. When Bill urged him to back out, he committed to running for the position. Floressa had professional signs made to replace the ones she'd written by hand. She did all she could to make Mills look corrupt, and Will even felt sorry for the sheriff, who appeared to have aged a great deal in the past months. Will, on the other hand, was young, could serve the county for years, and Floressa said he'd have much of the Black vote, which should result in a win since this was a majority Black county. Sam still had not returned, and the grief Will had observed in Zeke and Floressa troubled him. Zeke, in particular, cut a sad figure, seeming a husk or apparition of himself. Once ready to smile at anything, the man now appeared hollowed out with worry and uncertainty. It seemed to Will that victory at all costs was not always worth the pain and struggle. Defeat, loss, surrender. Those could be gifts; they could be guidelines to a life otherwise too free and open to survive. The campaign seemed to give them all a purpose, a distraction, and Will often wondered how he had become a source of hope for them. He often thought of Sam out there and hoped he was making his way. He'd developed a habit, after his mother's death, of praying not to God but to her, believing she could hear his thoughts. And now, though Sam to his knowledge was still among the living, Will spoke to him in this way, hoping Sam would know his heart and forgive it. Maybe Sam was doing well. Maybe he was better off without Will. Every time Will called Caleb at Dixie Insulation, he was told there had been no sign of Sam. Will avoided Richmond for some time. Instead, he focused on the campaign.

ONE DAY in late October Sheriff Mills called Will into his office. The department had been quiet in comparison to those wild weeks of July, starting with Tom's death, and the two men had spoken awkwardly, professionally.

"Shut the door and sit down," Mills said. "I want to make you an offer."

Will stood, and the sheriff continued: "You drop out of the race, and I'll be honored to have you to stay on as my deputy."

"That's an offer?"

"Well, I want to be honest with you now. I got something that proves you were harboring a fugitive, giving him drugs. I got evidence that I don't want to use, and you can control all that. I always tried looking out for you, son. But you've made it hard. After all this job has cost me, I'm going to need to be reelected. It's just the only thing I can tolerate. I was born for this office."

"Why don't you admit you broke in, conducted an illegal search?"

"That's a baseless accusation. It's offensive is what it is."

"How else would you get it?"

"That won't make no difference to anybody here."

"Look," Will said. "You can search my house. You won't find Sam Hathom anywhere. Truth is, I don't know where he is."

"Ain't that a crying shame. Look here, son. This is some truth for you: I told your daddy I wouldn't use that evidence against you long as I'm sheriff. And I'm gonna keep my word. So run against me, I don't care. But if you get elected, you're gonna have to answer to the facts."

Will thought about telling Mills he knew about Ricky Pace, the trapper from the Snakefoot, but what was the point? It was all a struggle, fighting uphill against every force natural and man-made, and Will was tired of it.

So he dropped out of the race. He was unable to explain his decision to Floressa and Claudette. He had to admit it looked as if he were ungrateful for all their help. He wanted to say, "There was never any point. You'd still end up with me as sheriff at best, and at worst . . ." But you can't make someone feel better by reason. And you can't reason with a person's hopes. He felt worse for them and all the dreams the campaign had given them than he felt for himself.

WILL CALLED HIS SISTER, but no answer. She never answered, not since she had left home, skipping even their mother's funeral. But they had grown up together. They had both known the mother they had lost. They could help each other, but she had left school and gone away. He saw in her some of his mother's traits. She was independent, brave, could do without others. She could push everyone else away, and Will missed her. Will then called Bennico, getting the voicemail and wishing he hadn't called. She was getting on with her life, Will thought. And he was calling her, who knew why, maybe because she understood something about him he didn't, or because he trusted there had been a partnership, a teamwork, that had mutually led to Zeke's acquittal. Reaching out to others did little good. You couldn't depend on anyone, really.

Will sat in a chair in the dark corner of the parlor and looked at the old peeling wallpaper hanging down from the ceiling like cobwebs, felt the years that had made the place, years that were killing it. The trees swayed outside. He could hear them groaning. Walnuts falling with their thudding weight like cannonballs. He forced himself to sit there, gripping the armrests on the old chair, trying to remember. He could smell her food, could still conjure the taste of her sweet potato biscuits and pie made with the pecans from the trees in the yard, the cookies and all the pastries baked in the old range, the salt-cured ham his father used to bury and then smoke in the smokehouse and hang on hooks in the basement kitchen, and which she would then boil and scrape and pair with her biscuits, feeding Will always, even when he wasn't hungry, the answer always in the comfort and nourishment of her food.

He could remember her cooking, but he had forgotten her voice somehow, all but a tone in it and the pitch of it, but he couldn't remember it, and in the early days it was her voice that had stayed with him, haunting him, making him play hopeful games with himself, going to school, telling himself she'd just happen to be home when he got back because that was the way it had only just recently been, and the familiarity of everything else guaranteed that regularity. He wanted to stop thinking and focus on the wind, on the distorted windows that made it look like he was staring out into the air from underwater. But nothing then could save him from his thoughts, and he remembered school nights when she would play the piano, and sometimes a man or woman with an instrument would accompany her, and her voice would rise into the upstairs of the house. He'd leave the door to his room open, listening, and he listened now, as if she might somehow return.

O N DUTY ONE DAY, Will went all the way back out to the Snakefoot. It was more impulse than thought. It had been dry and warm, and he could smell the swamp as he approached the Sunoco. The swamp was low, and the odor filling the trapped air spoiled any of the sweet residual fragrance of the tobacco harvest curing elsewhere in the county.

He came to the turn where he'd seen Day's brake lights that night in July. It was lunchtime now, bright and hot, and it was far worse seeing it in the hard daylight. He'd felt a surge of courage when he'd made up his mind to return. To see it again. To see where she had lived. Where she had died. Where they'd killed her. But as he turned onto the clay-dirt track, as red as any blood, and saw the little house, white and sagging and ruined, he regretted the decision, deciding just as impulsively to retreat.

He swung around in the broken yard, where the sheriff's truck had parked that night, and put his cruiser in reverse. But something gave him pause. On the stoop where the baby had been found, clawing and crying at the vines and treetops above, he saw small bouquets of swamp flora spread out on the steps, hanging from the railing and from the doorway, withered and wilting in various stages of decay—one was even fresh—all of them hanging like charms of nothing, gathered of a place where beauty must be harvested with imagination, with an eye for the unseen. Someone missed her, mourned her still, even after these months.

He climbed out of the cruiser, a sense of urgency overtaking him, and heard the shutter click before he even realized he had photographed a scene that should not have been captured, a house all but ruined that offered an aesthetic only of a kind of patient, wounded defiance, even in grief, of something infected by love of a kind, untamed and rough, entirely without the varnish of blood kin or ceremony.

FTER THE SHERIFF was reelected in November, Bill
Seems came to Euphoria County and stayed for a few days,
a week. He stayed at Promised Land this time, and he and
Will began working on the house. They pried the boards off it, and
they even called Granddad to come on down and help. The old man
brought Jerome Davis and Terrell Bloom with him. The hard work
was good. At first, Bill and Granddad stepped warily around each
other, like drunks who might fight over a woman. They had not
seen each other since Hannah's funeral. But Jerome and Terrell had
a carefree and humorous ethic that seemed to remove any tension
that would have been there otherwise. And the work brought them
all together. There was a job to do, and Granddad worked three days
with them before returning to Emporia with Jerome and Terrell.
Will saw the old man shake Bill's hand before leaving.

The night before Bill left, he and Will drove out into a field,
sat above the wheel wells in the truck bed like they used to, seeing
if they could spot deer, sleek and muted under the moon, the grass
still waist-high before the first frost. They sat a long time without
speaking. Bill did not look like a lawyer anymore, but in his rubber
boots, jeans, and flannel, with a cigar in his mouth, he appeared

to be some kind of good-natured frontier ruffian. Will felt closer to him than he had in some time.

"Maybe you ought to think about finding someone," Bill said, looking out over the land. "Settle down, make a life. You got the house."

"It's your house."

"Not anymore it isn't. It's yours." In the moonlight, Will could see his father leaning over his knees. The man continued: "What I've seen is you got what it takes, what this house needs. Without you it would just keep falling apart. I want you to have it. Your ancestors would be proud as hell of you coming back the way no one else could. I'll bet she's proud too."

"I couldn't," Will said.

"Next time you come to Richmond, I'll sign it over. You deserve it."

Soon they could see a doe, green with moonlight, not far. She turned her neck, gracefully, and out of the woods emerged a broad buck, evasive, bright as mist, a shadow floating across the ground. He caught up with the doe, and they moved together until they had vanished like spirits lost together without a sound.

CHERRY STARED at her expanding belly, which would only continue to inflate with the burden of another life. "Do you have family?" the doctor said. "Anyone can help you with the baby?"

She nodded, remembering those nights "riding," when he would open up and tell her about his troubles. He'd talked to her about everything, wanting to run off. Then, in the weeks before he died, there wasn't that smile, and she wondered if she could have done more to prevent his death, to protect the man she loved. She used to believe there was such a thing as a coincidence, but now she wasn't so sure, though she did know her life was going to have to change. But no daddy. There wouldn't be a daddy, just as she had never had one, and maybe she had turned out okay, maybe not, but she knew what that was like. Daddy. She remembered calling Tom that. He seemed to like it, said his woman wouldn't ever call him that, but he liked that Cherry did. He loved her when she said it. And she wondered if it is something in us that wants to love the things we create, if that's what he liked about it, the thought that he was responsible for her, her daddy, the daddy she'd never had, so in a way the only daddy she had ever had was Tom Janders, also the daddy to what was coming now. A long line of daddies, with their

337

title "father" and nothing else, all powerless in their absence, filling families with their conspicuous vacancies. She was scared, prayed to Tom the father, God the Father, the Almighty, saying, *Why you do this to me?* No answer. Didn't know where he was or if he was watching over from his place up there. But she didn't feel him now. She could not even feel him at all. It was as if he had never been there, except for the evidence he'd left to grow within her. Just like a man to leave you with a cross to bear. To carve some initials on a tree, a tree that had no use for them. She could feel what he had left her, the beginning of a long process.

Claudette offered to help when the young soon-to-be mother showed up at her door. There was no doubt Cherry's baby, when it came into the world, was also Tom's. He was a big baby, a boy Cherry called Tom right away. That meant the world to Claudette. Brother Tom and sister Destinee grew up together, playing on the carpet and out in the yard, praying every night for the spirits of the dead. They were raised in a world of Mamaw Claudette's and Mama Cherry's making, where you did not need a memory, only an appetite for God and family. One day Tom would earn a football scholarship, and he'd take it. He would end up owning a restaurant in Richmond, in the Fan, and on Sunday mornings he would deliver food to the homeless at Monroe Park. Destinee would turn to nursing, and she would never leave Southside. Something held her to it, something magnetic and sad and beautiful. A world of the spirit and of the flesh that needed saving.

SOMEWHERE, on some road, a man shivers in a kind of thrall. He considers calling home. He dreams of calling an old friend. He knows he could return home anytime. He doesn't care about the warrants. He could return. He thinks of all the things they could say, he and Will. He is not bitter any longer. He thinks of friendship. But he does not want to be seen. He does not call his parents. He does not want to smell his mother's food, hear his father's voice. He does not want to meet the eyes of men and women who come from where he comes from but have not seen the things he has seen. It should not have turned out like this, he knows. And he would rather not have to explain what he already knows. There are small triumphs every day. He knows he is not too far from home, and he feels it, them, waiting to gather around. He looks out at many roads, feels a kinship of possibilities. He has menial jobs. He paints, he buffs floors, he cleans bathrooms. He uses, knows this emptiness is the life he was born to complete, is soul, is what he has always known he would follow like a blood trail. He thinks he would like to see Will again, as they once were. He will call him, but not now. When things are better, when he gets on his feet. He stares along a road toward a direction he doesn't know. There is a kind of conversation he has with that other voice, and they always seem to understand each other. He has not returned because a return should be a victory, not a retreat. As if in some great awful womb, the two somehow exist, somehow see each other, somehow engage in that silent dialogue that could never be spoken. *To drive home myself,* the man thinks. *To drive home sober, and in my own car.*

A SEASON PASSED. The leaves were long fallen, deer and football seasons finished: that bleak age before spring. Will left Promised Land one evening for that long retreat to Richmond, after eating dinner, once again, with Tania. Actually, he had barely touched the food she had prepared. Something had developed between them since they'd been out to the Snakefoot that night, the night Mills shot Ferriday Pace, the night of Tom's first funeral, something rooted in the sins of others, but this evening, he didn't want her to stay over. He told her a truth: he needed to be alone. He left his gun at the house he still didn't own simply because he hadn't signed the papers.

He considered on his drive reaching out to see Bennico again, or Bill, or anyone, but that would have defeated his purpose. They would try to talk him through. He could hear Bennico or Tania or Bill calling him crazy, and he didn't need that right now. He needed to be alone to keep her headstrong courage.

The sky had been cloudy, swirling with a depth that blocked all blue sky beyond it, any stars that might show themselves this night. He thought of his father, his house full of books, the dull droning of America like a preacher no one is listening to. What was life if not one small unheroic sacrifice after another, until all you saw was your own failed selves like trees against the horizon. He thought of the Southside crew, gathering at the bars. He thought of his ancestors, starving and wounded raw, recovering slowly from war and the poverty of a region, a renegade nation, patriots and traitors both. He thought about two boys playing basketball against a white church, of a warm creek waiting where night would fall into it. He knew he was hungry but had no appetite. He thought of his mother. He thought of that special feeling on a Friday afternoon of getting out of school, of the whole weekend's potential. Of the choices. Things he would not have again anyway. Nostalgia, the worst drug of all.

It was late night, early morning, and a crisp air flowed across Richmond. He stopped at a dive bar where the bouncer watched him closely, and he took a shot and ordered another.

Will left the money on the bar, talking to no one. He thought again about his father. Then about Tom, busting out of the tobacco, clearing the scene, and carrying Sam, that little cumulative weight Will had carried since. He thought of a little girl in a muddy dress, expelled out into the broken yard of a house in the swamp, staring out at the Sunoco lights that illuminated the world around her like a dream, that world that now was hung with pert, defiant bouquets. The same girl he would see as a woman from across a parking lot or gas station or the square, knowing she perceived him as well, a reminder each to the other.

He found himself at the James River, close by the old Tredegar Iron Works and the canal between it and Brown's Island. He looked out to Belle Isle across the water and followed a little walkway that ended abruptly over a series of rapids. In the distance: Hollywood Cemetery, though he couldn't see it now. He brought out the bundle and emptied the remainder—most of what there had been when he bought it—into the river like pale ashes of the dead. It looked pure, like some distillate of bone or moon, and faded without a sound against the night river.

He rode around for some time, not even hoping but looking anyway for Sam, until she spoke. It was a vivid and sudden memory, like a smell, her accent true and melodic, a voice soothing and of the heart, a heart as big as Euphoria County, so big it had to break.

He parked his truck somewhere in Church Hill, got out, and walked up streets where he normally would not have walked, and the old chipped white brick townhomes rose like headstones, and the vacant field devoid even of grass stretched beyond a chain-link fence to his left. You could tell by the style of the homes that once, some time ago, this had been a respectable neighborhood. He approached the huddle, the men he saw each time but never on foot. They lifted their shirts like shrouds, and he continued toward them anyway.

"Ya boy ain't here," B said. "You hear me? The fuck you doing?"

Will pressed on in a haze like a high.

"Yo, back off," B said. "Get gone."

He heard their voices.

*"Look at this white nigger."*

*"I done told you not to come 'round here."*

*"Back away. Yo, go back to where you belong. Crazy mo'fuck. What the fuck?"*

*"White nigger."*

He marched on, and the circle formed around him in a strange fellowship he knew, something choreographed by the variables of history. He felt a strange cold relief like a drug (China White, dynamite), the release from old heavy chains. Anything was possible. Finally, action.

It began with fists and pistol whips, and he understood something all too late, that he could be free of fear and that his own lack of it now had instilled it in these men around him. They were afraid. They were afraid because he was not. He had crossed that boundary. And there was much to fear, but he was not afraid. Only the regret for him remained. The regret that there had ever been such fear. That it had come to this. That thirteen years ago he had stood still, and it had come to this. He was the danger, yes. The weak, tremendous threat.

He rose, glowing somehow above himself, and watched over that Holy City sprawled out across bluffs and eager hills. Sheets of an early morning fog like a strange flag were beginning to burn away in the dawn over the dark water of the James yet hung around the buildings and the Confederate monuments, and all the years feared, regretted, forgiven, gone, stood like buildings themselves, old vacant boarded-up structures, and the weathered gangrenous figures appeared to move on horseback through the fog. It was possible someone would call him a man of courage (*H* for hero), a man who had fought against drugs, addiction, crime. But no one knew because no one could that this was the sickness, the treatment. That someday those platforms would stand vacant, riderless and bare, the abandoned pedestals of the ghosts of men long dead and innocent of self-defense.